Bringer Unleashed

Book #2 in the Logan Bringer Series

Jaz Primo

RUTHERFORD LITERARY GROUP

www.rutherfordliterary.com

Novels by Jaz Primo

The Sunset Vampire Series
Sunrise at Sunset: Revamped
A Bloody London Sunset
Summit at Sunset
Wicked Sunset
Sunset Rising
Sunset Burning **

** Additional Titles Forthcoming

* * *

The Logan Bringer Urban Fantasy Series
Bringer of Fire
Bringer Unleashed
Bringer's Law *

* Additional Titles Forthcoming

* * *

Gwen Reaper
(A Young Adult Paranormal Romance)
Winner of the Paranormal Romance Guild's Reviewer's Choice Award for Best Young Adult Novel of 2012!

* * *

All titles published by Rutherford Literary Group

This is a work of fiction. Names, characters, places, and incidents either are the product of the author's imagination or are used fictitiously, and any resemblance to actual persons, living or dead, business establishments, events, or locales is entirely coincidental. The publisher does not have any control over and does not assume any responsibility for author or third-party websites or their content. Any trademarks mentioned herein are not authorized by the trademark owners and do not in any way mean the work is sponsored by or associated with the trademark owners. Any trademarks used are specifically in a descriptive capacity.

Published by:
Rutherford Literary Group
1205 S. Air Depot, PMB #135
Midwest City, OK 73110-4807

Cover Art by Brandon Acree

Edited by Laura Matheson

ISBN 0-9885690-8-6
ISBN-13 978-0988569089

DEDICATION

For the readers...who waited so patiently for book 2 in the Logan Bringer series. This is for you!

CONTENTS

ACKNOWLEDGMENTS

As always, my heartfelt thanks to Tabby, who injects her youthful exuberance into both my life and my writing process, often with equal parts mirth and aggravation. Both she and my dearest friends remind me there's much more to life than creative writing. My sincere thanks to my loved ones for supporting me through the protracted creative process for this book. As always, a huge thank you to my dear friend and publicist, Vicki Rose, for her continued support and encouragement.

An enormous "Thank You" to my editor, Laura Matheson, for her marvelous editing and mentoring skills. You're such a sincere joy to work with! Special thanks to Brandon Acree for his polished cover art and creative zeal and wizardry for all things graphic and fonty.

Last but not least, a hearty thank you and a big hug to my dedicated readers for your continued support, encouragement, and steadfast promotional assistance. Thanks so much for all you do!

CHAPTER 1

"He who fights with monsters might take care lest he thereby become a monster. And if you gaze for long into an abyss, the abyss gazes also into you." - Friedrich Nietzsche

* * *

I'm an all in—or all out—type of guy.

I've never been good at moderation.

At the moment, I was definitely all in.

I was jostled back and forth while shrugging into my bulletproof vest as sirens wailed outside our panel van.

Our intended destination was yet another crime scene; our ninth over the past six weeks.

Across from me, my quasi-partner, FBI Special Agent Megan Sanders, struggled to maintain her balance.

The van lurched as a loud horn sounded outside, tossing Sanders toward me.

I caught her in my arms as her hands landed atop my shoulders, her hazel eyes staring into mine with a mix of surprise and something else.

Intensity.

For a split second, I was tempted to kiss her.

It would've been one hell of a first kiss for us.

However, she regained her footing and pulled away from

me to perch on the opposite side of the van, securing her vest in place.

The contingent of police tactical members momentarily looked at us and then returned to checking their weapons and equipment.

"Christ's sake! Damned drivers don't even give way to the police anymore," complained the officer driving. "Like we're an inconvenience or something."

"Yeah, until they need us," said the officer beside me.

Lately, the police, as much as many other state and federal agencies, had been busy on a daily basis.

It was exactly fifteen days since I had prevailed in my knock-down battle against a crazed guy with telekinetic abilities near the FBI office building in Nevis Corners, a corporately managed city in Iowa and my city of residence in recent years.

My duel had resulted in dozens of people—both innocent bystanders and authorities—either killed or wounded, not to mention numerous buildings nearly leveled.

The carnage had surpassed Hollywood disaster film levels.

Since then, the world had not only changed, it seemed to have gone to hell even faster than I had thought possible.

"Fifteen minutes to scene, people," said the driver. "Lock and load."

Weapons had rounds chambered in quick succession.

"Where exactly are we going again?" I asked.

"Browns Point Boulevard," said the sergeant across from me. "It's near the coast."

"That's over near Marine View Drive," said the officer beside him. "Really nice neighborhoods."

I'd never been to Seattle, Washington, but it was one of those scenic destinations that I had always wanted to visit.

It was disappointing that my arrival there had nothing to do with a vacation.

"What's the sitrep?" asked Sanders.

"Not sure, exactly. The initial teams were setting up

when the scene turned hot," replied the sergeant. "We're the backup tactical team and were told to pick you two up at the airport on the way out there."

"Anything else?" I asked.

"Command's already onsite. They'll brief you when we arrive," he said. "Sorry, that's all I know for now."

Great. Nothing like stepping into a hot zone without any intel.

Although, I was quickly getting used to that.

I listened to the radio traffic, but it was a jumble of team positioning and unit arrival announcements.

Closing my eyes, I gently opened my mind to listen in on the thoughts of those around me.

Nothing unusual; mostly curiosity mixed with silent prayers and anxious thoughts.

…running around like chickens with our heads cut off, came Sanders' thought.

I opened my eyes to see her frowning back at me.

…better not be getting in my head again, she thought.

I barely contained my amusement.

Our van slowed and then lurched to a stop.

"Aw, hell. You've gotta be kidding me," said the driver.

"What?" asked the sergeant.

"Sarge, we're blocked in tight before hordes of press and a crapload of empty cars," he said. "This is about as close as I can get us."

"Good enough. Let's hit it," the sergeant ordered.

Two officers near the back doors burst outside with assault rifles at the ready. The rest of us followed them.

I could smell seawater from not far away.

The blazing orange and yellow hues from the waning sunset caught my attention, followed quickly by the pandemonium surrounding us.

Helicopters flew overhead amidst the buzzing and thrum of their engines. Various makes and models of vehicles from what must have been practically every governmental law enforcement agency sat hastily parked, their lights flashing and strobing in a psychedelic array of colors.

More surprising was the throng of onlookers who had gathered like a flowing mob while scant numbers of police officers tried to hold them at bay before crime tape, orange cones, and impromptu cordons.

"Hey, there he is!" shouted someone in the crowd.

"Aw, crap," said the sergeant.

In a matter of seconds, you couldn't throw a rock in any direction without hitting a member of the press.

A sour feeling formed in the pit of my stomach as I immediately became the central target of their attentions.

Just great.

A commotion ran through the crowd.

Then eerily hushed silence.

It seemed to me that when you're a famous celebrity or athlete, people want your autograph, or even to have a photo taken with you. Crowds might even scream questions and accolades from every direction.

But with me, most people simply stared as I walked by, typically saying nothing at all.

Many people openly gawked at me.

However, their eyes spoke louder than any words; they told me everything I needed to know.

"Hey, you! What the hell are you, anyway?" demanded a bystander.

I pointedly ignored him.

It wasn't that I resented his question. In truth, I just didn't really have an answer for him.

Tell me and we'll both know, pal.

"He's a superhero!" yelled a young boy not far from me.

I turned and grinned at him, but then winked and shook my head.

Sorry, kid, I'm no superhero.

At least, not like in the comics.

"He's the devil!" shouted an old woman to my left. "The end days are coming! Protect us, Lord Jesus!"

Her, I also ignored.

If I had a nickel for every crackpot religious nut in our country…

"Hey, hero," prompted the sergeant. "C'mon, they need you up front."

Of course they did.

I was the only bad-ass monster in their inventory; and they were leveraging me at every opportunity.

Am I really a monster to them?

"Bringer," Sanders said, grasping at my forearm. "You okay?"

"I'm golden," I said. "Let's go."

As we proceeded at a trot down the street toward ground zero, a newswoman with a cameraman in tow managed to dodge past the barricades.

I had to give her credit, she was moving pretty fast for a lady in heels.

"You're Logan Bringer, aren't you?"

I didn't even look at her.

"Get her outta here!" the sergeant ordered.

"Have they cornered someone like you up there?" the reporter asked. "If so, what powers do they have? Can you match them?"

Fortunately, two of the tactical team members intercepted her and her cameraman as we proceeded up the street.

"I hope so," I said.

If it was anything like the past six weeks of action, it might be just another bunch of crazies stockpiling weapons and ammunition for the perceived coming apocalypse, or a terrorist group that had somehow moved their way up to the top of the federal target list.

We hadn't encountered anyone else with telekinetic abilities yet. They seemed to have fallen off the radar entirely.

While I should've found that comforting, I was certain it was only a matter of time. There had to be more of them out there.

I couldn't prove it, but I had a feeling that the shadow group calling themselves Continuance Corporation, or Bestand Gesellschaft, was out there somewhere, waiting to rear their ugly heads again.

We passed no fewer than two armored personnel carriers and four Humvees with machine guns mounted atop them.

A week ago, the President had declared martial law and suspended the writ of habeas corpus. Some members of Congress objected, but they were quickly labeled as unpatriotic and obstructionists to national security for their opposition. For the moment, fear and paranoia ruled the day.

Following that, the Department of Homeland Security had established tactical control centers in each state to act as leads with state authorities on all surveillance, investigations, and mobilizations of law enforcement for any activities deemed related to the Continuance Corporation scare.

Nearly every state governor had activated their National Guard units, ordering them to mobilize to support Homeland Security and local authorities.

It had become a scary time in our history, and not simply because of potential terrorists with telekinetic abilities.

As we rounded the street corner, I saw a small army of law enforcement and government tactical teams surrounding a cul de sac containing less than a dozen large homes against a backdrop of heavy woods.

Sanders and I proceeded toward, and then into, a nearby mobile tactical command vehicle, a veritable armored mobile home.

I didn't bother trying to remember the series of names of FBI, Homeland Security, ATF, local police brass, and National Guard officers who introduced themselves to us.

Hell, it felt just like some sort of wearisome meet-and-greet event. And it was crowded beyond belief. They definitely needed a bigger trailer.

During the introductions, everyone warily looked at me like they expected me to explode or something.

"The house at the back of the cul de sac is where they're holed up," said an Army National Guard colonel.

"We've secured a complete perimeter, including the western edge of the woods bordering Commencement Bay," said the local tactical team captain. "They're not getting out without engaging us."

"Any telekinetics?" I asked.

I got a round of blank looks.

"You know, people with abilities?" Sanders asked.

"We don't know yet," said a man wearing a Homeland Security jacket.

"You don't know yet?" I asked. "Okay. How many people are we facing out there?"

"We're not sure precisely," he replied. "We've engaged at least six, wounding one. But we pulled back when we encountered heavy weapons."

"You're not sure," I repeated. I gave Sanders my best perturbed look.

"Okay, how would you like to proceed here?" Sanders asked, hiking her hands atop her hips.

"We're in a sound position with control of all possible egresses," said an ATF agent. "Fortunately, now that you're here, we also hold the element of surprise."

I stared at him as if he was crazy. "Surprise? You're kidding me, right?"

"Well," he said. "They don't know you're here."

Incredible. Where did they get these people?

A television perched on the wall just over his shoulder caught my eye. It displayed streaming news coverage of the event.

Then I noticed the lady reporter who had chased after me.

"Wait. Turn that up," I said, pointing at the screen.

Everyone turned to stare at the television as someone reached for the remote.

"…mysterious man from the Nevis Corners battle just arrived on scene and was moving into action," she said. "We're standing by to see what happens next."

I cast a sour look at everyone.

"You were saying about your element of surprise?" I asked. "Did you happen to have cut the power to that house?"

"Done," said the tactical team commander. "However, they've got a backup generator that kicked in as soon as we did."

"Just great," I said. "We're losing daylight and there's a good chance they already know I'm here."

"I'm betting anybody with a mobile phone in there already knows you're here," Sanders said.

She made an excellent point. That's why she's the FBI agent instead of me.

I turned and headed toward the exit.

"Bringer, where the hell are you going?" Sanders demanded.

"Well, somebody's gotta get something done around here," I said. "It may as well be me."

"Wait, Bringer," she said, chasing after me as I briskly exited the trailer onto the street.

The remainder of those in the command trailer followed closely behind her.

I pointed over to a nearby personnel carrier.

"Get behind that, Sanders," I said. "Keep your head down until the smoke clears."

"But—"

"Now!"

Then I heard her footsteps retreat toward cover.

I'm getting better at this.

A flurry of activity happened all at once as I heard more chatter from nearby police radios. All manner of law enforcement officers and officials were in motion, either moving into tactical positions or heading for cover.

I conjured an invisible shield before me as I rounded the corner of the street and trod into direct view of the two-story house at the end of the cul de sac.

A hail of small arms fire erupted from in and around the house, all headed downrange at me as I walked forward.

Most of the rounds impacted my shield, but rather than ricocheting off of it, I'd learned to catch and envelop them to minimize collateral damage.

Louder shots sounded, followed by heavier rounds buffeting against my shield. Though I caught them like the others, I felt small pangs of pain in my head as each one clobbered me.

So far, so good.

I can handle this.

I was halfway to the house when a loud whistling sound erupted.

A large explosion smashed against my shield, nearly knocking me off balance as intense pain shot through my brain.

Oh, shit. Rocket propelled grenade?

I strengthened my shield just as two more large hits arrived. This time, both of the projectiles ricocheted off my shield.

One slammed into a nearby vehicle, causing it to explode in a shower of hot metal and flame. It flipped end over end into the air, even as the other round struck a large nearby tree, felling the top of it onto the street below.

I dropped to one knee as throbbing waves pounded through my head.

I hadn't expected that.

"Bringer!" yelled Sanders.

I held up my hand, in case she was thinking of doing something bold and stupid.

Like I just did.

I got to my feet and shook my head to clear it as the pain subsided slightly.

Small and medium arms fire hammered into my reconstituted shield.

"Fine," I said. "Let's see how you like being on the receiving end."

I conjured a fireball as I briskly resumed my stride toward the house.

Seconds later, I cast it downrange at the house. It collided with the home's exterior in a shower of flame, setting fire to the wooden façade.

Oops, too big of a fireball that time.

I heard the whistle from another small missile, but it sped past me and walloped a power pole just behind me.

"What the—"

A middle section of the pole exploded in a shower of sparks and wooden shards as the upper half of it fell toward me. I strengthened my shield as I stepped aside, but some sort of erratic electrical discharge cascaded across the outer portion of my shield.

My body felt like it was on fire and my skin felt like ants were crawling all over it, even as aching rocked through my head.

All I could see was bluish-white light before me as I fell toward the pavement.

I scarcely managed to thrust one arm outward to break my fall. My teeth chattered as my body flopped uncontrollably on the pavement, sending wave after wave of pain rolling through my bones and muscles.

I gritted my teeth and shut my eyes as I used every ounce of strength I could muster to imagine a protective circle enveloping me.

Suddenly, the pain abated to reasonable levels, though my head felt like it was being squeezed in a vice.

I heard simultaneous shouting, gunfire, and commotion all around me. Then I heard a buzzing, sizzling sound.

To my astonishment, I opened my eyes to see blue-white electrical currents orbiting my shield.

At first, I was afraid to move. Then I gingerly pushed myself up while concentrating fully on maintaining my shield.

"Bringer!" Sanders yelled.

I staggered up and away from the transformer that lay on the pavement next to me, waiting until the electrical currents dissipated.

More small rounds battered my shield, and I turned to look at the house before me.

I saw more than a dozen muzzles flashing at once,

including a large machine gun from an upstairs window.

"Bullshit."

I reached out with imaginary hands to grasp a nearby pickup, and concentrated on levitating it off the ground.

It raised a couple of feet into the air and I cast it toward the upstairs window where the machine gun was firing.

I heard a scream as the truck imbedded itself in the house.

"One down," I said, looking over to where I last saw Sanders.

She waved at me. "Are you okay?"

I motioned for her to stay where she was and concentrated on the house again.

"This ends now," I said.

I conjured two fireballs, one in each hand, and focused on maintaining my shield before me.

My head felt like it was going to split wide open.

More rounds impacted my shield, but I had difficulty capturing most of them; numerous rounds ricocheted off in various directions.

I cast one fireball toward the garage and the other toward the front door.

Each fireball exploded in a shower of flames, setting fire to two more areas of the house.

"Throw down your arms and come out with your hands up!"

Oh, I've always wanted to say that.

The gunfire ceased.

"Get out here before I get really pissed off!"

For a moment, nothing happened.

Then, one by one, men and women exited the house with their hands over their heads.

A mass of various law enforcement officers and tactical team members rushed forward to take custody of them.

Some of my opponents appeared to be in their mid to late twenties, though others were definitely older, perhaps in their sixties.

A small part of me couldn't help wondering what their story was. However, my head hurt far too much to care enough to find out.

I staggered aside and leaned against a nearby car.

Sanders rushed to me with a group of paramedics and agents in tow, even as fire trucks raced past us toward the burning house.

"My God, that was incredible," said a Homeland Security official.

"No, that was a fiasco," I said.

I knew damned good and well that my ego had gotten the better of me.

I had been stupid, displayed too much hubris.

For a moment, the tactical team commander appeared speechless and just shook his head at me. Then he turned and ran over to the officers surrounding the house.

"Anybody have any fluids?" I asked, of nobody in particular.

Sanders handed me an already opened plastic energy drink bottle.

I gulped it down.

Two paramedics stared at me, as if not sure what to do.

I took a few final swigs of the orange-flavored substance, appreciating the cold liquid flowing down my throat.

"Um, can we do anything for you, sir?" one paramedic asked.

"Yeah, you looked like you were being electrocuted," said the other.

I looked at each of them in turn. "Nope, fine now."

"You two had better go check on whoever else might be injured," Sanders suggested.

They looked at each other and then moved away from me in an almost grateful-looking manner.

Everyone else alternated between staring at me and then gaping at the commotion around us.

"So, Agent Sanders and I are done here?" I asked, my eyes sweeping the faces standing around me.

"Well—" replied the Homeland Security official.

"Er, sure," said the FBI agent in charge. "Agent Sanders can see that you file the appropriate field reports. Won't you, Agent Sanders?"

"Right," she said, grabbing hold of my forearm. "Let's go, Bringer."

I permitted her to lead me away in the direction of the command trailer.

"Hey, where are we going?" I asked.

"Somewhere out of the public eye," she said as two news helicopters hovered overhead.

I looked westward toward the waning sunset. "Great. While we're at it, I could use a vacation. You know, somewhere distant, preferably out of the public eye."

"Ha, fat chance," she replied.

* * *

After checking into our hotel that evening, Sanders and I walked to a nearby restaurant for a late dinner together. I was half-surprised that the press hadn't located us yet.

Sanders looked as weary as I felt, and she picked at her food, even as I wolfed mine down.

"What happened to you out there today?" she asked.

I was an idiot, that's what.

"I know where you're going with this," I said. "I was impulsive."

"I'm glad you're willing to admit that much," she said. "However, I was referring to the power pole. I thought I'd lost you out there when that transformer almost landed on top of you."

I looked up at her.

She said, 'thought I'd lost you.'

Her sentiment meant a lot to me.

Though it went without saying that I was undoubtedly attracted to Meg Sanders, I'd also grown to care about her in recent weeks. We'd been through a helluva lot together.

And maybe I was just being gullible, but part of me liked to think that I mattered to her, too.

She frowned. "What?"

I shook my head. "Nothing. Just a passing thought."

"Well?" she asked.

I shrugged. "Yeah, well, I've never been hit with electricity before. At first, I thought I was a goner, too. But I adapted, and I think I could manage it again if I had to."

She shook her head. "You and your 'adapt and overcome' mindset. You're like an overgrown Boy Scout sometimes; admittedly, one who can cast fireballs at people."

I wondered if I could do the same with electricity with some practice.

I'd ask Maria Edwards when we got back to Nevis Corners. She was a physician's assistant with a chemical engineering background who had helped me understand my abilities. She was the closest person I had to a scientific advisor about my condition.

Even better, she was someone I could trust.

"Have you given any more thought to Clive Bernard's offer?"

With everything that had been happening the past few weeks, I'd almost forgotten about that.

Clive Bernard was the president of Nuclegene Corporation, the company responsible for the cancer treatments that had conjured my telekinetic abilities. Recently, he had approached me about becoming a company man.

I looked up from my plate. "Sign a contract in blood with Nuclegene? What sort of choice is that? I don't want to be owned by some mega-company for the remainder of my life."

"I know. I wouldn't either," she said. "Though, in truth, working for the federal government doesn't feel much different."

I nodded. "Maybe so. But, hey, at least they're paying for our dinner tonight."

She stared back at me as I chewed a chunk of steak.

"I really don't get you sometimes, Bringer," she said. "You're sitting on one goldmine of an opportunity right now and you seem completely oblivious to it."

"Listen, I read through that painful, tree-killing tome they called a contract, and despite all the legalese, I actually understood the gist of most of it," I said. "In the end, I didn't exactly like their terms. Left up to them, I'd practically become a lab rat part of the time, and a contracted suit for the Feds the remainder of the time. It'd be almost like being in the military all over again…owned body and soul. Hell, at least then I liked wearing my battle fatigues better than some damned suit and tie."

"So, what? Make Nuclegene strike the parts of the agreement that you don't like," she said. "Haven't you ever heard of contract negotiations?"

I contemplated that as I dipped another piece of steak into some barbeque sauce and then bit down on it.

She shook her head. "Your colon probably hates you, you know."

I swallowed and absently pointed my fork at her. "First, my colon and I get along just fine, thank you. I've got one helluva hearty metabolism nowadays. And second, I'm not a rabbit like you."

She glanced down at her plateful of salad. "Maybe not," she said, looking up with narrowed eyes. "But I do know that if you keep pointing that fork at me, this rabbit's going to stick it somewhere painful."

My eyebrows rose. "Hey, what gives? Somebody sure turned all pissy on me all of a sudden."

"Pissy? I'm pissed because I don't think you're thinking things through carefully enough," she said.

"What? Because I'm not some contract specialist like you seem to be?"

"Maybe, but it's not just that," she countered. "Take that full frontal assault earlier today, for example. What were you thinking? You were reckless and could've easily gotten a lot of people killed. Hell, you practically got fried on some electrical lines."

I hated to admit that she made a good point.

What was worse was the look on her face spoke volumes, too. She knew she was right.

I shrugged. "Fair enough. I'll try not to rush into things in the future."

Her tight facial muscles appeared to relax somewhat.

I started to take another bite of steak, but stopped.

"So, how would you feel about taking a quick peek at that Nuclegene contract for me? Maybe help me out with that negotiations idea of yours a little bit?"

She gave me a satisfied look. "Sure, Bringer. I'd be happy to."

We returned to eating, and the remainder of our dinner was much more agreeable. However, as I reflected on our conversation, I couldn't help feeling like a guy who'd just been subtly handled.

Usually, I resented that feeling.

What really struck me as strange was, in this case, I didn't really mind all that much.

CHAPTER 2

Nevis Corners was beginning to haunt me.

We landed at the airport the next day, and hadn't even finished our portion of the field report paperwork when Sanders received a call from her FBI field supervisor, Chuck Denton, telling us to hightail it back to the Nevis Corners office for an important meeting.

I wasn't sure which I disliked more, paperwork or meetings.

Despite our orders to report directly to the city's administrative offices, I insisted on stopping by my house to pick up the proposed Nuclegene contract that Clive Bernard had given to me. I didn't want to give Sanders time to change her mind about looking it over for me.

When we arrived at the tall, modern-looking office building, we waited for a brief pre-meeting to end before heading up to the conference room.

It was never a good sign when a meeting had its own pre-meeting.

I only hoped there wouldn't be a post-meeting following it.

Sanders and I took up positions outside, taking advantage of the vacation-worthy weather. The relative sense of normality around us was welcome, too.

No sirens. No explosions. Just the ordinary sounds of a

city teeming with people absorbed with jobs, errands, and a host of other who-could-care-less distractions.

I remembered when those days were the norm, but it seemed like forever ago.

I heard a deep rumbling noise and one of the army's new main battle tanks rolled past us and proceeded up the street. My vision of normal promptly evaporated.

Sanders' smartphone chimed.

"Logan," she said, lightly touching my elbow. "They're ready for us now."

I took a deep breath and looked up into the clear blue sky, savoring a few fleeting seconds of warm sunshine against my skin.

"Can't the bureaucrats just sort everything out by themselves?" I asked.

"Yeah, that'll be the day," she said. "But then, you're the man of the hour, Bringer, and everyone wants to see your shining face."

I responded with a growl from deep in my throat as I followed her inside the building.

"Try not to set anybody afire," she added dryly.

You're a real comedian, Sanders.

The offices of the city's administrator reminded me of what I had previously only seen in a high-rise law office building in downtown New York City. Add to that, the conference room that we entered held an air of privilege and entitlement; not surprising, considering that some of the nation's largest mega corporations were the city's founders.

Regardless, I had rarely enjoyed sitting in conference rooms, particularly ones where I was the center of attention.

Feeling rebellious, I studied an oversized aerial photograph of the city hanging upon the far wall, all the while trying to ignore the roomful of eyes boring into me.

"…and half the city is terrified out of their minds over the prospect that another freak hell-bent on destruction is going to stroll into town and start blowing up the place…seeking him," said the city's chief administrator.

I looked at him just as he pointed an accusing finger in my direction.

Most cities had publicly-elected officials such as mayors and city councilmen running the various local government services and offices. In corporate cities like Nevis Corners, managers representing the local influential corporations served on the city's Board of Directors, rather than a city council. In addition, corporate cities appointed an administrator in lieu of a mayor.

As such, Gerald Prievus was appointed to govern Nevis Corners.

I already didn't like him. He struck me as a rather self-important, ladder-climbing weasel of a man.

"There were fourteen people killed in this city just two weeks ago," Prievus complained. "And no fewer than thirty-two others injured; many seriously, others maimed forever. I speak on behalf of the Board of Directors when I say that Logan Bringer's continued presence poses an immediate danger to the continued safety of the city."

I ground my teeth in an effort to curtail some smart-ass remark.

Still, there was very little that I could say to that. My failure at mastering my talents caused many to rank among the killed and injured. I would have gladly done more if I could have.

Hell, I never asked for this.

What began almost six weeks ago as an FBI investigation into a supposed terrorist attack against the cancer treatment center that I had been attending as a patient quickly turned into a giant load of crap. I was swallowed up by a global conspiracy involving shadow corporations left over from the Cold War, including experiments seeking to menifest telekinetic abilities in humans.

These were all matters that I felt completely out of my depth to adequately negotiate. Much of what I had learned was literally acquired as I went along, honed by trial and error.

Sometimes, many errors.

Regrettably, what was done was done. All that I could hope to affect was the present, or perhaps even the future.

"We're still trying to repair all of the damage in and around the city's central park," Prievus continued. "Not to mention the four buildings and vast expanse of street infrastructure that was heavily damaged two weeks ago. And where are the funds supposed to come from for that? We may have to order an increase in city residents' user fees to earmark for the repairs."

The resident user fees were nothing short of a tax, in my opinion. Each resident paid annual user fees in lieu of federal and local taxes for maintenance and upkeep of the city, which conservative politicians crowed was a tax decrease for those residents compared to the usual federal and municipal taxes.

What wasn't clearly communicated to the public was that the user fees curtailed the state and federal government's influence to interfere with the city's corporate-led operations and management, since little if any traditional tax dollars flowed into the city's coffers.

"Just take a breath, Prievus," cautioned FBI Deputy Director Mark Wainright, a person who I counted as one of my supporters, and a man who I had grown to respect during the short time that we had known each other. "Logan Bringer is the only reason that you still have a city left standing to administrate."

I liked Wainright. He might, in fact, be the central reason that I wasn't already being whisked away to become a resident in some government lab for closer study.

Sanders bit her lip; though I still caught the subtle formation of a smile. I also noticed the frown that her supervisor, Denton, cast in her direction.

"Bringer is the reason that the city was attacked in the first place," Prievus said. "He's drawing unhealthy attention to Nevis Corners. The press has practically camped out here since day one covering this situation."

"And by situation, you mean—" Wainright said.

"*Him,*" Prievus said, pointing to me with a finger that looked far lengthier than any normal human finger should. "He's the situation. Just this morning, one of the cable news networks reported that a church congregation from Kansas was on their way up here to demonstrate outside the city because of him. They're practically calling him the Anti-Christ. They're claiming the city is suffering a penance from God for our iniquities."

Oh, brother. You've got to be kidding.

While I had tried to stay away from the network news channels in recent weeks, my sister and mother had been more than happy to fill me in. Despite that, I hadn't realized that I was labeled with the mark of the beast already.

"Wait just a damned minute," Denton said. "If, by church, do you mean those extremist yahoos who demonstrate at soldier's funerals? Give me a break."

"They attract attention," Prievus said. "And negative, undue attention matters whether you like it or not."

"Hey, I'm for the first amendment and all," I said with a shrug. "That being said, those nutty bastards can kiss my ass on their way to a deservingly fiery hell. But then, that's just my personal opinion."

"Ditto," Sanders muttered.

I gave her an appreciative wink.

"I think we should make better use of our time by focusing on the core matters at hand," suggested Cheryl Henson, Iowa's State Attorney General. "Namely, identifying the perpetrators and quickly locating their command structure before they have time to initiate further destruction. Our governor is very concerned by what's taken place and has charged me with assembling a state task force to secure our state's infrastructure."

"Those are excellent points," agreed Bob Tevin, the Deputy Director of the National Security Agency/Central Security Service. "Federal agencies will happily collaborate with your efforts."

"Yet, this still involves a sensitive matter of national

security. There are topics that we may not be able to share at this time," said Yasmine Prichard, Special Agent in Charge of Domestic Affairs for the Central Intelligence Agency.

I wasn't one of Prichard's biggest fans, and I was betting I was still at the top of her shit list, as well.

"The core matter at hand here today should be ensuring that one of America's newest and premier corporate city isn't turned into rubble," Prievus insisted. "Both the state and federal governments, in accordance with the Land Reclamation and Investment in America Act, are obligated to provide proper protection for Nevis Corners."

I didn't much care for that historic piece of land-grab legislation. Unused, privately-owned land all across America was seized by the federal government and parceled out to corporations who promised to construct modern cities to serve as shiny bastions of new private sector jobs for the nation.

What they became were taxpayer-fronted, yet corporately owned and controlled, utopias where corporations had virtual run of the place, tax-free and with minimal government intervention.

Granted, Nevis Corners had become my home in recent years, but that was primarily because my cancer treatments were here. If not for having secured a job from one of the city's sanctioned supporting businesses, I wouldn't be authorized to be a permanent resident.

The conference room door abruptly opened to reveal a cadre of business suit clad individuals.

"My apologies for being late," said a middle-aged man at the head of the group. "Our flight was delayed due to some foul weather in Washington."

"Who are you?" Prievus demanded.

The man extended his hand toward Prievus.

"I'm Roger Beck, Deputy Secretary of Homeland Security," the man declared. "I'm here to take command of this situation, as well as secure this city."

Everyone rose to greet Beck and his entourage.

I extended my hand. "I'm—"

"Yes, Logan Bringer," Beck interrupted. "Oh, I know of you all too well already, Mr. Bringer. You and your unique set of abilities were quickly and prominently affixed on my radar."

Somehow that didn't inspire my confidence in him. Granted, I'd been on the FBI's radar immediately following the destruction of the Wallace Building; former host of, among other services and offices, the Nuclegene Cancer Treatment Center. But this fellow conjured a vision of shadowy government figures sitting in dark rooms making all sorts of impactful decisions that few were privy to.

"You've created quite a mess for us, Bringer," Beck continued, taking a formerly empty seat at the head of the table as if it were intended for him.

"As had been mentioned earlier, Secretary Beck," Deputy Director Tevin smartly interjected. "Bringer is the reason that there's something left for you to actually clean up."

Like Deputy Director Wainright, Tevin was another one of the few government bureaucrats who had earned my respect.

"That may well be," Beck coolly conceded. "However, the fact remains that, by the order of the President, federal authorities are being installed to ensure that if further unexpected and destructive surprises appear, we're prepared to handle it."

My recent experiences with a hostile telekinetic suggested that they were already in well over their heads. But then, nobody asked me.

The room fell eerily silent, though Prievus appeared quite satisfied with Beck's revelation.

"The city's board of directors will be very pleased to hear that," he said.

Beck's stare shifted to Deputy Director Wainright.

"Now, Wainright," he prompted. "First, what are the FBI's next steps in pursuing those responsible? And second, what are you anticipating Mr. Bringer's role to be?"

Frankly, I had to concede that both were excellent questions.

Wainright diplomatically assured everyone that the FBI had mobilized their resources and was making progress. As for me, he stated that I was a civilian collaborating with the investigation.

Somehow, I found that a less than satisfying classification for my participation.

Two hours later, the meeting concluded. However, government bureaucracies being what they were, it was merely the conclusion of one meeting and followed by yet another meeting hosted at the downtown offices of the city's corporately-managed police department.

In the aftermath of my duel with a telekinetic madman, the Nevis Corners' federal building housing their FBI office was damaged beyond use until expansive repairs were completed. As such, the FBI had temporarily relocated to office space inside the local police department's facility.

As Agents Sanders and Denton and I exited into the hallway, grateful to leave the roomful of bureaucrats behind, I mulled over the tentative plan sketched out during the meeting.

According to Deputy Secretary Beck, by the order of the President, a special joint FBI/NSA taskforce established under the title Telekinetic Anti-terrorism Surveillance and Interdiction Taskforce, or TASIT, was co-led by Deputy Directors Wainright and Tevin, to root out the sources and participants involved with both the destruction of the Wallace Building and the attack on the downtown federal building.

"What happens next?" Sanders asked her supervisor.

"That's what the next meeting is about," he replied. "The Secretary issued his marching orders and it's up to the Deputy Directors to put everything together. What I do know is that our local FBI office is to be involved. We're a key piece of this pie."

"Involved? Aren't we the choice center of the pie?" she

countered.

Denton pointed at me. "No, he's the center; we're just the flaky crust around the edge."

"All this talk about pie is making me hungry," I said.

"Well, it's almost four o'clock, so we'd better go get something to eat while we can," Denton suggested. "I have the feeling that our long day isn't over by a mile."

"I could eat," I said.

Sanders gave me a long look. "When are you not hungry?"

"Usually, right after I eat," I replied.

Denton chuckled.

We walked outside the building, and had no sooner stepped onto the sidewalk, when a shiny black stretch limousine pulled up to the curb before us.

The rearmost tinted window rolled down to reveal the smiling face of Clive Bernard, a multimillionaire in his own right and the President of Nuclegene Corporation.

"Good day, Mr. Bringer. Agents," he greeted. "Mr. Bringer, I don't suppose that you would be so kind as to share a ride with me?"

"We're on a bit of a tight schedule, Mr. Bernard," Sanders said.

"I understand," he replied. "However, I think that what I have to discuss is worth just a few minutes of Mr. Bringer's time."

I had to admit that I was curious as to what Bernard wanted to discuss. My initial guess was it was about his recent contract offer.

I suddenly wished that Sanders had already had a chance to read over the documents.

"We're on our way to an early dinner," I said. "Why don't you join us?"

"Normally, I might. However, I'm afraid that my topic of interest is intended for your ears only," Bernard replied. "But I promise that you won't go hungry."

"Go ahead, Bringer," Denton said. "We'll meet you at

police headquarters. Be there by six o'clock sharp."

As if on cue, the front passenger door opened and a giant of a man, one of Bernard's personal body guards, stepped out of the vehicle to open the rear passenger door for me.

"Mr. Bringer," the man—who I knew simply as Scott—offered with a polite nod.

It hadn't been that long ago that I almost propelled the guy through a wall with my skills. Glad to see that he didn't appear to hold a grudge.

I nodded back at him while ducking into the roomy interior. Sandra Yalesin, Bernard's assistant, sat beside him, so I commandeered the empty seat across from them.

"Do you have a restaurant preference, Mr. Bringer?" Bernard inquired.

"Surprise me," I replied.

"Very well," he said. "I'll endeavor to do just that."

Not one for too many of the wrong sorts of surprises, I opened my mind to listen in on stray thoughts.

…only hope that he likes what I have to say, came a thought that had to be Bernard's.

…can he look so relaxed after all that's happened?

I nodded at Ms. Yalesin, who responded with a welcoming smile.

…very handsome, came an immediate thought.

After only a brief journey, we stopped in front of the one of the city's most exclusive restaurants. As I waited for Bernard and Yalesin to exit the limo, I spied a non-descript dark sedan just down the street from us. Two men sat in the vehicle, both wearing sunglasses.

I was willing to bet they were government agents, though I couldn't discount the idea that they might also represent the Continuance Corporation.

Rather than take matters into my own hands, I texted Sanders.

Ten minutes later, I sat in a private dining suite with Bernard and Yalesin reviewing a menu that listed numerous exotic dishes; likely at outlandish prices.

"See anything that you like?" Bernard asked. "I highly recommend both the Roasted Duck Magret or the Baked Skate 'En Papillote.'"

In the end, I ordered the largest rib eye on the menu. "Well done, please."

"Well done, sir?" the waiter asked, his disapproval all too evident.

I stared him in the eye with the best hard look that I could muster. "Burn it. Or I will."

Yalesin nearly choked on her mineral water, while Bernard adopted an amused expression.

"Of course, sir," the waiter replied with a hard swallow before slowly backing away from the table.

Was it something I said?

Then again, he'd likely seen the various film footages that the news kept rerunning around the clock.

Looked like the joke was on me, after all.

"Speaking of burning," Bernard began once the waiter had left. "Your performance has been nothing short of amazing. In Seattle, as with here, you appear to have handled an untenable situation with remarkable skill."

"Very charitable of you," I said. "However, the truth is that I almost had my ass handed to me…on both occasions."

"You merely need additional practice," he said offhandedly, as if we were casually discussing my golf game.

Still, I conceded that his suggestion for practice was credible. The little amount that I had done at one of the construction sites outside of town had been remarkably helpful. Hell, in the army, we practiced until we could execute skills in our sleep.

"Nuclegene Corporation can be quite helpful in that area," he offered. "In fact, we can do even more than help you refine your talents; we may even be able to strengthen them. We are, after all, the inventors of the beneficial drug that made your abilities possible in the first place."

While the drug had certainly eradicated my brain cancer,

in my mind the jury was still out on the whole blessing versus curse argument regarding my newfound telekinetic abilities.

"Rest assured, we've already made some excellent progress in understanding some of what's manifested inside of you," Bernard continued. "Though we lost some key researchers and project data in the treatment center explosion, we have already reassigned some of our company's leading engineers and staff onto the project."

"Like Maria Edwards?" I promoted.

Maria had been one of the few survivors of the explosion, a clinical assistant whose chemical engineering knowledge was sorely underutilized for her role in the project. Not to mention that she had been the one person who helped me to understand the nature of my abilities.

I wondered if Bernard had figured out that Maria had also been supplying me with a daily regimen of injections that helped sharpen my abilities.

"Yes. Ms. Edwards is still involved with the project," he confirmed.

"Give it to me straight. I've read through your contract proposal, though it practically gave me headaches. What is it exactly that you're offering me, Bernard?" I asked. "And more to the point, what's the catch if I were to accept?"

He quietly considered me while his assistant impassively watched.

…*important that he accept*, came a useful stray thought.

"Nuclegene Corporation is facing a remarkable opportunity to help shape the course of world events in a number of important ways," he began. "As you've seen firsthand, we've found new ways to treat, and even cure, cancers. But more importantly, we've proven that humans have latent abilities at their grasp, and, as with you, we're very close to activating them on a larger scale."

"What you've done is open Pandora's Box," I countered.

Then it hit me.

"Wait a minute," I said. "Continuance Corporation was also researching those latent abilities dating all the way back to the Cold War. And I can't help wondering if they might've even done it before Nuclegene Corporation."

"You're merely speculating," Bernard said. "Our formula could just as easily have been stolen and reproduced elsewhere after our achievements were already well under way."

I didn't dare add that Maria had already told me about the numerous deaths resulting from Nuclegene's repeated failed attempts at success.

"Ah, then how do you explain the guy who took apart a portion of the city a couple of weeks ago?"

Bernard frowned. "What do you mean?"

"I can tell a beginner from a pro. That guy was adept at what he did," I explained. "Unlike me, he was no amateur. He demonstrated a firm grasp and control of his abilities. That tells me that he'd been using his skills a lot longer than me. No, not using, practicing."

I could see the muscles in Bernard's face tighten.

…does he know, and how much?

"Continuance Corporation," I said.

"What about them?" Bernard asked.

"They beat you to it, didn't they?" I challenged. "They may have stolen Nuclegene's early research, but they were successful first, weren't they?"

Bernard's fallen features said it all.

"It's entirely possible," he conceded. "But it would be better if that information remained between us."

"So, let's be honest with each other, shall we?"

"Fair enough," he said. "After what just took place in this city, the U.S. government is spinning on its head right now. They're afraid that more telekinetics are out there waiting to strike again. Whether on behalf of foreign governments or terrorist organizations, it makes no difference.

"The point is the U.S. wants to lead the way on this and not get left behind. However, other world governments feel that way, as well. This situation has quickly escalated to a battle between world powers, both preeminent and burgeoning," he said. "And right now, our company is the only legitimate organization who can offer the U.S. government what it desires most…foot soldiers with telekinetic abilities."

"And what if an organization like Continuance wants to compete with you?" I asked.

"By long-standing tradition, the U.S. doesn't negotiate with terrorists," he replied.

"Yeah, right," I said. "You ever heard of Iran-Contra? The U.S. may not officially negotiate with terrorist groups, but they damned sure cut deals with them on occasion. In my experience, political expediency trumps ideology nearly every time."

"Fair enough. However, in this case, let's say for the sake of argument that I'm right," he said. "If Continuance is out of the equation, per say."

"Based upon what we know, which I believe isn't a helluva lot, that might leave only your company then," I said.

He nodded. "That's right, Mr. Bringer. Nuclegene Corporation is the only company who's solely positioned to supply the U.S. with what it wants most."

"What's to keep old Uncle Sam from taking your formulas and research from you? Developing it themselves?" I asked.

He shook his head. "They won't. It's too expensive a venture for them. Besides, there are all of those unpleasant rules and regulations they'd have to negotiate."

I hated to admit that he was probably right about that.

"No, the government will let us continue unabated," he said. "They'll permit us take the risks and front the expense, plus they'll have plausible deniability if things go horribly wrong. Nuclegene would be their scapegoat."

"Things have already gone horribly wrong," I said. "So, I'll ask again, just what are you expecting from me?"

He smiled. "Join our Nuclegene family," he said. "Let us study you and your abilities to help us refine our replication process."

"In case you hadn't noticed, I'm a little preoccupied with working alongside the FBI right now," I said. "Plus, Continuance made the mistake of threatening my family, and I plan to bring them to account for that."

"I don't see that as a problem," he said. "The government is anxious to take advantage of someone with your abilities. I'm sure that a mutually-beneficial arrangement can be established between all parties."

"I'm working with them already," I said.

"Yes, working perhaps, but for no compensation whatsoever," he countered. "By contrast, we'll make it worth your while to come aboard. And let's be frank, Mr. Bringer, the U.S government's radar is rather full at this time with much larger concerns. They don't exactly have you or your family's best interests at heart."

"And you do?" I challenged.

"Unlike the government, we happen to think that you're the most important person on the planet right now," he said.

"On the contrary, the government seems rather interested in me as of late," I said.

"Because they need you. You're their only hope against the unknown telekinetic threat. Of course, they're equally scared about what you can do, or what you may grow to become," he said. "Granted, you're not proving to be an overt threat in their eyes quite yet. Right now, you're an asset."

"I've already proven quite helpful to them," I said.

"They may appreciate your assistance, but they're hardly focused on meeting your needs or even investing in a commitment to you for compensation of any kind.

"For example, what would happen if you became injured during your exploits? I suspect that the prospects of your meager employment with the tag agency is all but finished, which changes your eligibility status as a prospective resident in Nevis Corners. Then consider how long you can maintain even a Spartan lifestyle with no source of income," he challenged. "With Nuclegene, your every need would be our concern. We can provide you with a full-featured and sizeable compensation package. And there are other favorable terms. For example, we can, and will, protect your family, Mr. Bringer."

I almost laughed. "Seriously? You expect to protect them from somebody like me, or worse?"

"A reasonable challenge," he replied. "However, at least we will do far better than a sole patrol officer in a vehicle parked outside of your family's house."

Something in the way that he said that irritated me. "Just how closely has your company been keeping an eye on me and my family?"

He appeared momentarily unsettled. "I can assure you that we have maintained a courteous and respectful distance from you and your family," he carefully replied. "Although I can well imagine that Continuance Corporation and agencies within our government, or other governments for that matter, might be tracking you and your relatives. Yet another reason to accept my company's offer of protection. Think of the array of resources that we can place at your disposal."

Before I could say more, our food arrived, and aside from small talk, I spent the majority of the meal silently contemplating what was said, including topics relating to the continuing threats to my family.

My appearance on the world stage, along with my agitation to Continuance, was the reason that my family had become a target. If anything happened to my parents, my sister or her husband and children, I'd never forgive myself.

But I felt ill-equipped to negotiate on any prospective contract until I had time to discuss it with Sanders.

She was not only smart, but perhaps savvier than anyone I knew. And I trusted her advice.

By the time we finished eating, I realized that I needed to stall for more time. Not surprisingly, I didn't need to read Bernard's mind to know that he was anxious for my decision. If I hadn't reminded him of my six o'clock meeting, he might have sat there all evening pressuring to convince me.

"Give me a couple of days," I said. "I'll give you a decision by this Friday."

He nodded, but I could tell he was disappointed. He appeared reflective as we walked outside to the waiting limousine.

"Nuclegene Corporation is receiving significant pressure from the government. They're insistent about seeing our project come to fruition again with live subjects," he said.

"They want people to deploy into the field," I said.

"Very perceptive, Mr. Bringer," he said.

"It's less perception and more simply field tactics," I said.

"In case you hadn't noticed, Mr. Bringer, we have a security-conscious administration in the White House. And a primary focus of theirs is perception, particularly when it comes to national security," he said, lightly rubbing the opposing tips of his fingers against one other. "Add to that, the President's party narrowly controls both houses of Congress. They can't afford any national security mistakes on their watch; not with mid-term elections coming up next year. There's much more riding on this than you may realize; much more than merely money.

"What I'm offering you, Mr. Bringer, is not only an opportunity to be part of something lucrative, but something historic," he said.

My eyes narrowed. "What exactly is the government promising your company, Mr. Bernard?"

His response ended upon the arrival of Agents Sanders and Foster, who had pulled up behind the limo in their government-issued sedan.

I scanned the immediate area for the vehicle that I had spotted when we arrived. "Great timing, guys. Trouble?" I asked as they exited their sedan.

"Nope," Foster said. "We're clear here."

"Denton was afraid that you might forget our appointment," Sanders said.

I turned to Mr. Bernard to shake his hand.

"Thanks for dinner, Mr. Bernard, but I'm afraid I have to go now," I offered. "I enjoyed our chat."

"As did I," he replied, handing a business card to me. "Please think seriously about what we talked about. My personal number is on the card, so please call me anytime, day or night. At the very least, I hope to hear from you by Friday."

I pocketed his card. "I don't know any other way to take this but seriously. Either way, as promised, you'll have my answer by Friday."

* * *

As Foster and Sanders sat up front, I sat in the back seat staring out the side window mulling over everything Bernard had said during dinner.

"Did you intercept whoever was sitting in that car down the street from the restaurant" I asked.

"Nope," Foster replied. "They had already left the area by the time our folks arrived on scene."

I couldn't help but wonder who 'they' might be. CIA, perhaps? Continuance?

It was enough to make a person paranoid.

One of my army buddies had once told me, "Just because you're paranoid doesn't mean that someone's not out to get you."

"How was your dinner?" Sanders asked.

I broke from my reverie. "Great," I replied. "Had a tasty well-done filet. How about you?"

"Something healthy. Nothing you'd probably ever eat," she replied dryly. "So, did he woo you again?"

I saw Foster's curious gaze in the rearview mirror.

"Yeah, he said something about the latest Republican plan to outsource the FBI, and he asked if I wanted to be in on the ground floor of the civilian contract."

Sanders glared back over her shoulder at me.

"He wants my answer soon," I said. "I need you to be in a reading mood, and sooner rather than later."

"Fair enough," she said. "I'll start reading tonight."

CHAPTER 3

Conference rooms are a lot like the Gulag; they make me feel trapped and I can feel my life wasting away in them.

The conference room we entered was smaller and more functional, and a lot less corporate looking, than the one we had been in earlier that day, but it was still a conference room. The chief of police for Nevis Corners sat near the head of the table alongside NSA Deputy Director Bob Tevin and FBI Deputy Director Mark Wainright.

Chuck Denton and a host of FBI agents were there, as well as a couple of high-ranking police officials and a handful of NSA agents.

The group filled the room to capacity.

"Cutting it kind of close, aren't you, Agent Sanders?" Wainright asked, looking down at his watch.

"Well, Bringer had a very important dinner to attend," she quipped.

Wainright looked at me, but I merely shrugged.

"What can I say? I'm in high demand nowadays," I said.

"We should probably start this meeting," the Chief urged. "It's getting late and we're already a little behind schedule. And some of us haven't had the opportunity to break for dinner yet."

I ignored the hard look he gave me.

"Ladies and gentlemen, you are officially members of a

joint FBI/NSA taskforce called TASIT, the Telekinetic Anti-terrorism Surveillance and Interdiction Taskforce," Wainright began. "Deputy Director Tevin and I have full co-operational command of this taskforce, which will be based in Nevis Corners, and more specifically, in this building."

"That is, until your FBI offices in their former location are no longer exposed to the elements," Tevin quipped.

A number of chuckles proliferated throughout the room as Wainright shook his head.

"There is that," he conceded. "That aside, I realize that our team was put together in a rather hasty, impromptu fashion, but time is a rare luxury in unique situations such as this. The severity of what we're now facing required a near-instantaneous reaction on the government's part, so we'll all need to observe patience as we get up to speed together.

"Some of you may already be familiar with Mr. Logan Bringer from his assistance to the FBI on the Wallace Building bombing investigation, though others have likely become acutely aware of him and his unique set of abilities during recent events. Once again, Mr. Bringer has graciously offered to volunteer his services to us."

Wainright politely nodded in my direction and I responded in kind, though I didn't like his use of the word 'volunteer.'

"Pardon me, Deputy Director," interrupted one NSA agent. "Could one of you please clarify what Mr. Bringer's exact role and status is with this taskforce?"

"At this time, Mr. Bringer is a VIP civilian operating under the protection of the FBI," Wainright clarified, glancing over at me in a meaningful manner.

Had he learned of my meeting with Clive Bernard?

Tevin leaned forward. "We in the NSA extend our appreciation to Mr. Bringer. The remainder of our team will take further shape over time. Resources will be added or removed as deemed necessary. However, our central concern will remain focused on locating and immobilizing whatever threats we may encounter as we proceed with our investigations."

As I listened to the briefing, it sounded familiar, like the numerous situational briefings that I had sat through in the military. Approaching boredom, during the drone of formalities, my thoughts wandered to my earlier conversation with Clive Bernard.

Bernard had made a number of good points in our discussion, not the least of which was the need to secure adequate protection for my family during this ordeal. While I shared his opinion that the authorities were less concerned with diligently protecting them, I nevertheless didn't like the idea of getting in bed with the same company whose researchers had used me as an involuntary, overgrown guinea pig during my cancer treatments.

One thing was certain: I had a big decision to make and, as Wainright had just stated, the luxury of time wasn't mine.

When the briefing ended, I barreled out of the room. I felt pensive and my mind filled with a host of concerns, ranging from my family to paying my monthly bills with no active income source.

I had barely made it to the elevator at the end of the hallway when I heard, "Bringer! Wait up."

I turned to see Sanders and Denton quick-stepping after me.

"You in a hurry to get somewhere?" Denton asked.

"Yeah, home," I replied. "I hear some cold beers in my fridge calling to me, as well as a pillow on my bed."

"I'll drop you off," Sanders said.

I punched the button to call for an elevator car.

Upon its arrival, the three of us stepped inside and, as the doors partially closed, a hand grabbed at one of them and Deputy Director Wainright stepped inside. He waited until the doors shut to say anything.

"Listen, there's something I wanted to mention to you three, but I didn't want to say it in front of everyone else," he began. "Bringer, I think it would be a good idea if you don't talk to too many people about the true scope of your abilities.

In fact, let's just keep it between the four of us."

Sanders and I exchanged a curious look.

"Makes sense, but why the urgency?" I asked.

"To be honest, there's a large number of interested parties focused on you right now, and I'd rather we don't add to your allure," he said.

"Like who?" I asked.

"Well, the military, for one," he said. "I was in a recent meeting with members of the Joint Chiefs of Staff and a couple of them voiced interest in you."

I frowned. I wasn't sure I wanted back into the military under my current circumstances, particularly if some power-hungry general had his sights on me.

I opened my mind and heard multiple voices chime in.

…never heard him talk like this, came one voice.

…glad I'm just an agent at times like this, came another.

…putting my cards on the table. Hope Bringer will trust me.

"In addition, word has it that you've received a job offer from Nuclegene," he added.

"Who'd you hear that from?" Sanders asked.

"Believe it or not, one of those same generals," he replied. "Listen, I realize it's none of my business, but it might not be a bad idea for you to consider their offer."

I frowned. "Why would you care?"

"I like you, Bringer, and I appreciate all you've done," he said. "But I've been in this business a long time, and I've seen people get used…badly sometimes."

"Why not make me an offer yourself?"

He arched one brow. "Honestly? I'm not sure the agency would give you a fair shake."

Both Denton and Sanders looked at him with surprise, but he shrugged.

"Listen, Bringer, I've asked you to trust me, but keep in mind that I'm not the top dog in our agency. And the scary truth is, I don't necessarily trust the politics above me right now, if you catch my meaning."

The elevator doors opened and Wainright reached out to

shake my hand.

"Just think about what I said. Look, we haven't known each other all that long, and I realize that you don't have any reason to fully trust me yet, either," he said. "But I hope to secure your trust over time. You're a good egg in my book, and I'd hate to see the system eat you up."

I shook his hand. "Thanks."

Wainright nodded to Sanders and Denton and then walked away.

"What the hell do you think prompted that?" Denton asked.

"I don't know," I said. "But I'm damned sure gonna keep what he said in mind."

We no sooner took five steps away from the elevator when a door burst open behind us.

I turned, expecting trouble, but saw Deputy Director Tevin waving and hurrying to catch up with us.

"Hey, wait!" he called.

He seemed almost out of breath as he placed a small briefcase onto the floor beside him.

"Did you just run downstairs?" Sanders asked.

"Yeah," he huffed. "Couldn't catch the elevator...but had...to talk to you."

"You want to sit down?" Denton asked.

"Nah, I'm okay," he said, finally taking in a deep breath and letting it out. "I've spent too many years behind a desk, I think."

"You ever hear of a treadmill?" I asked.

"Funny, Bringer," he said. "Listen, I need to talk to you three, but I—"

"Didn't want to say anything in front of everyone else?" I asked.

His expression was priceless. "Yeah, how did you know? Do you read minds or something?"

"Me? Nah," I said.

To their credit, both Sanders and Denton adopted great poker faces.

Then I opened my mind again.

...good idea speaking out in the open like this?

...have any idea if he'll believe what I have to say, but I've got to try.

...kick him in the balls if he's reading my thoughts right now.

I carefully avoided eye contact with Sanders.

"What were you going to tell us?" Denton asked.

Tevin looked around and then focused his attention on me.

"Bringer, I've got word that there's some politicians, and even the CIA, with their eyes on you," he said. "You need to be careful who you trust with, shall we say, sensitive information about yourself."

"Politicians and the CIA?" Sanders demanded.

"Yes, and there may be others," he replied. "Though I'm not privy in all circles, I will say that a couple of the Joint Chiefs mentioned interest in you, as well. That was during a recent high-level meeting that included some of the President's cabinet."

I looked at Sanders and then Denton, who each had grave expressions on their faces.

"You should also know that I've also heard from two senators that Nuclegene has offered you a job," he added.

"Which senators?" Sanders asked.

He looked at her. "Ben Conway, a republican from Utah, and Penelope Savage, senator from Oklahoma."

"Those are both key members of the Freedom Party," Denton said.

Great. More ultraconservative nutjobs.

"Why would they have an interest in Bringer's employment options?" Denton asked.

"Nevis Wallace, the founder of Nuclegene Corporation, is a key campaign contributor to Senator Conway, who was a co-author of the Land Reclamation and Investment in America Act," Tevin said.

"Without which, Nevis Corners wouldn't have been established," Sanders said.

"Precisely," Tevin said.

"Geez. Tell me again then why I'd want to get into bed with Nuclegene."

"They might be able to shelter you from some undesirable influencers," Tevin replied. "But you'd still need to be careful with them, as well."

I rubbed my temples with my fingertips. "This is getting friggin' confusing fast."

"You'd practically need a program to keep track of all these players and their connections," Denton said.

"Why are you telling me all of this?" I asked. "What's your angle?"

I listened in for any stray thoughts.

...dangerous time for us all.

"You three need to understand that, even with what little information I've managed to piece together, there's a lot of unknowns surrounding Continuance Corporation, telekinetic research, and our government's interest in both," Tevin said. "Right now, Bringer, you're the only person in this country who can even remotely challenge any other telekinetic adversaries. We can't afford for you to become compromised."

"Listen, are you sure you should be saying this in the middle of a public lobby?" Denton asked.

Tevin shrugged. "Of course. I'm NSA. I always think about that. The best place to talk is where nobody expects you to. But we shouldn't talk much longer or we will earn unwanted attention."

His cool sense of confidence was impressive, yet another reason I liked him.

"What do you recommend?" I asked.

Tevin looked me straight in the eye. "There's a lot of unknowns right now, and we need to be careful who we trust. If you didn't mind, for the time being I'd like to keep the scope of your abilities and any revelations you might encounter along the way between the four of us. We should be cautious about what we share, even with our own TASIT team members. And Sanders, I like Wainright, but I'm still not sure which side he falls on just yet."

I nodded. "Okay, but I think there's someone that you should talk to, and soon." I looked at Denton and Sanders. "Am I right?"

They both nodded.

"I'll go get him," Sanders said. "He may even still be in the building."

"Who?" Tevin asked.

"You'll see," I said.

Sanders hurried across the lobby in the direction that Wainright had headed earlier.

Denton helped me struggle through small talk for a few minutes until Sanders strode back across the lobby with Wainright in tow.

I caught Tevin's frown as Wainright approached.

"Wainright?" Tevin asked.

"Yep," I replied. "I think you and Wainright here will find discussing what each of you said to us very enlightening. And while I'm thinking about it, were you two separated at birth or something?"

Both men appeared slightly confused.

"Don't you two already talk?" I asked.

"Both of you do seem awfully chummy in meetings," Sanders added.

"Well, sure, we do see eye to eye on a lot of things, I think," Wainright said. "But, I mean, this. We haven't exactly talked much about—well, you know."

Tevin looked at me. "You sure about this, Bringer?"

I pointed to my head meaningfully. "Trust me, gentlemen. I have skills. You should talk more. And we need all the help we can get, right?"

"Bringer's right," Sanders added. "Don't let paranoia separate you from potential allies."

Both men appeared intrigued.

"All right, then. Coffee, Tevin?" Wainright asked.

He looked at his watch. "It's nearly eight o'clock now.

44

How about Cuba Libre instead?"

Wainright shrugged. "Well, Cuba's not yet free, but I'd take the drink. Throw in a steak and you've got a deal."

"Done," Tevin agreed.

They both turned and walked away from us.

"Oh, and Wainright, just for the record, the Bay of Pigs isn't on us," Tevin said as he walked alongside Wainright. "That was a CIA fiasco, not NSA."

"True enough. Suffice to say, we can always prod Special Agent Prichard about it at our next meeting," Wainright conceded.

Tevin laughed. "Oh, I like how you think."

As we watched them, I couldn't help thinking that they looked like two future brothers in arms. At least, I was convinced that we needed them to reach that point.

I had learned to trust my instincts; it had frequently saved my life in combat situations. And while I was never a pessimist, I had the oddest feeling that things were about to turn shitty.

Sanders shook her head. "Well, now I've seen everything, Bringer. You actually can bring people together."

Denton chuckled, breaking me from my grim thoughts.

"Go ahead, get your digs in now," I said. "Just don't forget that you've got a lot of dry reading ahead of you tonight, Sanders."

"Don't push your luck," she warned.

I sure as hell wasn't about to do that.

I couldn't afford to.

CHAPTER 4

The next morning, Sanders appeared at my door not long after I awoke. I had remembered to actually set my alarm, as well as start the coffee maker.

She handed me a small sack as she strolled past me, just like she owned the place.

"Breakfast is on me this morning," she said.

She made her way to the dining room and slapped a thick sheaf of paperwork and a steno pad onto the table.

"Long night?" I asked.

"Long enough," she said. "Mm, coffee."

As she raided my cabinets for a coffee mug, I sat down at the table and peeked inside.

"What magical treats await me?" I asked. "Breakfast biscuits, maybe?"

Instead of sausage and egg biscuits, I found, to my dismay, containers of piping hot oatmeal, yogurt with granola, and fruit smoothies.

"What's all this?"

She sat down across from me and savored a sip of coffee.

"That is my reward for spending half the night pouring over your contract," she replied.

"This is a reward?" I asked. "Wait, there's two of everything in here."

"Oh, yes, Bringer," she said. "Not only do I get to enjoy a

nice breakfast, but I get to watch you eat yours, too."

I looked up at her and noted her wicked smile. Admittedly, it was kind of sexy.

"You've been letting your diet slip," she said. "And now it's time for restitution. I need you to stay alive long enough to stop Nuclegene."

I grimaced. "You're really evil."

"Oh, you have no idea," she said.

Admittedly, there was a time not so long ago when I had been a much healthier eater. Perhaps it was time to moderate a bit.

"I used to eat stuff like this, you know," I said.

"What happened?" she asked, stirring her oatmeal.

"My taste buds got bored," I replied, quickly thumbing through the contract, noting highlights, notes in the margins, and lots of little sticky notes placed in various locations throughout.

She reached out toward a stack of information to retrieve her steno pad. "Now, we'll go over my notes while you eat your breakfast."

I shriveled up my nose as I opened the oatmeal container.

"Every bite or I stop talking," she said. "Have you had your morning injection yet?"

"Uh, not yet," I replied. "I've just barely woken up."

She got up and went to the refrigerator to retrieve the formula that Maria had concocted for me.

Despite the fact that Sanders had grown up helping her father in a local neighborhood clinic, I wasn't sure I wanted her sticking me with needles when she was obviously feeling a sadistic streak.

She tapped the end of the syringe and thumbed the plunger. "Which arm today, Bringer?"

* * *

After breakfast, I placed a call to Clive Bernard's mobile phone, and he was anxious to meet with me.

Scarcely two hours later, I sat in his office, awaiting his arrival.

I reached inside my sport jacket pocket for the notes that I had scribbled during my so-called breakfast, which admittedly had been tastier than I had anticipated.

In addition, Sanders had goaded me into dressing up for the meeting. I momentarily reflected on the unusual influence she was having on me as of late.

"My apologies for the delay, Mr. Bringer," Bernard said, entering the office with two ladies in tow.

He shook my hand with enthusiasm.

"This is Ms. Judy Wren. She's from Legal Affairs," he said. "And, of course, you already know Ms. Yalesin."

Each of us took seats around a nearby conference table.

"I'm so happy that you decided to accept Nuclegene's offer," Bernard said. "I hope you'll agree, this is a wonderful opportunity for us both."

"Yes, but I'd like to negotiate some changes to the contract before I'm willing to sign."

Bernard's expression darkened. "That's a bit unexpected, given how generous our terms are, but certainly we can discuss them."

"But then, you already anticipated that, or why else would Ms. Wren be joining us?"

Bernard offered a tight smile. "Very perceptive of you."

I glanced down at my notes and opened my mind to catch stray thoughts.

...wonder who's coached him?

"Let's begin with corporate surveillance," I said. "I don't like people shadowing me, so let's just consider me off-limits, moving forward."

Bernard frowned. "Are you being followed? I can assure you that it's nobody from Nuclegene."

He looked at Ms. Yalesin, who shrugged and shook her head.

"Well, that's one possibility down. Either way, I'll take care of the problem," I said.

"As you say," he replied. "Other concerns?"

"Next, in the section covering the formation of a medical support team, I want a clause added stipulating that Maria Edwards is to head the team and has final say on team member selection and coordination."

"Ms. Edwards—"

"Is the closest thing you have to an expert," I interrupted. "And I trust her."

He nodded and glanced at Ms. Yalesin. "Very well. Next?"

"The contract indicates the preferred location of residence for my family to be Nevis Corners, specifically in a corporate housing complex," I said.

"It's best for their protection," Bernard replied.

"Our housing is custom-built with many amenities, including furnishings, if desired," Yalesin explained. "And our on-site security patrols a secured outer perimeter. We also have high-quality in-addition services for residents' convenience."

"Ms. Yalesin is one of our residents and can attest to our residency experience," Bernard added.

"I'm sure, but I want it left up to my family as to whether or not they relocate," I said. "Insert language into the contract specifying that your best security services will be provided, no matter the location; all subject to my approval and satisfaction."

Bernard took a deep breath and slowly exhaled. "Fine. Done."

Ms. Yalesin appeared surprised, while Ms. Wren calmly took notes.

"There's a benefits section where medical care is simply called 'Corporate Complete.' What does that mean, exactly?"

"Mr. Bringer, you're the only successful, surviving member from our telekinetic research project," Bernard said. "Our teams of doctors and specialists will see to your every medical need, from common colds to any advanced medical treatments you may require. Naturally, a regimented testing and examination process will be conducted as part of our continuing research and your continued well-being."

"I'm not going to become a lab rat," I insisted.

"Perish the thought," Bernard assured me.

"Fine, but only if all activities will be overseen and preapproved by Maria Edwards."

"You're placing a lot of your welfare into the hands of someone who isn't exactly experienced with that level of responsibility," Bernard cautioned.

"Then you need to make sure she's prepared for it," I said. "And she and her family had better receive the same protection you'd give my family, including a salary commensurate with her responsibilities. Of course, she needs to be able to negotiate that for herself."

Bernard appeared momentarily unsettled, but quickly regained his composure.

"Mr. Bernard, we'll need to review these and run them by—" Wren said.

He held up his hand. "Mr. Bringer drives a hard bargain, but I'm prepared to meet his demands. We'll adjust his contract terms."

"There are two more issues, Mr. Bernard," I said.

"Really?" he asked.

"I want the contract to reflect that I only receive my marching orders from you," I said.

Bernard nodded. "I see the efficacy of that, though it will need to include Nevis Wallace, as well."

My eyebrows rose at that. "I thought that Nevis Wallace was only the corporation's founder and chairman of the board; a figurehead nowadays. He still takes an active role in day-to-day operational activities?"

"You'd be surprised how active his hand is in corporate activities," Bernard said. "Naturally, our intent is to subcontract your services to the FBI, which means you're under their immediate stewardship. However, your primary oversight will be from me or Mr. Wallace."

That was interesting.

"I see," I said. "All right."

"You had one more item?" Bernard asked.

"Yes, you'll need to add a conscientious objection clause," I said.

All three of them appeared shocked, though not so many years ago the mere mention of such a thing would have seemed equally surprising to me.

Since then, my values had matured considerably.

"Conscientious objection? I must say, I'm rather astonished to hear something like that from a former soldier like you," Bernard said.

I shrugged. "I've seen and learned a lot since then. Let's say this is a deal-breaker of sorts."

"Objection to what, precisely?" he asked.

"Anything," I said. "Anything I deem unconscionable."

Bernard leaned back in his conference chair and steepled his fingertips against each other before him.

"This is…highly unusual," he said.

"In my twenty years of experience with Nuclegene, it's absolutely unprecedented," Ms. Wren added.

Then I heard the thoughts begin to flow.

…*does he think he is?*

…*put Mr. Bernard in a difficult situation.*

…*better let Wallace handle this*, came a prominent stray thought.

Bernard rose from his chair and made his way over to his desk. He picked up his phone receiver and dialed.

"Sorry to bother you, Mr. Wallace," he said. "No, sir, we're still negotiating. There's a sticky point. Now? Yes, sir."

He reached down to press a button on his phone base and hung up the receiver.

A widescreen video display at the head of the conference room came on to reveal a white-haired old man in a stately looking business suit, sitting at a desk before a scenic ocean view.

Despite his obvious advanced age, his blue eyes still held a piercing quality.

"Hello, Mr. Bringer. Thank you for coming in to meet

with us today," announced the man with a determined and steady voice. "My name is Nevis Wallace, founding father of Nuclegene Corporation.

"I apologize for not meeting you in person, but I'm currently in the Mediterranean on important corporate business. And since I wasn't certain if you'd entertain our offer, I didn't see the need to remain stateside," he said. "What seems to be, as Mr. Bernard puts it, the sticky point?"

"Hello, Mr. Wallace," I offered. "Our current topic revolves around conscientious objection."

"Hm. Interesting," he said. "What is it, precisely, that you conscientiously object to?"

"Nothing, yet," I replied. "But I'd like the opportunity to make that determination, if necessary, in the future."

"Ah, but not merely to determine, rather to declare," he clarified.

"True."

"Mr. Bernard, why not bring me up on the other items of negotiation," Wallace prompted.

As Bernard relayed our previous discussion items, Wallace patiently listened, nodding here and there. I desperately wished that I could poll the old man's thoughts from a distance.

But then, it occurred to me that over the span of thousands of miles, the additional millions of minds of feedback would probably drive me insane.

"Mr. Bringer," said Wallace. "I hope you realize and appreciate how much effort this company—my company—is engaged in to accommodate you. Some of your stipulations are unusual, to say the least."

"Mr. Wallace, I do indeed appreciate your company's consideration," I conceded, staring intently at him onscreen. "However, I believe you'd agree that these are unusual and quite dangerous times for both your company and the rest of the nation."

The sober expression on Bernard's face was priceless.

"Undoubtedly. You understand that better than most

anyone, I'd venture," Wallace agreed with a knowing look. "Well, Mr. Bringer, you do drive a hard bargain, but I'll agree to your stipulations, including your right of conscientious objection. All that I ask is, should the situation arise to exercise that particular clause, that you will permit either me or Mr. Bernard the opportunity to discuss the matter."

"That sounds reasonable enough," I conceded.

"Good. That being said, and unless you have any further concerns, I believe we have a deal, Mr. Bringer," Wallace said. "Mr. Bernard and his team will draw up the final contract paperwork for us."

"That sounds like a wrap for me, as well," I said.

"Congratulations and welcome to Nuclegene Corporation, Mr. Bringer," Wallace said. "Do shake his hand for me, won't you Clive?"

"My pleasure, sir," Bernard said, reaching out to firmly grasp my hand. "Welcome to Nuclegene, Mr. Bringer."

A flurry of emotionally charged thoughts filled the air around me.

…entirely unbelievable.

…never thought I'd see something like this.

…historic occasion for us.

"Call me Logan," I said, returning Bernard's firm grip.

"Logan, just for contractual purposes, when can you start?" asked Wallace.

I smiled. "I believe I just did."

Bernard turned toward Yalesin and Wren.

"I need contracts, now. Top priority, no delays on this. Bring in everyone that's required to get this done asap," Bernard ordered. "I'll need the federal paperwork for the FBI, as well."

"Certainly, Mr. Bernard. I'll also schedule his two-day corporate orientation immediately," Ms. Wren replied.

"What? Two days?" I asked. "I'll just take the Cliff's Notes version, if you don't mind."

Bernard held up his hand. "Mr. Bringer is correct. We're working under very time-critical circumstances here, so we'll dispense with the usual formalities."

"I see," said Ms. Wren, obviously displeased.

My mobile phone rang and I whipped it out of my pocket. It was Sanders.

"Bringer," I said. "What's up?"

"I know you're probably in the middle of your meeting, but something important just fell into our laps," Sanders said.

"Fell?"

"Sorry, figure of speech," she said. "But it's big, and you'd better get down to the office fast."

"Be right there," I promised.

"Is everything okay, Mr. Bringer?" Bernard inquired.

"I'm sorry, but I've really gotta run."

"Logan," prompted Nevis Wallace.

"Yes, sir?" I asked, turning toward the monitor.

"I admire your sense of commitment, and I suspect there's no time for delay," Wallace said. "Due to the situation at hand, we'll need to proceed under a handshake agreement. But rest assured, you're a Nuclegene man now. We're one of the most powerful companies in the world, and we don't stand still while others vacillate or cower. You're our company's right hand now, and you have the discretion to use either a handshake or a fist."

I held out my open palm and conjured fire above it. The room fell silent and I knew I had everyone's rapt attention; even the old man's eyes widened and he leaned forward as if compelling his body to enter through the wall-mounted display.

"Sometimes, I use neither a handshake nor a fist," I said. "For those who threaten me or my family, I have other means at my disposal."

"Incredible," Wallace muttered.

I waved my hand, extinguishing the flames.

The old man chuckled. "Well, I suppose you shouldn't have to worry about any breach of contract on our part, then."

Much to my surprise, I found the guy somewhat

charismatic.

"And I don't do hidden agendas," I said.

Wallace's eyes narrowed. "Good. You'll find that I don't either, Mr. Bringer. My agenda is keeping this company intact and flourishing, while also assisting in securing our country's national security. That's a big job for one man, even one as powerful as you."

I nodded. "I'm fine with those objectives, though the order may vary by the situation. However, my primary objective is the safety of my family and eliminating any threats to them."

"Understood," Wallace said. "Fortunately, those appear to be mutually inclusive objectives for us. Let's hope that continues, for both our benefits. In the meantime, proceed as you see fit, but please check in with Mr. Bernard, or me if he's not available, to keep us appraised of your progress. In the immediate future, and per your agreement, you'll be subcontracted to the FBI."

"Sounds fine," I said with a nod.

I hastily shook Bernard's hand before barreling out of his office toward the elevator.

I left the meeting with a hopeful sense that at least a few things in my life were finally falling into place at a manageable level.

Experience had taught me that was typically about the time that everything went to hell.

But most of all, I hoped that I hadn't just sold my soul to the devil.

CHAPTER 5

When I walked through the FBI office doors, everyone looked up with expectant expressions.

Agent Denton stepped outside of his office and rested his hands atop his waist. "Sorry to interrupt you on draft day, Bringer. I hope we didn't rush you during your stock options negotiation. Did they give you a healthy signing bonus?"

I grinned and flipped him my middle finger, resulting in sporadic laughter throughout the office.

"What's going on?" I asked.

Denton inclined his head toward his office door. "In here."

Sanders looked up with an expectant look. "Well? How did it go?"

I held my arms wide open. "You're looking at your newest contract employee."

Wainright and Tevin were also there, and joined Denton in shaking my hand and congratulating me. Sanders seemed especially pleased.

"How was the steak and rum dinner?" I asked Wainright and Tevin.

"A good time was had by all," Wainright replied.

"A good meeting of the minds, as well," Tevin added.

"Good all around," I said. Then I turned my attention to Sanders. "While I'm at it, thanks for the contract advice,

Sanders," I said. "You're even better than having an agent on retainer."

She flashing me a cute, and rather rare, smile. "Hey, I am a federal agent, thank you. But your sentiments are appreciated and, as such, you owe me the industry standard fifteen percent of your contract value."

I shook my head. In all honesty, at that moment, I wanted to give her a lot more than fifteen percent…and it had nothing to do with money.

Denton cleared his throat. "We better get to it now. This could be the break we've been waiting for."

He definitely had my attention. "What sort of break?"

"An American agent in Europe made contact with a Russian investigative reporter out of Moscow who witnessed an unsettling event at an abandoned mental institution in Belarus," Tevin explained. "Fortunately, she took video of what she saw. Even better, the agent she made contact with was NSA and not CIA, otherwise we probably wouldn't have a crack at it this yet."

"CIA's keeping secrets from us now?" Sanders asked.

Tevin shrugged. "They always have. It's been a pissing contest between us and them for some time now. However, it's become even worse since the last presidential election."

"I thought policy under Homeland Security after 911 changed all that," I said.

"Yeah, but 911 was a long time ago. When it comes to interagency rivalries, policy and practice are two different things," he replied. "That aside, things changed a lot soon after President Graydon took office. He seems to have a different vision regarding his favorite federal agencies."

It figures.

I couldn't help wondering if the Wallace Building explosion could've been thwarted if all the government's intelligence agencies had been working together from the start.

The door to Denton's office opened and a young man who couldn't have been older than his mid-twenties peeked inside.

"Sorry to interrupt, but I've processed the new intelligence and it's ready for your review," he said.

"Agent Wilson's one of mine," Tevin said. "Route it to the main conference room, son."

"Yes, sir," he replied.

We'd no sooner closed the door to the conference room than Agent Wilson brought up a grainy video image on the widescreen mounted on the wall. It was past dusk. A grayish, decrepit-looking building sat amidst overgrown hedges and encroaching trees.

"What are we looking at?" Tevin asked.

"This is the abandoned mental asylum outside of Minsk, Belarus," Wilson replied. "I've run it through filtering software to maximize image and sound clarity."

"That place?" I insisted. "It looks like something post-apocalyptic."

"Yeah, I'd have to agree with you on that," Denton said.

Wilson increased the volume and we heard breathing, rustling leaves, and gruff voices shouting in the distance.

The person taking the video, a woman by the sound, muttered something indistinguishable.

"Russian, you said?" I asked.

"Yes," Tevin replied.

"Her name is Nika Veselov. She said she was on the north side of the building," Wilson said. "She's also the contact who provided the video."

A bright flash illuminated every visible window around the building and the crackle of energy sizzled, drowning out all other sounds.

Part of the roof exploded outward as flames shot in all directions from various breaches.

The frame momentarily froze before the image jerked back and forth, and then resumed toward the building.

More shouts in the distance preceded a high-pitched sound and another flash of white light that pierced into the sky through the roof and windows.

A woman cursed as the windows burst and flames jetted from the openings.

The video turned jerky again and the image rotated in what must have been the opposite direction.

I almost got nauseous watching branches slap at the videographer as she barreled through the brush.

As loud explosions permeated the audio, the woman eventually fell forward. The ground loomed large and a resounding crashing noise abruptly ceased.

"That's it," Agent Wilson said. "Veselov said she was too scared to do anything more than hold her camera and run."

"How old is the video?" Wainright asked.

"Seventeen days," Wilson replied.

"Why did she turn this over to us?" Sanders asked.

"We weren't her first choice," Wilson replied. "She's a patriot and she first looked into the possibility that it was a secret Russian government research project."

"And?" Tevin pressed.

"She said that, as closely as she could determine, it wasn't," Wilson said.

"Why did she decide to seek out one of our agents?" Tevin asked. "Let me see the report."

Wilson handed him a red folder filled with printouts, which Tevin immediately began thumbing through. "According to Veselov, the Russians weren't pleased with her footage. She feared for her life and sought our assistance."

"I don't see how the video helps us, except maybe that they hid someone there. What she captured was probably caused by the Balkan-sounding guy I faced off with downtown," I said.

"No, can't be," Sanders insisted, shaking her head.

"Why the hell not?" I asked.

She gave me a flat stare. "Because the video is seventeen days old. That's the same day you were tearing up Nevis Corners with that telekinetic. It couldn't have been him."

Her revelation hit me like a cold splash of water.

"If that's true, then just as we feared, there's more

telekinetics out there somewhere," Wainright concluded. "And based upon the video, they don't appear too happy."

"According to this field report, after Veselov saw the news coverage of Bringer's showdown with the telekinetic, she knew there had to be a connection between that and what she witnessed," Tevin said, flipping through pages in a flurry. "She was confident enough that she bargained for asylum in the United States and full citizenship in exchange for the video and her testimony."

"I wonder if whoever was at that abandoned site is still there," Denton said.

"That would be one of a number of million-dollar questions right now," Wainright agreed.

"I'll mobilize some of our European agents," Tevin said.

"No," I insisted. "We need to get out there ourselves. More to the point, I do."

"Belarus is in the heart of Russian territory, and they won't like our agents just showing up unannounced," Wainright said. "Hell, they'd probably like to comb through the place themselves, if they haven't already discovered it."

"Wainright's correct," Tevin said. "We'll need to do this clandestinely."

"Aw, bullshit," I said.

Something occurred to me, and I withdrew my mobile phone.

"You know, I'm not officially a subcontracted employee for the feds just yet," I said. "I'm still just a private citizen right now. And I'm due a vacation to Europe, don't you agree?"

"Oh, yeah, like the TSA's going to put you on a flight to Europe after all that's happened," Wainright countered.

Sanders gave me a look of pure recognition. "Yeah, and I'm way overdue a vacation, too. I think I'd like to take some annual leave now, Denton."

"Just what the hell do you two think you're up to?" Denton demanded. "Federal agents don't just fly off to Belarus for no reason, Sanders."

I reached over and wrapped my arm around Sander's shoulders. "Gentlemen, I'm taking my girlfriend on a European trip to Belarus. Denton, how does the FBI view interoffice relationships?"

Sanders elbowed me in the gut.

"Bringer, you can forget government flights, and customs probably won't let you board any commercial jets destined for there," Tevin said. "Under the circumstances, the State Department will want to regulate your departure from the country. As such, I'm positive that the TSA is already watching out for you.

I winked at him as I dialed my phone.

"Hello?" answered a familiar voice.

"Clive, this is Logan," I said. "Listen, I need to take an impromptu trip for two to Minsk, Belarus. Any chance you could arrange something?"

"It's an unusual request, but I think something could be arranged," he replied. "Do I detect that time is of the essence?"

"Faster is better," I said.

"Do you have a carrier in mind already?" he asked.

"Funny you should ask. Any chance that Mr. Nevis might loan us one of his private jets? I'm willing to bet he has at least one."

Wainright looked at Tevin. "We'd better get on the phone to State before these two are wheels up."

"Pack a bag, Sanders," Denton prompted. "Looks like you and your new boyfriend are headed to Belarus."

The astonished look on Sanders' face was priceless.

CHAPTER 6

Life seemed to be coming at me from all sides. I'd no sooner walked through my front door when my mobile phone rang.

"Hi, Maria. How are you?"

"How am I?" she asked. "I'm astonished, that's what."

I froze. "Is that a good astonished or a bad astonished?"

"Logan, it's a *dream* job," she assured me. "I can't thank you enough for what you've arranged for me here at Nuclegene. Oh, and the salary. You can't imagine what this means for me and my children. And we're moving onto the corporate campus, which is heavenly, even compared to the nice neighborhood that I'm living in now."

"Great," I said. "I'm happy for you. And hey, I'm happy for me, too. For example, I'm looking forward to working with you."

"Yes, but why me? The company has teams of doctors and scientists who are far more knowledgeable than I am. Some have even worked on the project since its beginning."

"It's a matter of trust," I said. "I trust you. And don't discount your abilities. Hell, you're the one who fine-tuned my daily supplement injections. They work well, by the way."

Reminded, I headed toward the refrigerator to retrieve some doses for my trip.

"Logan, it goes without saying that you're one of a kind,

though in a far better way than seems obvious," she said. "When can we meet and talk? I want to make sure we're on the same page before a medical support team is put together for you. Naturally, we'll need to negotiate times when you can come in for observation and readings—"

"Uh, yeah," I interrupted her. "I'm going to need a rain check on that right now. I'm packing for an impromptu trip."

"Trip? Where?"

"Out of the country," I replied. "But I should be back in a few days."

"Is this related to the investigation? Are you in any danger?"

"Just following some leads, that's all."

"Be careful. You know I care about you, Logan," she said. "You mean the world to me."

"You mean a lot to me, too, Maria," I said. "Listen, I better get going. I have to be outta here within the hour, and I've still got to find my passport. It wasn't long ago that I'd thought I'd never need it again."

I was relieved that we had recovered her before she'd been killed, or worse, by her Continuance abductors.

Once, cancer had wiped future plans from the forefront of my thoughts. Upon reaching stage four, I had thought only about my unfulfilled dreams.

While I'd beaten cancer, it was quickly replaced by the threat posed by Continuance Corporation, followed by any number of threats yet identified.

My dreams and desires would remain on hold, but they were merely on hold, not lost forever.

"Well, don't forget to pack syringes with your formula," she said. "And please be careful. You're my most important patient."

"Will do," I said. "Hey, wait a minute. I'm your only patient, right?"

She laughed and hung up.

I shook my head as I got my ass into gear, hastily packing a suitcase and heading to the refrigerator where I stored

Maria's formula.

My phone rang again.

This time, it was Bernard.

"Bringer here," I said.

"There's a private Lear jet fueled and ready for you at the airport," he said. "One of my personal aides, Calvin Strutt, will meet you there. You're in competent hands. He's proven to be both trustworthy and dependable. Good luck, Mr. Bringer."

"Whoa, wait a minute. I didn't say anything about needing an aide."

"You've said that you need to get to Belarus, and I'm confident it's not for a vacation," he said. "And unless you speak either Belarusian or Russian, you're going to need someone who does."

"That's probably helpful," I conceded.

"Strutt is also familiar with our operations in Odessa," Bernard said.

"Yes, but that's in the Ukraine, isn't it? What's the angle with Odessa?"

"That will be your closet Nuclegene support site, Mr. Bringer," he said. "You're in luck, of sorts. Since Russia acquired and fully controls Ukraine, you can easily make your way there from Minsk."

"Acquired? You have a way with words, Bernard," I said dryly. "The Russians rolled tanks into the damned place over a decade ago. I think I'd call that *invaded*."

"Invasion, acquisition, liberation, it's really just a matter of semantics. Functionally, it's the much the same when it comes to corporate interests," he said. "We have strong ties within Eastern Europe, which could be helpful in a pinch if you run into trouble. Either way, Odessa provides you with Nuclegene corporate influence in the region. You'll like it there. They have wonderful beaches."

I hated to admit that he made a valid point about corporate influences being helpful. Still, I didn't share his corporate view about the Russians and Ukraine.

"You know, corporations have a bad habit of ignoring the plight of ordinary people, including those who were badly affected by the Russian takeover in Ukraine."

"I must say, your sensitivity to the topic surprises me somewhat. I had no idea you were such a passionate Ukrainian advocate," he said.

"Let's just say I've recently increased my awareness of users of arbitrary power," I said. "Both governmental and corporate."

"Human history is replete with instances of growth and advancement through the uses of arbitrary power. Be that as it may, I might point out, Mr. Bringer, that ordinary people do matter to corporations. In fact, they've influenced countless balance sheets and income statements dating all the way back to ancient times," he parried. "People, politics, and profit are remarkable bedfellows, and it's a shortsighted company that ignores any one of them."

I had to hand it to him; Bernard was quite the spin doctor.

"You should do speaking tours. Anyway, I appreciate your assistance, Bernard," I said. "I'll be in touch again soon."

"Happy hunting, Mr. Bringer."

As I pocketed my smartphone, I couldn't help but wonder if Continuance Corporation applied many of the same ideological principles that Bernard had just shared.

If so, could that give me additional insight into their game plan?

It seemed the same no matter the source: whether corporate or governmental, the goal was to horde and control all of the marbles on the game board.

The question was, precisely which marbles did Continuance want?

Sanders pulled into my driveway in a government sedan just as I stepped outside and locked my front door.

I stowed my luggage in the trunk and plopped onto the passenger seat.

"Ready for Europe?" I asked. "I'm told they've got sunny beaches in Odessa, so I hope you packed a bikini."

She slammed on the brakes while backing out of my driveway, bouncing me in my seat.

"Odessa? Why would we go to Odessa?"

"You never know."

She gave me a hard look.

"Never mind. I'll fill you in on the way to the airport," I said.

"You better," she said. "But rest assured, Bringer, there'll be no bikinis on this trip."

"No problem," I said. "A one-piece is fine with me."

"Oh, shut up."

* * *

By the time we arrived at the airport, I had received a text message from Bernard telling us to meet Calvin Strutt inside the terminal.

Between what appeared to be an Ivy League haircut and youthful face, Strutt looked like a guy fresh out of college, ready for his first corporate job.

Great, I thought. *A greenhorn.*

Still, he had a firm handshake, which was encouraging.

"Mr. Bringer, Agent Sanders, I'm Calvin Strutt," he offered.

"Are you sure you're old enough to fly without your parents?" I asked.

To his credit, he seemed to take my jab in stride.

"I get that a lot. It's in my genes. My mother looks twenty years her junior," he said. "Rest assured, despite my appearance, I'm actually twenty-seven and seasoned in international business negotiations, including Eastern European linguistics."

I wasn't terribly surprised. Bernard wasn't the sort of fellow who surrounded himself with amateurs.

Then again, at times, I felt like a rank amateur with my telekinetic abilities.

"Your expression suggests you don't believe me, Mr.

Bringer."

"What? Nah, it's nothing to do with you, just a passing notion," I said. "Would you care to show us to our plane?"

To my surprise, we experienced an expedited TSA processing. Frankly, I was pleased to see that I hadn't made it onto any of the Do Not Fly lists.

We boarded an impressive Gulfstream jet, brightly painted with Nuclegene's corporate logo. The decked-out interior screamed luxury. I had never been inside an aircraft that impressive before.

"Please make yourselves comfortable," offered Strutt. "The crew is prepared to meet most any need you have, including a well-stocked galley and bar."

"I could get used to this," Sanders said.

"Hell, this makes my house seem like a shack," I said.

"It's brand new, specially built to Nuclegene's specifications," said a familiar voice. "They don't come much nicer than this."

I turned to see Bernard's primary bodyguard, Scott, standing just inside the cabin door.

"What the hell are you doing here?" I asked.

He shrugged. "Mr. Bernard said that I should accompany you on the trip."

"Aw, I didn't know he cared," I quipped.

"Don't let it go to your head, Bringer, but you're the golden child right now," Scott said. "Enjoy it while it lasts."

"I could say the same about Nuclegene in my mind," I said.

Strutt and Scott exchanged glances.

Sanders gently grasped my upper arm. "Bringer, let's pick out our seats."

We settled in and were airborne within the hour.

The plane was designed for long-duration flights, so we only had one brief layover at New York City's John F. Kennedy International airport to top off our fuel tanks.

Inside one of the airport's lounges, a nearby television caught my attention. According to the scrolling text, a press conference was taking place regarding the terrorism threat and the effect on the economy.

I nudged Sanders and motioned for a server to turn up the volume.

The conference was at the behest of the so-called Freedom Party, a block of conservative war hawks in Congress. Two party leaders, Senators Benjamin Conway of Utah and Penelope Savage of Oklahoma, stood before the cluster of microphones.

"…Americans to rise to the occasion during this time of crisis. The Freedom Party stands firmly with the President in his continuing efforts to protect the nation while mobilizing our nation's resources to root out and eliminate these terrorist threats. That's why we're advocating an emergency funding package for the Central Intelligence Agency to strengthen their recent anti-terrorism efforts," said Conway. "Standing together at this crucial moment, I'm confident that justice will ultimately prevail."

He leaned forward, with his hands gripping the sides of the podium. "Future generations may judge us favorably by our convictions for success. Yet, for me, conviction and posturing aren't enough, and failure is not an option. We must act decisively and succeed today to ensure a peaceful and prosperous tomorrow," added Conway before stepping back from the podium and gesturing to Senator Savage.

Savage stepped confidently forward, her expression determined. "Thank you, Senator Conway, for your inspiration and effective leadership," she began. "I share the senator's stance on the terrorist threats before us, and I support the CIA funding bill. In addition, I also advocate a proactive stance to secure a strong economy for our nation.

"In recent weeks, our economy has suffered some temporary setbacks from the shock shared by so many Americans over terrorist threats," she said. "But the stock exchange's recent plummet is only a temporary reaction that should rebound, given adequate time. However, some of the opportunistic liberals in Congress are using this momentary setback as a blatant opportunity to curtail years of productive, pro-capitalist growth programs that have set our nation's economy on a path to future prosperity. Such regressive efforts come from backward-thinking socialists who want to derail our promise of prosperity."

"All of the tired rhetoric bores me," Sanders muttered. "Bringer, I didn't figure you for a news hound. Why can't you just watch sports like a normal guy?"

I gave her a wan look.

"...requiring reasonable income tax participation by America's citizens is only fair. After all, that's how their desired and essential government services are paid for. However, corporations are not typical citizens; they're the engines of our advancement and prosperity. As such, they should not be taxed, or America's prosperity falters, and eventually, evaporates," Savage continued.

"That's why I oppose any of the recently proposed liberal legislation to increase corporate taxation to fund already bloated social programs. We must encourage the less fortunate in our country to improve their job skills, and motivate them to achieve better standards and quality of life. We must not be enablers for them to continue their path of social welfare dependence," she said. "Thank you, and now we'll take a couple of questions from the press."

"Senator Savage, today's press conference seems an odd pairing between Senator Conway's terrorism stance and your view on economic legislation. How do you explain the direct correlation between terrorism and taxation legislation?" asked one reporter.

"Oh, the two are quite connected," Savage insisted. "Senator Conway and my fellow Patriots in the Freedom Party measure terrorism on a broad scale. First, shadowy foreign entities are perpetuating lethal attacks against our nation. Meanwhile, leftist politicians are attempting to tear down our nation's domestic economy from within. I think you can easily see how the two are equally dangerous to our country's well-being."

Sanders looked up from her cola with a wide-eyed expression.

"And you said rhetoric was boring," I teased.

"Pardon me, Senator, are you claiming that liberal politicians are actually terrorists?" demanded a reporter.

Senator Conway quickly stepped forward.

"I think what Senator Savage means is that regressive domestic economic policies threaten our nation as much as external threats from terrorist groups abroad," Conway replied.

Senator Savage smiled and leaned toward the microphone. "I think some of you may have misunderstood my response. What I'm saying is that our institutions should be engines of industry and advancement, not enablers of either public apathy or socialist benefit programs that undermine our nation's security and prosperity."

"But Senator Savage, if you're advocating against tax increases, where do you expect the emergency CIA funding to be allocated from?" asked another reporter.

Savage gave the reporter a measured look. "Obviously, some tough choices will need to be made to trim excess funding from social programs or reallocate funding from other government agencies. We must each make sacrifices for our nation's safety and security or we'll have no nation remaining to concern ourselves with."

"I think that's all the questions we'll take for now," Conway said. "Thank you all for coming."

Sanders gave me a sober look. "Bringer, we really need to focus on the task at hand."

"Oh, I am," I assured her.

"And, pray tell, how was watching that pitiful stage craft helpful to us?"

"Well, for one, we just learned that the CIA has garnered political support from the war hawks for additional funding," I pointed out. "I didn't hear Homeland Security, the FBI, or the NSA mentioned, did you? That means they're placing all their eggs in one basket."

Sanders frowned. "Hm. And the CIA gets the eggs."

I winked at her and took a final swig of Jack and Coke.

"Good catch, reading between the lines there, Bringer," she offered.

"I'm learning," I said with a shrug.

Once we were inflight again, Sanders received a text message from Bob Tevin informing her that firsthand NSA satellite data of the abandoned facility near Minsk was available.

Minutes later, Sanders booted up her notebook computer and we viewed impressively crisp top-down images of the facility and surrounding area.

As reported, it appeared both remote and abandoned. Tevin had also included multiple maps of the most accessible routes to the site.

"Tevin's very helpful," I said.

Sanders received another text message.

"He estimates that we've got a head start on the CIA," she said. "But he expects they'll have operatives in the area within the next twenty-four to thirty-six hours."

"Strutt," I prompted.

The young man's head shot upward from his mobile phone. "Sir?"

"How fast can this luxury bird tote us to Belarus?"

He grinned. "Fast, Mr. Bringer. This plane was designed to break the sound barrier."

I had to admit that impressed me.

"Good. Make sure the pilot burns feathers off the wings for as long as possible."

He nodded and practically lurched from his seat toward the front cabin.

Sanders gave me an amused look. "I'll bet you were a handful on family road trips growing up."

"Family trips are one thing. This has suddenly turned into a competition between us and the CIA," I said. "And I, for one, don't like having to bat against our own team."

"I don't like it, either," she agreed. "Of course, given

recent events, it's rather hard to determine exactly who *is* on our team."

That sobering thought plagued my mind for some time afterward.

CHAPTER 7

The pilot must have been running the engines hot. It took less than eight hours for us to touch down at the Minsk International Airport. Despite a short flight, considering the forty-five hundred miles traversed, I experienced some serious jet lag by the time we arrived.

Given the successive years of depressed Russian economy, I had expected more humble surroundings. Instead, the airport was a large and surprisingly modern complex in its own right.

While the United States had managed to barely keep its head above water during a decade-old worldwide recession, many European nations had suffered greatly. As such, Belarus seemed like a rich prospective location for operations by Continuance Corporation.

Our journey through customs took a lot longer than I'd anticipated, though Sanders did a great job posing as the consummate girlfriend. That included brief instances of holding my hand, which I had to admit felt surprisingly comfortable.

As we handed over our passports for review, I felt cautiously optimistic.

That was, until one official stared at the terminal before him and then back at us with a terse look.

Fortunately, Strutt immediately proved himself useful by

stepping forward to negotiate our processing using native Belarusian, which momentarily seemed to make the customs official more at ease.

Strutt leaned over to me. "I explained that you're here on a blend of company business and vacation with your girlfriend."

The customs official gestured over to a nearby office door. "If you and your companion would please proceed into that office, we will complete your processing," he said in clipped English.

I noticed he retained our passports in his hand and I looked at Strutt, who conversed with the official in Belarusian. The man frowned and shook his head while gesturing for Scott to proceed to a nearby processing station.

"They're not going to let me or Scott follow you from here," Strutt said. "I think they realize now who you are, but I'm not sure that there's any hostile intentions. However, I'm going to start placing some key calls to influential resources just in case. Try to remain cordial."

I nodded and grasped Sanders by the hand to lead the way.

"I don't like this, Bring–," she whispered. "Logan."

"You really don't like my first name, do you?"

"What? No," she countered. "It's just something new for me, okay? It's takes getting used to."

"My first name or having a boyfriend?"

"Maybe both," she quietly murmured.

I curtailed a growing smile.

A guard opened the office door for us and waited for us to step through before closing it. The lock clicked into place behind us.

Two middle-aged men in black business suits stood to one side, projecting an air of authority, while a younger man wearing a Belarusian customs uniform moved from behind a desk and gestured to two Spartan-looking chairs before him.

"I'm Major Uladzimir, local administrator for the Customs Service. Please take a seat, Mr. Bringer and Ms.

Sanders," he said.

We sat as the official took his seat behind the desk.

"And your two friends are?" I asked.

"They represent other Belarusian authorities," he replied.

I wasn't sure that I liked his answer.

He diverted his attention to a computer screen before him, likely reading our entire life histories, as viewed by Russian intelligence services.

I opened my mind to listen in on stray thoughts, but was surprised by what I overheard.

...*bad feeling about this.*

The other thoughts were strangely in what sounded like Slavic, though they could have easily been either Russian or Belarusian. As I knew nothing of Balkan languages, I had no way of knowing for certain.

A major shortcoming of my mindreading ability stunned me; I had to be able to understand the languages used by the subjects I was listening in on.

Shit.

"So, you are here on business *and* pleasure, then?" Uladzimir asked. "I see that you claim to be under the employ of Nuclegene Corporation, Mr. Bringer. While you, Ms. Sanders, appear to be a member of American federal law enforcement?"

"Yes, the Federal Bureau of Investigation," she replied.

"Yes, the FBI, as you say," he said. "However, you'll pardon me if I say that it is an interesting pairing when you claim to be the companion to one of the most dangerous men in your country, yes?"

By then, I was feeling increasingly annoyed.

"Ah, my reputation precedes me, I see," I said. "But again, we're only here as tourists."

The major offered a tight-lipped smile, though the two gentlemen standing to the side appeared wholly unamused.

"It goes without saying, given your recent history, Mr. Bringer, that our security services have you on our watch lists," said the major, glancing at a computer terminal before him. "I find it surprising that you would suddenly be taking a vacation to our country at such a critical time. You were involved in a well-publicized incident in Seattle, Washington, were you not?"

"Ah, well, the press blows everything out of proportion nowadays, doesn't it?" I noted.

"Perhaps, yet you could also share with us why your government has really sent you to Belarus, hm?"

I gave the major a level look and then spared another for the two men standing nearby.

I leaned forward, placing my forearms onto the major's desk, and felt Sanders' hand grasp my thigh.

"Major, I'm going to share something with you and your two associates that's entirely the truth," I offered. "First, I'm not here at the behest of my government. I am here to see some interesting sights in your fine country with my companion here, and maybe even forget that my life's been a bit too hectic recently.

"Second, I have no interests in causing trouble for you or any of your citizens or government. In fact, in a couple of days, we'll peacefully board our plane and be on our merry way again," I said.

"I see. And where will you go when you leave Belarus, if I may ask?"

I shrugged. "It's been recently suggested to me that the beaches in Odessa are really nice," I said, glancing over at Sanders. "And beaches go hand in hand with romance, wouldn't you agree?"

Sanders dug her nails into my thigh.

The major appeared amused while one of the two guys in suits leered at Sanders.

One of the men—he had what appeared to be a chemical burn scar on his forehead—leaned down to whisper something in the major's ear.

The major nodded. "Mr. Bringer, this is—how might we say?—a delicate situation. You could be telling the truth, in which case, Belarus welcomes your patronage. However, if the alternate were to prove true, it might be dangerous for both you and for Belarus."

I leaned back in my chair. "So, the question becomes, what do you plan to do?"

The major appeared uneasy while the man with the scar intently watched me.

"We could always take you and your companion into protective custody until we're comfortable with the matter," offered the man with a sober expression.

"I'm sure that would only escalate to an uncomfortable international incident for everyone involved," Sanders said.

"I'm certain you would find your circumstances equally *uncomfortable*, Ms. Sanders," said the man with the scar.

I didn't like the way he said that.

I nodded. "You know, my girlfriend makes an excellent point. Of course, you probably should consider the additional complications that might arise."

All three men frowned.

"What sort of complications?" asked the man with the scar.

"For example, attempting to take us into custody on what might be perceived to be false pretense, not to mention threatening my girlfriend, as you just did," I said.

"That is hardly a complication for us," he replied.

"Perhaps," I said. "Though if you'll consider my recent history, you'll realize what I'm capable of. Suffice to say I handle neither antagonism nor hostility particularly well."

I felt Sanders' grip on my thigh tighten.

The major and the other two men stared at me.

I stared right back at them. Their game was getting old fast.

"The time has come to make a choice, and I'll give you two to select from," I offered. "Either you admit us into your country, in which case we see some sights, sample some local cuisine, and purchase some souvenirs, or you ask us to leave and we peaceably board our plane and depart."

"I challenge that you neglected a number of other

choices," the formerly silent man said. "We are the ones controlling the options here, Mr. Bringer."

I focused my attention on him. "Perhaps. Although mine were the only two that end with you arriving home safely after a long day at work."

Sanders gave me a hard, sidelong look. "*Logan*, let's not be hasty."

The tension level in the room ratcheted up after that, but I played it cool and acted as if I wasn't overly concerned. I had no intention of being bullied, and I was fully prepared to make that known.

Uladzimir's desk phone rang, causing both Sanders and him to jolt slightly in their seats.

He picked up the phone and spoke in Belarusian, then gave me a curious look and handed the phone to the guy with the scar.

After a few moments, the major took back the proffered handset and briefly conversed with whoever was on the line. Afterward, he took a deep breath and nodded to the man with the scar.

"Mr. Bringer, it seems that our Ministry of Foreign Affairs favors your visit," Uladzimir said, handing our passports to us across his desk. "Welcome to Belarus. I hope that you have an enjoyable and peaceable stay. I strongly recommend you conduct yourselves under the best of behaviors."

I stood up. "Oh, rest assured, Major; I always dish out my best."

* * *

We made our way through the terminal, trying to locate Strutt, Scott, and our luggage, in no particular order.

"Has anyone ever told you that you're a really crappy poker player?" Sanders asked.

"Actually, you're the first," I replied.

"What would you have done if they had called your

bluff? Burn down the airport?"

"I'm pleased that we won't have to find out," I said.

"What were you thinking back there, Bringer?"

"That I wasn't about to let anyone harm you, Meg."

She looked up at me with a thoughtful expression. "You know, it sounds strange, you calling me Meg."

I reached out to grasp her hand in mine. "Maybe, but I sort of enjoy it."

Her eyes widened slightly and she quickly looked away.

"There's Strutt by the escalators," she pointed out.

"Happy to see you two," he said.

"Should I presume that I owe you a debt of thanks for a timely phone call?"

He nodded. "None needed. The Ministry of Foreign Affairs came through for us."

"Do I want to know how you managed that?"

He shook his head. "Um, not really. At least, I'd rather that Mr. Bernard share that, if he chooses to."

"Fair enough, I suppose."

"Where's Scott?" Meg asked.

"Oh, I sent him down to the luggage retrieval, just in case you appeared there first."

"Well, lead on, then," I suggested.

As we collected our luggage in the main terminal, I reflected upon our recent office visit with Major Uladzimir.

I couldn't help feeling that a phone call wasn't going to be the end of our intrigue while in Minsk.

* * *

It was early evening by the time we pulled up before the upscale Hotel Chagall in our rented sedan. The hotel, conveniently located in downtown Minsk, was supposed to be one of the finest in town; and was namesake of a famous Belarusian painter and composer, or so the information on the airport's complimentary pamphlet indicated.

"Just so you know, we're still being tailed," Scott warned.

"Yeah, I half expected as much after our customs interview," I said.

"Everyone unload the luggage and head inside while I park our car," Scott said. "I don't want to turn it over to anyone while we're here. I'll have to sweep our rooms for bugs, too."

"You brought some equipment that can?" Meg asked.

"Yes, Ma'am," he replied. "Strutt sneaked it in with the flight crew's gear, along with some other handy items."

I gave the young man a sidelong glance. "You're turning out to be pretty handy after all."

He inclined his head in silent appreciation.

Before Strutt went inside, he handed me a credit card.

"I almost forgot to give you this," he said. "Mr. Bernard asked to make sure you understood this card is specifically in your name for any expenses you may incur related to company activities."

"Like dinner?" I asked.

He nodded. "Dinner, hotel stays, travel expenses, and most anything you may require in pursuit of your objectives."

"Most anything?" I asked.

"I'd imagine you could even purchase a tank if you needed one," he said.

"Thanks," I said. "But just so you know...I am the tank."

He grinned. "Actually, that sort of occurred to me after I said it."

We proceeded to our hotel rooms, including a grand romantic suite for Meg and me.

"I'd like to remind you this is just for show," she insisted as I opened the door for her.

Meg set down her luggage just inside the suite's sole bedroom and fell backward onto the king-sized bed with a bounce and a sigh.

I eyed the living room's couch with resignation; likely my relegated sleeping accommodation during our stay.

I made a mental note to procure an extra blanket or two

for myself later that evening.

"Logan?" Meg called. "Are we heading out to the site now?"

I turned to see her leaning against the bedroom door looking both tired and somewhat cute with stray strands of hair hanging down across her forehead.

I shook my head. "Daytime is better. Besides, we're already under scrutiny and I don't want to raise suspicions so soon after leaving the airport. Let's be tourists for one night and head out at first light tomorrow."

"But what about the CIA? What if they beat us to the site?"

"Don't worry," I said. "I won't let the spooks get ahead of us. We'll start extra early. Besides, we'll need time to evade our inquisitive shadows outside, too."

She gave me an appreciative look, which was all the confirmation I needed that she approved of my idea.

"I'll let you exercise your super-governmental powers for that," I added.

"Sorry, the FBI doesn't evade other people," she countered. "They're usually evading us."

I couldn't help but chuckle.

We freshened up before dinner, and I told both Scott and Strutt to enjoy an evening of diversions. If anything, I mentioned them assessing the area within a few blocks of the hotel, just to get a feel for the landscape.

Acting on inspiration, I managed to arrange for a cozy table for two at a small restaurant called Oleg's Kafe around the corner from the hotel. Fortunately, Sanders seemed pleased with my initiative.

For the first time since I'd met Megan Sanders, the two of us casually enjoyed each other's company without the fear of bombs, terrorists, or issues of national security. It was just she and I chatting over nothing of consequence…but it was precisely what I needed.

Honestly, it felt so very refreshing to experience a semblance of normality; or, at least, more normal than I'd felt in a long time. I almost didn't want the evening to end.

Then I felt guilty, first for permitting my focus to ebb from our mission at hand, and second for actually feeling happy that I had.

As we walked back to the hotel later that evening, I felt more at ease than I had in quite some time.

"That was wonderful," she said. "I almost forgot—"

"What it was like to relax again?" I interrupted. "Yeah, me too."

She smiled and reached out to gently intertwine her fingers in mine. I curled my fingers between hers in return.

"Thank you for dinner," she said.

"You're welcome," I replied. "Although, I apparently get an expense account, so this one's on Nuclegene."

"Lucky man," she said.

"You don't know how right you are," I said with appreciation.

She frowned at me and returned an inquisitive look.

"Why, Mr. Bringer, are you hitting on me?"

I shrugged. "Can't blame a fellow for trying."

She appeared reflective. "Hm."

As we rounded the corner and approached the hotel, we spotted Scott outside, visiting with two hotel concierges. As soon as he saw us, he disengaged from them and walked toward us.

"Have a nice dinner?" he asked.

"Yeah, we did. Any trouble?" I asked.

"Just scoping out the place," he said. "We've got two groups of surveillance that I've located so far."

"Two, huh?"

"Yep, though I don't have any idea who they're with."

"I'd guess both Belarusian and Russian," Meg said.

"That's my inclination, until I know differently," he agreed.

Scott held open a tourist map before us. "Just act like we're talking about the map."

I nodded and absently pointed to a random spot.

"Where's Strutt?" I asked.

"Upstairs making arrangements for a second rental car for in the morning."

"Good," I said. "Now, if we have an idea where our observers both are, we can plan for tomorrow morning. And I'll need you and Strutt to run interference while Meg and I make our way to the site."

"Hey, neither of you speak the language," he reminded us.

"True," I said. "I was hoping that you two could split up, and then we'll meet up with Strutt somewhere else. While you're at it, maybe you can act suspicious and keep at least one group occupied."

"Sure," he agreed.

"Don't worry, we'll decide upon a location to meet up when we're done and then come looking for you if you don't show," I assured him.

"I'm happy to hear you're one of those 'leave nobody behind' sorts of guys," he said dryly.

"Damn straight," I said with a nod.

Sanders shook her head. "We need more women on this mission. You sound like two stereotypical guys from a cheesy action movie."

Scott gave her a wry look and pressed the map into her hands.

"Funny. I'm gonna take one more walk and call it a night. Call my room in the morning when you're ready to head out. I'll be up and ready by 4am," he said. "G'night."

We watched him walk away.

"You're all heart, Sanders."

She started walking toward the hotel lobby entrance.

"What can I say? Dad watched those lame films when I was growing up," she said with a shrug.

"No action movies for you?" I asked, catching up to her.

"Ballet and musicals," she replied.

"Ugh."

"Stow it, Bringer."

CHAPTER 8

I woke before Sanders.

Though I had managed a reasonable amount of sleep, the couch was less comfortable than I'd imagined, so I wasn't averse to rising early.

I roused Sanders, who groaned at me. "You're a real bummer, Bringer. Remind me never to go on vacation with you again."

I brewed coffee and called Scott and Strutt.

By 4am, Meg and I made our way down a staff service hallway on the first floor to the back of the hotel while Scott and Strutt spaced their departures through the main lobby entrance and headed in opposite directions.

Meg and I were remarkably successful in our departure by following the best advice I'd ever received: act like you belong there, or at least like you know what you're doing.

Nobody bothered us as we walked out through the shipping and receiving area at the rear of the hotel and into a nearby alleyway.

It was surprising how much traffic and activity there was in the city for that time of morning, but it only helped to further mask our activities.

"I hope Strutt makes it to where he's supposed to meet up with us," Sanders said, clutching her notebook computer closely to her.

We briskly made our way three blocks away from the hotel, though not in such a hurry that we garnered unwanted attention.

Outside of a still-closed bakery, we waited only about ten minutes before Strutt pulled up in a black, compact rental car.

"Any problems?" I asked, pushing forward the passenger seat for Sanders to get in.

"Hey, why do you get to sit up front?" she asked.

"Can you make the fireballs, if needed?"

She shook her head and squeezed onto the back seat. "Point well made."

"No problems," Strutt replied to my earlier query. "I took extra turns down two side streets because I thought I was followed for a time by two men in a white sedan. I lost them, for now."

"Well, let's not linger until they catch up," Sanders urged.

We made our way through town and then back-tracked through the city using an electronic map that Sanders brought up on her notebook.

"Remind me to thank Tevin for that when we get back," I said.

The NSA deputy director had proven very helpful recently. While it was hard determining who to trust, it was nice knowing that we could at least rely on Tevin and FBI Deputy Director Wainright.

Unfortunately, that still left a large number of prospective powerful enemies on the table.

We need to narrow that list down soon, too.

"Bringer? You awake?" Sanders asked.

"Huh? Yeah, what?"

"Should we take the most direct route or bypass the site and double back once we're sure we're not being followed?"

"Direct route," I replied. "I don't want to give the bloodhounds any more time to find us than necessary."

Sanders gave Strutt directions while I contemplated Continuance Corporation. I needed a way to get inside their heads, to figure out what it was they wanted and what their next targets might be.

Since I was the only person with the abilities to counter others like me, it was imperative that I located them before they struck again.

I stifled a yawn.

Hell, I don't even have any clue as to what targets they might want to strike.

I felt like I was struggling to solve a mystery without any tangible clues or leads. Of course, I hoped that would all change once we arrived at our intended destination.

We pulled up outside a locked security gate within the hour, just as a predawn glow formed in the east.

"Strutt, drive the car up the road and park on the next side street you come to. Then walk back down here and meet up with us inside," I ordered. "Meg will bring the notebook with us."

"Yes, sir," Strutt replied.

Sanders and I exited the vehicle and watched Strutt drive away.

"I don't suppose you know how to pick a padlock?" I asked.

"Actually, no."

I shrugged and extended my right palm toward the gate, drawing on my power and imagining a giant wrecking ball swinging forward.

The gate propelled inward like a truck had impacted it, snapping the chain that secured it closed.

"Show off," Sanders said.

We walked along the asphalt driveway. The grass and foliage had overgrown the edges of it like some unruly monstrosity that was progressively pressing past its containment area. The early morning shadows lent the environment an eerie mood.

"This is a grim place," she said.

I had to agree.

After following the winding route, we made our way up

to the front of the abandoned facility, which looked like a throwback to the dark days of turn of the century asylums and sanitariums.

The reinforced steel front doors, though rusty, were ajar, and creaked loudly as I pressed past them. A musty, decayed smell permeated the area.

Sanders and I produced flashlights, though I was half-tempted to conjure a fireball in one hand, just for reassurance and peace of mind.

The place looked like the perfect hangout for all manner of spirits, restless and otherwise.

Upturned and broken old furniture and paint-peeled walls were the décor of the day. The tiled floor was in disrepair, though a variety of fresh-looking scuffs and footprints were evident.

"People have been rummaging around here not terribly long ago," Sanders ventured.

"Yeah, but who, I wonder," I said. "Vagrants, maybe?"

We proceeded through the main lobby and into nearby areas that appeared to be clinic rooms and offices. More dated remnants were strewn here and there, as if some creepy asylum museum had been ransacked and then forsaken.

However, as we proceeded deeper into the facility, through patient rooms and surgical areas, the place appeared much more recently utilized.

In fact, though abandoned, some offices and patient rooms had viable furniture inside them.

At the end of one central ward, we discovered burned areas and breached places along the walls, as if exploded outward.

At one point, the roof was peeled back, revealing blue sky and the glow of the sunrise above.

"What the hell happened in here?" Sanders asked. "I mean, it looks like someone was testing explosives or something."

"Nah, they were testing someone, or a number of *someones*," I countered. "This wasn't munitions. This was people like me."

She gave me a hard look.

"Yeah, this is exactly what I feared when I saw Tevin's video," I said. "I just wonder how many were here."

"Crap," she muttered.

I shone my flashlight against a far wall where it looked like lightning had struck the area; rivulets of cascading lines in the wall and floor suggested that electricity had coursed throughout the room.

Another patient room was completely marred with scorched and burned patches, including nearly incinerated furniture. The windows had been completely blown outward, as well.

"Bringer, who are these people?"

I shined my light on a nearby wall. There was the outline of a human body with arms extended outward. The wall itself was blackened, like charcoal.

"Looks like somebody got pissed off at someone else," I remarked.

Sanders started taking photos with her smartphone, the flash highlighting eerie-looking imagery at intervals.

Muted footsteps sounded in the distance, prompting Sanders to cease taking photos.

I motioned for her to stay put and turned off my flashlight while quietly making my way back down the hallway.

Holding out my hand to generate a fireball at a moment's notice, I peered around the corner of the hallway.

"Bringer? Sanders?" Strutt called.

I relaxed. "Strutt, we're down here."

He joined us as Sanders resumed taking photos.

"Jesus, this is horrific," he said.

"Let's look around and see if there are any other clues or paperwork left that's useful," I suggested.

Though we didn't find anything of merit, I did begin to piece together some of the evidence surrounding us.

"Well, it looks like we're still in the dark," Sanders said.

"Sorry, pun not intended."

At least the sun was beginning to generate a glow through the breaches in the ceiling and wall, as well as the nearby windows.

"Actually, we know some things," I said.

"Such as?"

"By the damages here, I'd say we're dealing with people who can channel or manipulate electricity, fire, brute forces, and maybe something else that I haven't seen before," I said.

"Brute forces?" Strutt asked.

"Yeah, I don't know how else to describe it," I said. "Like when I imagine something big and propel it against a structure, or maybe levitate and throw objects."

"What do you mean by 'something else you haven't seen before'?" asked Sanders.

"Something like an explosion, but with heat and force, though not like fire," I estimated. "I dunno. It just doesn't look like fire."

"This all seems fresh, too," Strutt said.

"Yeah, fairly recent," I agreed.

"Maybe we got lucky and they incinerated each other," Strutt offered. "There's a lot of damage here."

I shook my head. "No. Look closer. There's places here and there where you'll see faded circles on the floor or against a wall. That's where shields were generated. Those people are still among the living."

"So whoever did this is out there somewhere," Sanders said.

"Yeah, I'm thinkin' that's the case," I said.

"Why were these people here in the first place?" Strutt asked.

"There's a lot of ruined medical equipment strewn here and there, and you'll notice that some of these patient rooms look like they were occupied," I said. "I'm willing to bet this is where people were either tested or experimented on."

"You think this is where their abilities were created or manifested?" Sanders asked.

"Maybe," I replied. "At least, that's as good an explanation as any."

"Ground zero for Continuance Corporation's telekinetic programs?" Strutt asked.

I gave him a suspicious look.

He gave me an innocent shrug. "Mr. Bernard explained what we might be up against here. In addition, I helped put together persons of interest lists for Nuclegene following the Wallace Building bombing. Mr. Bernard has always suspected Continuance Corporation."

I relaxed somewhat. "Well, it might be ground zero, or just one of however many other locations around the world. Who knows, really?"

I couldn't help wondering if the Belarusian authorities knew that Continuance had been operating here.

Of course, even if they had, I realized that, if they were facing telekinetics who could do what I saw before me, what could the Belarusian government have expected to do against them with any effectiveness?

"I think I have about all the images we need," Sanders prompted. "What now?"

I gave the immediate area one last look.

"Well, let's wrap it up before others arrive," I said. "And when I say others, I mean most anybody."

We made our way to the front of the facility and cautiously peeked out through the main doors before proceeding back toward the main gate. In truth, I felt happy to be leaving that dreary place.

When we arrived at the main gate, a lone man stood in the middle of the driveway. The hard edge to his expression was at odds with what I considered to be rather youthful-looking features. He folded his hands calmly before him, striking a non-hostile pose.

"Mr. Bringer, I presume?" he asked with a slight English accent.

Great, I thought. *Now who the hell is this?*

CHAPTER 9

I stared at the man before us, countering his hard expression with one of my own.

"Please, I'm not armed and I mean no harm," he stated. "I'm here on behalf of the British government to request your immediate assistance."

"The British government?" Sanders challenged. "And just who are you supposed to be, James Bond?"

"Agent Sanders, my name is Colin Fisk," he replied. "MI-6."

"I'm pretty sure you're not supposed to just blurt that out," she said. "And just how to you know me?"

He shrugged. "I hoped that my forthrightness might encourage a dialogue. And it shouldn't surprise you that MI-6 is familiar with many of the individuals that surround Mr. Bringer, though I confess, I don't recognize the gentleman with you."

"Calvin Strutt, Nuclegene Corporation."

I glanced over my shoulder at Strutt. "Let's not get chummy all at once here."

"Of course," Fisk offered, holding his arms out to his sides. "If you'd care to search me for weapons, perhaps I can set your minds further at ease."

Sanders handed her notebook to Strutt and stepped forward to pat down Fisk while I scanned the immediate area and opened up my mind to nearby thoughts.

…never met a British agent before. Sorta cute.

My attention lingered on Sanders.

…wait until Mr. Bernard hears about this.

…imperative that Bringer agrees to help.

Nothing else came up, so I felt more comfortable that Fisk might be alone. Of course, I wasn't exactly sure how far my sensory range might be, either.

"If you're looking for others, Mr. Bringer, I can assure you that I came here alone," Fisk offered.

"Fine," I said. "But let's not talk out here in the open. We really should be leaving."

"Of course," he said. "However, you may be interested to know that a CIA team arrived in theater this morning."

I looked at Sanders, who had stepped back from Fisk and nodded at me.

"Yeah, we'd like to keep this between us for now," I said.

"Shall we proceed?" Fisk asked, gesturing toward the road.

"All right, just stay with us," I said, taking the lead to walk toward the main road. "But if you try anything funny, I'll cook you where you stand."

"Ah, well then," he said. "I'm happy to oblige."

* * *

I felt relief as we finally drove away from the area. Strutt was at the wheel while Sanders sat up front. I shared the back seat with Fisk so that I could keep an eye on him for the time being.

"How about sharing with us why you've been sent to find me," I said. "You said something about needing my help, but with what, exactly?"

"British intelligence has located a small cell of what we've identified to be sleeper agents for Continuance Corporation," he replied.

"How do you know they're from Continuance?" Sanders asked.

"Two of the individuals photographed were cross-referenced in our databases with intelligence placing them at previous Continuance-related incidents."

"Why come to us?" Sanders asked, looking back at him over the front seat. "You should probably be taking this up with the NSA, or even the CIA, first."

Fisk gave her a long look. "Yes, we tried, but your CIA insisted that they didn't have enough evidence to substantiate conveying you to British territory given the high-risk status of conditions in your own country."

My gaze met Sanders' and I noted her look of surprise before I stared across at Fisk.

I opened my mind and focused on him.

…wrong with the United States today? Bloody bastards don't even care about their allies anymore.

I frowned. As a matter of fact, Fisk's concerns didn't betray any thoughts that I hadn't shared myself recently.

"How did you know we were here?" I asked.

The muscles in Fisk's face tightened. "Look, don't take this the wrong way, but you've been on our radar since the events in Nevis Corners. As soon as we learned that you were a person of interest, we started tracking everyone around you, in fact."

"Even Maria Edwards?" I asked.

He appeared surprised. "Well, yes, she was one of the central figures, I believe. However, I was assigned to watch you. Ms. Edwards was assigned to another agent."

"Are they still tracking her?"

"Bringer—" Sanders interjected.

"Well, yes, I suppose so," Fisk replied. "Though I don't understand what this has to do with—"

"Never mind," I interrupted. "Let's get back to those Continuance people you mentioned."

I wondered if British agents had observed Maria's abduction from her home and done nothing.

Still, what would that have changed? It wasn't as if the UK had any allegiance to go around saving people, save those deigned as valuable to their own interests.

It really wasn't any different with my own nation, I supposed.

The important thing was that Maria was safe once again.

"…they appear to be preparing for something," Fisk was saying. "As such, we couldn't wait for diplomatic channels. We need help, Mr. Bringer, and we need it now. Forget that we're British…we're allies, and innocent people's lives are at stake."

I frowned. The opportunity to strike at Continuance first felt highly tempting.

"Where did you say they were again?" I asked.

He appeared annoyed. "I just said, Cardiff Bay, across the bay from Bristol. Haven't you been listening to what I'm telling you?"

"Listen, Fisk, I've got a lot on my plate right now, so just back the hell off."

An uncomfortable silence grew as I alternated glances between Sanders and Fisk.

Each had tentative expressions.

"Mr. Bringer, we're being followed," Strutt said. "There's a dark sedan shadowing us less than a mile back."

I glanced over my shoulder, but couldn't see anything due to heavy trees at the bend we'd just passed.

"Speed up," I said. "Around the next bend, stop and let me out, then proceed on for a couple of miles before you stop."

"Logan, what are you planning to do?" Sanders asked, evident concern in her voice.

"Don't worry," I insisted. "I just want to lose our tail."

As soon as we rounded the next curve of road, Strutt brought the car to an abrupt halt. I quickly exited the vehicle and tapped on the window."

"Go!" I ordered.

As they pulled away, I rushed over to some nearby

bushes and tall grass that interspersed with the trees.

Moments later, a sedan pulled into view.

I used my abilities to grasp the car and elevate it into the air, rotating it until it was upside down. The car's engine whirred at high revolution before sputtering and stalling. I could see shock and panic on the two men's faces through the car's windshield.

I held up my right hand and wagged my index finger at them in mock-chastising fashion.

The driver and passenger windows opened to the sounds of what sounded like excited Belarusian, though I couldn't say for certain.

"Oh, shut up and enjoy the ride!"

I gently lowered the vehicle to the pavement until it balanced upon its roof. Just as a pistol was pointed toward me from the passenger, I gave the vehicle a spin, like a child might spin a top.

I paused to appreciate their shouts and what had to be colorful curses.

Then I jogged up the road until I saw our car slowly returning in my direction. They stopped as soon as they caught sight of what I'd done.

I opened the back car door and got in.

"All taken care of," I said. "Now, call Scott and tell him to get his ass back to the hotel. We're checking out. Oh, and I want our plane ready to go as soon as we can get to the airport."

"Yes, sir," Strutt said, turning our car around. "What shall I inform the flight crew? They'll want to know our destination for the flight plan."

"The UK. We're conveying Mr. Fisk back to Cardiff."

* * *

Scott met us at our hotel and within the hour we were headed back to the airport.

In a sense, it was a damned shame. After my enjoyable

dinner with Sanders the previous evening, and given our scenic location, it would've been nice to have stayed longer under more peaceable circumstances.

Unfortunately, it seemed that time was the commodity that we had the least ample supply of.

Much to my surprise, at the airport, we had no trouble processing for our departure from Belarus. Surely word of my encounter with those who had likely been associated with either Belarusian or Russian authorities must have spread by then.

Perhaps it was an indication of how happy they were to see us leave.

As we entered the departure wing of the airport and headed toward our private boarding area, I noticed the man with the scar who had interrogated us the previous day standing ahead of us with his arms folded before him.

He made no move to bar our way, instead staring at me with a sardonic expression and holding up his index finger, which he wagged at me in much the same fashion I had earlier in the day to those who had tailed us.

I slowed almost to a stop beside him.

"Happy hunting, Mr. Bringer?" he asked.

"Sorry, I left my hunting license back at home this time," I replied.

"You know as well as I that you carry your license with you wherever you go," he said. "It is a part of you, like any good predator."

I didn't know what to say to that, so I politely inclined my head toward him.

"Safe journey," he said. "But next time, perhaps you'll consider somewhere other than Belarus for your vacation. In fact, I strongly recommend it."

There was no misinterpreting his subtle warning.

"You have a beautiful country, and I like the food," I said. "But I suspect that, if I were to return here anytime soon, it won't be for either the sights or the cuisine."

He gave me a slight nod and looked in the direction of

our boarding gate; yet another subtle suggestion.

Sanders and the others had stopped and were watching us with curious expressions.

I conjured the most pleasant expression that I could muster at that moment and walked purposefully toward the boarding gate.

CHAPTER 10

During the flight to Cardiff, Fisk made contact with his superiors while Sanders cornered me in the plane's galley.

"As much as I want to help Fisk, you're aware that this takes us well outside of our arranged itinerary," Sanders said. "I need to consult with the home office on this."

"Okay, I get it. Give them a call now," I said. "Bear in mind that we didn't find any credible leads to go on while in Minsk, and we'd just be heading back home scratching our heads if it hadn't been for Fisk."

She nodded. "True enough, I suppose. Still, this could be a real political hot potato that might go a lot higher than either the FBI or NSA."

"Now you sound like Wainright," I said. "I don't have time to worry about politics."

"Bringer, grow up," she said, giving me a wan look. "You know as well as I do that politics are at the center of everything at stake here."

I shrugged. "Fine, then, let the damned politicians handle the politics. That's what Wainright and Tevin do for a living, in case you've forgotten. But while we're at it, doesn't it bother you, even just a little bit, that it was politicians who decided to forgo requests for assistance from the UK, even despite evidence that Continuance was determined to be active there?"

"At least, that's what Fisk said happened," she countered. "We have no way of knowing if he's even playing straight with us."

I pointed to my head with my forefinger. "Oh, no, I have high confidence that he believes what he told us."

"Yes, but that only indicates he believes what he's been told," she said.

"Okay. What are you getting at?"

She massaged her temples with her fingertips. "Look, I don't know. This whole mess has me looking at everything from so many angles, I'm not really sure who's playing straight with us anymore."

I reached out and gently grasped her hands in mine. Her hazel gaze had an almost helpless air.

I reached up with my right hand and gently ran my fingertips across her cheek. She closed her eyes and leaned into my fingers slightly.

I used my free hand to encourage her to turn away from me. Then I reached up with both hands and gently massaged her scalp and back of her neck.

A soft moan escaped her lips. "Oh, man, where did you learn that?"

I smiled. "One of my physical therapists during my chemotherapy days. It helped relax me a little bit. Maybe it will help you."

"Yeah, I'm all about this," she whispered, leaning her head back against my hands.

Such a simple gesture, and yet it spoke volumes to me. What surprised me was how much I enjoyed doing it for her, doing it to her.

I felt good easing her discomfort, if only for a few moments. And, frankly, I enjoyed the physical contact with her, if only in that limited fashion.

Maybe under different circumstances…

"There you two are," Fisk interrupted, parting curtain separating us from the main cabin.

Sanders turned with a start and I quickly withdrew my

hands from her.

"Oops, sorry to intrude," he apologized. "My mistake."

The curtain fell back into place, and I heard Fisk's footfalls retreating away from us.

Sanders looked at me with surprise. "Oh, priceless. I bet he thinks we're a couple or something."

"Well, partners at the very least, right?" I asked.

Her look of astonishment faded slightly and her eyes took on a suddenly distant look. Then she blinked and nodded.

"Yeah, partners," she agreed with a shy expression. "Thanks for the massage, partner."

I nodded. "Anytime."

I followed her back into the main cabin and over to where Strutt and Fisk sat.

"My superiors have arranged immediate clearance to land at Cardiff upon approach," Fisk said. "They'll meet us at the airport. Meanwhile, they're mobilizing additional law enforcement and tactical teams to deploy as soon as we're ready."

I looked at Sanders. "Feels like Seattle all over again."

She arched one brow at me. "Yeah, but this time let's not play with the electrical grid while we're in London."

Fisk gave us a cautionary look. "Electrical grid? Anything I should know ahead of time?"

I shrugged. "Hey, I'm a guy who already plays with fire and who likes to dabble. What more do you need to know?"

Sanders gave me a wry look.

"Lovely," Fisk replied. "I was barmy to ask."

Within the hour, Sanders set up her notebook computer for our secure conference with the home office. For additional privacy, she used a writing table in the small bedroom in the plane's aft section.

I appreciated a few minutes of reclining in one of the comfortable chairs positioned beside a small window.

"I just spoke with Mr. Bernard," Strutt said, walking from the gallery at the fore of the plane. "He's aware of our situation and encourages caution."

I nodded. "He means, 'try not to level the city,' I think."

"Perhaps a little of that, too," Strutt agreed.

"*Level the city?*" Fisk demanded. "Now see here—"

"It's ready," Sanders said, motioning with her hand from behind a curtain.

Strutt, Fisk, and Scott looked at her and then at me. For some reason, their expressions made me feel self-conscious.

"Teleconference with the home office," I said, hitching my thumb toward the curtain.

Strutt nodded and quickly looked down at the screen of the tablet he held. But Fisk adopted a mock-innocent expression.

"Oh, certainly, chat with the boss," he said. "I get it."

"Stow it, Fisk," I said, rising from my seat.

I parted the curtains to see Sanders staring at me.

"What was that all about?" she asked.

"Huh? Nothin'," I said.

I felt like a school boy who'd been caught playing hooky.

On the computer's screen, Tevin, Denton, and Wainright each appeared in their own windows.

"First, let's fill you in on what happened in Minsk," Sanders began. "I already uploaded some photos into the secure location on the FBI's storage network for you to review."

Sanders explained everything we did, or encountered, during our time in Belarus and with an impressive level of detail. She did a damned better job than I could have, anyway.

When we got to the part about Fisk and what was going on in the UK, Tevin appeared irritated.

"Yes, the CIA trumped us on that," Tevin said. "According to information that surfaced while you've been away, given how serious the concerns were following your Nevis Corners battle, the President felt it was better to keep you on U.S. soil."

"While we've been chasing our tails stateside with no results, I could've actually been busy kicking Continuance's ass over here," I said.

"Hindsight is always twenty-twenty, Bringer," Tevin said. "Listen, the point it, we don't have any better leads, so it makes sense to proceed to Cardiff. However, be aware that I'll need to share this higher up the food chain."

"Should we be concerned?" Sanders asked.

"Not at the moment," Tevin said. "But this could be viewed as trumping White House interests, or something of the sort. Suffice to say, I should be able to convey that we're reacting in the field to changing conditions."

"What about this fellow, Fisk?" Wainright asked.

"From what I can tell, he at least believes what he's telling us," I replied.

"Ah, I've got his bio here," Tevin said. "He's showing up as MI-6 in my database, although I don't have recent assignment postings for him. Still, as with anyone not in our circle, proceed with caution."

"Don't worry," Sanders said. "I don't blindly trust much of anyone right now."

I gave her a long look, wondering if my own suspicious mindset wasn't rubbing off on her or something. She poked me in the thigh where the others couldn't see, and my attention reverted to the screen again.

"Yeah, we're being careful here," I said. "Strutt and Scott have both been quite handy, I don't mind saying."

"Yes, well, we need to be careful in engaging civilians with our investigations and field operations," Wainright said. "Neither of them are official government contractors."

"Yeah, well, I'm not entirely trusting of the government side of our house right now, either," I shot back.

"Hard to argue with that," Denton said.

"You, now, too?" Wainright asked. "Look, let's not get carried away here or paranoia will run away with us all."

"Hey, I trust the people I know," Denton said. "And frankly, thus far, both Sanders and Bringer have displayed excellent instincts."

"Thank you, sir," Sanders said.

Tevin nodded. "Yes, well, under the circumstances, I'd have to agree with that."

"Something you want to share with us, Tevin?" Wainright asked.

"Perhaps," Tevin replied. "Lately, I've grown more concerned about some key players on Capitol Hill. Granted, it's easy to discount things when it's just your own suspicions; it's more unsettling when others concur or when suspicious events transpire."

"Interesting. Like what?" Wainright asked.

"For one, I found it strange that the CIA didn't even bother to mobilize any contacts for follow-up on the British reports of Continuance near Cardiff. Yet they practically raced to Belarus," Tevin said. "Second, President Graydon seems to be leaning more and more toward the advice of his National Security Advisor, Hal Wilkes, who favors both the CIA and the Homeland Security Secretary, Roger Beck, as preferred sources of intelligence."

"That last part doesn't sound like news," I said. "I think those are sources a President would typically listen to. Although I can't say that I'm a huge fan of Beck."

"Yeah, well, if Beck rubs you the wrong way, wait until you meet Hal Wilkes," Wainright offered. "You'll pine away for your biggest CIA fan, Yasmine Prichard."

I made a sour face. "You're just full of good news, aren't you guys?"

"Like it or not, those are the people that the President is listening to," Tevin said. "And we need to bear those individuals in mind as we strategize our own efforts. Also, the President isn't listening much to either the FBI or NSA lately."

"What?" Sanders demanded. "We're the ones spearheading the damned investigation."

"Yes, but the information is being filtered by those other individuals before it gets to the President," Tevin said. "My boss, Director Gus Pearson—he's a good guy and very competent, but he wasn't exactly in the President's cheering section during the campaign. That's come back to haunt him since the election."

I let out a deep breath and groaned. "Correct me if I'm wrong, but you guys make it sound like Capitol Hill is almost as bad as Continuance Corporation. Politics have always been dicey in Washington, but now it sounds like we're fighting against our own even while fighting against Continuance."

"Don't you just love politics?" Denton asked.

"That's why we need to be on our toes. Even more so. As people on the outside of the power bubble, we need to avoid making any major blunders," Wainright said. "These are people who use the system to their advantage, and you often don't see them coming out of your blind spot."

"Are you talking about Continuance or our government?" I asked.

"Both," Wainright clarified.

Sanders and I looked at each other.

"Okay, guys, just be careful out there," Tevin said. "In the meantime, I'll pass this up the ladder. Wainright, you might want to do the same so that we're presenting similar perspectives from different agencies."

"Agreed. Denton and I are on it," Wainright said.

"Sanders, you and Bringer watch yourselves," Denton said. "Oh, and Bringer, I have your contractor paperwork ready to sign when you get back. Mr. Bernard and his staff have been especially helpful expediting the process through the government contracting and procurement folks."

"That seems fast," Bringer said.

"Actually, that sounds historic," Sanders interjected.

"Yeah, record time, in fact," Denton said. "It typically takes weeks or months for something to make it all the way through contracting. Heck, it's often weeks just to get it through legal, much less procurement."

"Bringer was already on the executive office's radar," Wainright said. "A matter of top national security. Apparently, Hal Wilkes worked closely with Senators Ben Conway and Penny Savage, as well as Congressman Rubicon and Congresswoman Vandersnoot to put pressure on the process."

"Wait, aren't those key members in—"

"The Freedom Party," Tevin said. "Yes, and they're close supporters of the President, which doesn't hurt their gravitas."

"Okay, let me get this straight," Sanders said. "The people who are key to the President want Bringer on board as fast as possible but don't care to listen to advice from the two agencies who are working closest with him?"

"That's about the size of it," Wainright said.

"What the hell?" I demanded. "There's a disconnect here somewhere. I mean, that's not exactly a formula for success."

"I never said they wanted you to be successful, Bringer," Tevin said. "They just want to hire you."

Everyone fell silent.

"I don't think I like the implications there, Tevin," I said. "Hell, that wouldn't even make sense."

"Now you see why I'm concerned?" Tevin asked. "Look, I hope I'm wrong but some things just aren't fitting into place like they should. I've been in the business a lot of years, and I've never seen anything remotely like this, much less conducted with such disturbing disconnects at key decision-making levels."

Nobody said anything after that, but my mind raced with a host of dark thoughts.

Wainright finally broke the ominous silence. "Well, that's all we can do for now, I think. Anything further just spins up wild conspiracy theories that we don't have near enough data to substantiate. Suffice to say, we need to keep our eyes and ears open moving forward," he said. "Everyone be careful. Get back in touch the first chance you get after you assess the situation in Cardiff."

"That may not be until after first contact," Sanders said. "They're mobilizing as soon as we're wheels down."

"Like he said, be careful," Tevin said.

"Hey, Bringer, one more thing," Wainright said.

"Yeah?"

"For the time being, I'd like you to limit operational information going to Clive Bernard at Nuclegene. I know he's your contracting supervisor and everything," Wainright said.

"Why? What do I need to know about Bernard?"

"Well, it's not so much about Bernard as his boss, Nevis Wallace," Wainright replied.

"Wainright's correct," Tevin added. "Wallace is a big political contributor to both Senator Conway and Congresswoman Vandersnoot."

"Wait, you're implying that Nevis Wallace is one of those Freedom Party cranks?"

"Not exactly," Tevin said.

"Both Conway and Vandersnoot supported the Land Reclamation and Investment in America Act, which enabled corporate cities like Nevis Corners to be built. We think Wallace's support to them is mainly tied to that. However, we'd rather not take any chances until we see who all the key players are batting for," Wainright explained.

My head felt like it was spinning. "Yeah, under those circumstances, that's probably not a bad idea. I'll limit what I tell Bernard for now."

"Much appreciated," Wainright said. "Listen, I hope I'm wrong about suspecting Wallace, but it never hurts to be cautious, especially at this stage in the game."

"Good luck, you two," Denton said.

The screens went blank and I looked sidelong at Sanders.

"Damn," I said.

"Double-damn," she agreed.

CHAPTER 11

By the time we neared Wales, life on our luxurious aircraft was starting to grow old. There was a good reason I had once chosen to enlist in the Army instead of the Air Force.

Stuck on the plane, I felt like I was trapped.

Upon landing at Cardiff International, as Fisk had assured us, British authorities met us on the tarmac. However, the terminal overflowed with tension as many people watched televisions and their mobile phone screens.

A group of individuals approached us with an air of authority. They appeared on edge.

"What's going on? What's happened?" I asked.

"Mr. Bringer, Agent Sanders," said an older man wearing a starched-looking police uniform. "I'm Robert Digginsby, Deputy Assistant Commissioner of the Metropolitan Police Service. I'm afraid your arrival has coincided with a remarkable rash of events in Cardiff during the past hour. Matters have escalated far beyond investigations into Continuance Corporation. We're trying to sort order from chaos at the moment."

A middle-aged uniform-wearing man stepped forward to shake hands with Sanders and me. "Hello and welcome to Cardiff. I'm South Wales Police Assistant Chief Constable, Geoffrey Hill, part of the joint tactical team working under

DAC Digginsby's leadership."

A series of introductions ensued. Honestly, I'd already forgot most everyone else's names, so I hoped Sanders could prompt me, if needed.

"Pardon me if I seem a bit hasty, but we really should proceed from the terminal as soon as possible," urged DAC Digginsby.

Personally, I was fine with that. I turned to Strutt.

"You and Scott can check us into a hotel," I said. "Then stand by until Sanders or I contact you."

Strutt nodded. "Certainly, sir."

Sanders and I fell into step alongside Digginsby as we proceeded through the terminal.

"About that rash of events?" I pressed.

"We're still trying to make sense of it," he replied. "It's as if every sociopath in the city decided to go on a spree."

Sanders and I exchanged dark looks.

"What do you mean by spree?" Sanders asked.

"You name it," Hill interjected, walking behind us and alongside Fisk. "Murders, aggravated assaults, motorway road rage, arsons, and all manner of spontaneous acts of civil disobedience."

"All at once?" I asked.

"Well, perhaps not simultaneously," he replied. "But certainly beginning around the same time, then steadily increasing by each hour."

"Could they be coordinated?" Sanders asked. "Perhaps going off in a timed series?"

"We're still piecing information together, but it seems not. Thus far, it doesn't appear that the perpetrators have had communication with each another," Hill replied.

"That doesn't make sense," Sanders said. "Could it be chemical in nature? Perhaps some psychotropic-induced mass hysteria?"

"Agent Sanders, you sound as if you've seen too many science fiction programs," Digginsby said. "It seems to me our best angle is some sort of terrorist-related event.

However, we simply don't know how they've perpetrated it. At least, not yet."

"What about our primary target?" I asked.

"We have a police tactical team working alongside our antiterrorism response teams," Digginsby replied. "They've established a perimeter and they're maintaining its integrity under the highest priority."

"Do you have estimates concerning casualties from the various events?" Sanders asked.

"That's a bit sketchy right at the moment," Hill replied. "Certainly, dozens of people either killed or injured. However, at the rate events are occurring, I fear that number will quickly escalate."

"Everyone at the Yard has been mobilized, and the entire MPS has recalled its officers to immediate duty," Digginsby said. "Order will be reestablished soon enough. We'll mobilize the army if we have to."

I glanced back at Hill to see a less than optimistic expression on his face.

We all got into police-marked SUVs, Sanders and I sitting in the back seat of one while Hill commandeered the front passenger seat.

Lights and sirens blared as we made our way through semi-congested streets. The entire city teemed with rushing people.

"Bit chaotic, as I said earlier," Hill said, glancing back over his shoulder at us. "Still, we're making the best of it. I wish that we had three times the force to leverage, though. Or maybe just three of you, Bringer."

"Oh, really? We've found that one is hard enough to keep up with," Sanders offered.

I gave her a sidelong look. Then I started thinking about some of the things DAC Digginsby had said.

"When did everything start happening?" I asked.

"Hm? Oh, just over an hour ago, I'd estimate," Hill replied.

"Where did it start?" I asked, though I had little to no

knowledge of the area.

I pulled up a map of Cardiff on my smartphone.

"The roaming charges are going to cost you your first year's salary," Sanders said.

I looked up at her with a sober expression and then back at my phone.

Damn, she's probably right.

"I'll write it off on my taxes as a business expense," I said. "Now, Hill, do you recall where everything began?"

"As best we know, somewhere along the Cardiff docks," Hill said.

"Pardon me for saying, sir," said our driver. "But, if I'm not mistaken, the first strange call was Grangemoor Park, not far from University Hospital. A man attacked two joggers and then started thrashing bystanders."

"Yes, yes, that was it," Hill agreed. "Well said, Officer Gibbons."

"Sir," he replied.

"Wait," Sanders said. "When did your tactical team get everyone into place?"

Hill frowned over his shoulder at Sanders and then looked out the front windshield. "Let me see. It's coming up on two hours ago. Isn't that about right, Gibbons?"

"Right you are, sir." Gibbons replied. "They were here well before chaos erupted throughout the city."

Hill's mobile phone rang. "Hill here."

Sanders looked at me. "Are you thinking what I'm—"

"A diversion?" I interrupted. "Yeah, that crossed my mind, too."

"But for so many people to be involved," Sanders ventured. "We're talking about a major cell here."

"What if they weren't involved? Just victims," I said.

"Virus? Contamination from something?" she asked.

"No, someone," I said.

Sanders' face reflected my own level of concern.

"We haven't met anyone who can do that," she said.

"Not yet. But after what we found our recent

sightseeing venture, I suspect there's a number of other surprises out there waiting for us," I said.

"Here's an update," Hill said. "There's more events occurring throughout the city now. What did I miss between you two while I was on the phone? Perhaps an epiphany of some sort? We could use anything right about now."

"Listen, didn't I read somewhere that the UK uses a camera system for monitoring the general public?" I asked.

"Yes, we do. But we're hardly Big Brother around here," Hill replied. "We still have nothing on your own NSA, eh, what? They know what you've had for breakfast before you've finished clearing the table, I hear."

Hill appeared quite pleased with himself over his quip.

"If only," I said. "Actually, it's the CIA we worry about nowadays."

"Oh, I see," Hill replied.

Sanders gave me a sharp look.

"We're almost there, sir," Gibbons said.

"Thank you, Gibbons."

"Hill, is there any chance that your folks could confirm if there's a common person in any of the areas around where the events are occurring?" Sanders asked.

"Our technicians are already working on that with inspectors from the Yard," Hill replied. "We're awaiting an update."

Our group of vehicles pulled up outside what appeared to be a warehouse and industrial area.

"Where are we?" I asked as I exited the SUV with Sanders.

"Business district," Gibbons replied. "Not far from Hill Snook Park."

DAC Digginsby approached us, along with a tactical commander wearing combat gear. Digginsby made the introductions.

"They're just inside that dark gray and white warehouse," Commander Yarborough said to Digginsby. "We have the perimeter secure and we're waiting to either engage in dialogue or move in on your orders, sir."

"Any movement?" Sanders asked.

"No, they're just sitting tight," the commander replied. "One of my snipers believes they may have spotted our team, but it's as if they're waiting on something. We've got the airspace locked up tight and we control all ingress or egress routes by street, so I'm confident they're not going anywhere."

"They're waiting for the chaos to overwhelm us," I said.

"What?" Digginsby demanded. "What do you mean by that?"

"I'm in the wrong place," I said. "At least, right at the moment."

Digginsby appeared dumbfounded while the commander watched me through narrowed eyes.

"Sir, precisely why have we been waiting here?" he asked. "What is it that Mr. Bringer here can do for us that we can't already?"

"I'm afraid that's strictly a 'need to know only' for now, commander," Digginsby said.

"Due respect, sir, but I'd say that my need to know is now," Yarborough said.

"I'm the heavy artillery, commander," I said. "You're here to take people with telekinetic abilities into custody. And, right now, I'm the only person who can counter those abilities."

"So it would seem," Digginsby said. "Point well made."

"Wait, you're one of them?" Yarborough demanded.

"No," Sanders said, arching her brow. "He's on *our* side. He's one of *us*."

I gave Sanders a proud look.

"But I suspect the telekinetic I need to be worried about isn't here right now," I said.

"Well, if not here, then where?" Digginsby asked.

"Out there," Hill said, giving me a meaningful look. "You think there's someone out there causing all these events, don't you? That's why you asked me if we've evaluated the camera footages."

I nodded. "Yep. Your mass acts of violence will stop when I find the person who's the source of the chaos and make them stop."

"You mean one person might be responsible for what's sending half the city of Cardiff off the rails?" Yarborough asked.

I shrugged. "That's my guess."

"Well, couldn't they be doing that from in there?" Yarborough asked, pointing toward the warehouses.

I considered his question. "Maybe," I replied. "But I haven't met anyone yet with that kind of range or scope. I'd wager they're still somewhere in the city."

"DAC Digginsby, can you permit us access to where they're studying video recordings?" Sanders asked.

"Of course."

"Wait. What about the people in that warehouse?" Yarborough asked.

"I'd recommend letting them sit there, but keep them surrounded," Sanders said. "As long as they think their plan is working, we've got a chance to apprehend the person causing the havoc."

"Sanders is right. If they figure out otherwise, we may lose our opportunity to take them into custody," I said. "These people are proven extremists."

"I'll have officers convey you to the nearest facility where you can access the video feeds," Hill said. "Perhaps you'll see someone who looks familiar. In the meantime, we'll stand down and keep this area secured. That is, with DAC Digginsby's concurrence."

Digginsby nodded. "Certainly. Do proceed."

"I'm going to stay here with the tactical team," Agent Fisk said.

The plan all sounded well and good to me, and I admired Sanders' confident tone, but I didn't have the heart to confess to them that Sanders and I were as much in the dark as they were.

By the look on her face, she must've been thinking something similar.

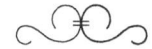

CHAPTER 12

I had been around large cities enough to know the difference between a hectic pace and out-and-out pandemonium. Cardiff had the look of the latter.

Gibbons and a fellow officer—Anson? —drove us to one of the nearest police labs where we could gain access to the video surveillance systems. The chatter on the vehicle's police radio was incessant. The mayhem had exceeded the ability of the authorities to contain it.

I wondered about the significance of Continuance Corporation's presence in the UK. Was it the location of one of their operational or logistical centers? Or did the shadow group have larger plans, perhaps even against the government itself?

Unfortunately, there was still too much I didn't understand about our foes and their objectives.

While we waited at a stoplight, a loud crashing sound, much like vehicles colliding, caught our attention.

"I think it came from the street to our right," Anson said, tightly gripping the steering wheel.

Gibbons started to report in via radio. "They're overwhelmed. Can't even get dispatch to respond."

Gunfire and screams followed. People ran for cover up and down the street.

I reached for the door handle. "Anson, take Sanders to

the lab. Gibbons, you're with me."

"Right, sir," Gibbons eagerly replied, already exiting the vehicle.

Sanders grabbed my upper arm. "You can't go out there, Bringer. We need you against the source."

"I'm not going to sit around staring at video feeds when I can be doing something useful," I said. "Call me when you locate somebody or some place of interest."

I slammed the SUV's door and ran headlong into a mob of frantic people who streamed past me. To Gibbons' credit, he pushed forward alongside me with his baton at the ready.

"Police! Move aside now!" he yelled, sounding authoritative and confident. "Seek cover! Get off the street!"

Two vehicles had collided in the middle of the street, one with what appeared to be small bullet holes in the back window and trunk. Both drivers appeared to be okay so we moved on.

Two more gunshots sounded as we rushed forward. By then, the crowds had thinned somewhat, many people ducking into nearby shops and behind vehicles.

Just ahead, I saw an older man wearing a hunter's vest. He'd just finished reloading a shotgun.

Not six feet away from him, two teenage girls huddled behind the trunk of a nearby car. The man lifted the shotgun, aiming at them.

"Police! Drop the gun now!" Gibbons ordered.

I admired the grit of a man holding only a baton who'd try to face down a gunman like that.

The man turned toward us instead.

I held up my hand and generated a shield just as the man pulled the trigger. The girls screamed.

Pellets appeared in a pattern, suspended in midair before us. The man fired again, but I caught the next round, as well.

I dropped the shield and pellets skittered to the pavement. I pushed my hand outward toward the gunman.

He flew into the air, landing about twenty feet away onto the street with a heavy thud.

"Bloody hell," Gibbons muttered, staring at me with mouth agape.

He quickly recovered, rushing forward with me to apprehend the gunman. I stripped the shotgun from the man's firm grip while Gibbons rolled him over and cuffed him.

The man muttered gibberish, so I took a chance and I opened my thoughts to him.

…must kill the zombies or they'll get me! I can't get away!

Then a wave of other excited and random thoughts invaded my mind, causing me to reel. I closed off my mind and pressed my palm to my forehead.

"Thanks ever so much. You okay, Bringer?" Gibbons asked.

"Yeah, fine," I said, appreciating the solitude of my own mind once again. "He thinks that everyone's a zombie."

"What? How can you—"

"Trust me, I know," I insisted.

I looked around at people who were starting to gather and come out from hiding places to stare at us, some commenting about what they had just seen.

"…threw the man into the air and down street right before my eyes."

"…see that? Just like the news said he did overseas."

Gibbons rose to stand, addressing the crowd. "See here now, move along! We're in a state of civil emergency! Get back to your homes and stay off the streets!"

I'd say one thing for Gibbons, he knew how to take command of even the most bizarre situations.

He tried his personal radio again to call in our situation.

"Suspect in custody. No injuries," he said.

"Hold until relief arrives. No free units at the moment," came the response from dispatch.

Then we heard more shouting and screams from around the corner and not far away.

Gibbons and I looked at each other.

"It's the apocalypse, it is," he said. "Help me get this

man over to that post and we'll handcuff him in place."

We ran toward the direction of the next commotion.

* * *

Two hours after apprehending two more violent suspects, Gibbons had run out of handcuffs and I was out of breath. He was kind enough to purchase a sports drink for me from a nearby convenience store as we paused to catch our breath.

"I'd been thinking about moving the wife and kids out to the country," he said between swigs from his bottled water. "Now I'm convinced to do it."

"There's no place safe from this until we stop who's causing it," I said.

"You're right, of course," he agreed.

"You're a brave man, Gibbons," I said. "Staring down a man with a shotgun like you did."

"Very kind of you to say, sir. But what you did is even more amazing," he said. "I'd be in bad way if you hadn't stopped those rounds."

"We both would," I said.

My mobile phone rang. It was Sanders.

"Tell me something good, this is probably costing me a million-dollar roaming charge," I said.

Gibbons chuckled.

"We've managed to correlate a common person at some scenes," Sanders said.

"Just a second," I said, putting my phone on speaker. "Go ahead. You're on speaker."

"She's a dark-haired woman wearing blue jeans and a dark-colored sweatshirt with a sports team emblem on the front," Sanders said. "No photo recognition for her on file. They're cross-referencing with Interpol now."

"Let's narrow it down a bit. Which team emblem is on her sweatshirt?" Gibbons asked.

We listened as Sanders and two other people conversed

in the background.

"Port Duckton is what the shirt appears to say," Sanders said.

I looked at Gibbons. "Duckton?"

He shook his head. "Someone's having a lark. At least, that's certainly not an English Premier team."

"Well, real or not, it's something to go on," I said. "Any idea where she's at now?"

"We have a recent image taken at Church Street and St. Mary's," Sanders said.

"That's not far from here," Gibbons said. "It's near the Central Market. We can make it on foot."

"Wait, that was almost an hour ago. We also have an image from about twenty minutes ago near Llwynfedw Gardens and—" Sanders said.

"Ma'am, look here," said someone at Sanders' end of the connection. "And there…"

"Oh, no," Sanders said.

"What is it?" I demanded.

"We've plotted her locations on a map by timeline. Unlike before, it now appears she's steadily making her way north through the city," Sanders said. "I'd bet she's heading in the direction of the warehouses and Commander Yarborough's team."

I looked at Gibbons, who was shaking his head. "She's far north of us now," he said.

"Dammit," I said. "Sanders, can you get anyone to pick us up? Helicopter maybe?"

"Hill and I are on our way from Cardiff Bay," she said. "Hang tight."

"Well, skip the red lights, okay?"

I hated waiting, but especially now that we had a specific target, it felt nearly intolerable.

"Our mark is on foot," Gibbons pointed out. "We'll intercept her yet."

Despite my misgivings, I admired his confidence.

Still, in the past we'd usually been one step behind our

adversary. It would sure be nice to reverse that trend.

* * *

Officer Gibbons helped things along by guiding us to a central roadway that he referred to as the A469. As we walked alongside the street, Hill and Sanders picked us up on the way north.

The roadway was less congested than it had been earlier. Apparently, the authorities had placed the city under martial law and established a curfew until further notice.

That's when I realized how out of control things were.

"Mr. Bringer, I can't thank you enough for pitching in until we had solid leads," Hill said.

"My pleasure. It kept me busy," I said. "You've got a good man here in Gibbons. He did stellar work in the field with me today."

"Well done, Gibbons," Hill said.

"Thank you, sir," replied Gibbons. "And just so you know, we just passed Llwynfedw Gardens on the right. The tactical team is just a kilometer or so ahead."

"Good," I said.

I could hardly wait to get onsite and prepare for the hopeful arrival of our visitor. The only problem was I didn't know how much more havoc she might wreak before arriving to us.

"Are we sure this lady is the one?" I asked.

"The video evidence is compelling," Sanders said. "There weren't any other people who appeared near multiple incidents as she did."

Aside from the continued heavy chatter on the radio, an unsettling silence fell among us.

Hill's mobile phone's ringing made me lurch in my seat.

"Hill," he said. "What? We're almost there. Contain, if possible."

A sour feeling formed in the pit of my stomach.

"Commander Yarborough just reported in," Hill said.

"There's activity around the warehouses. It seems that more chaotic events are stirring in the vicinity and some team members have been forced to intervene."

Officer Anson was at the wheel and he increased our vehicle's speed, passing the police SUV in front of us.

My previous years of field experience in combat zones kicked in.

"Your forces are being split up and lured away," I warned. "It must be an attempt to weaken your perimeter."

"Yes, well, there's not much to be done about it," Hill said. "We don't exactly have any surplus of force to supplement them right at the moment."

"Yes, but what if that was the idea all along?" Sanders asked.

"This is something we simply never anticipated at this scale before, and we don't have boundless resources to draw upon," Hill said, sounding quite defensive.

"ACC Hill, listen, we're not trying to be critical," I said. "It's frustrating for everyone involved."

I knew things were getting bad when I was the one trying to play peacemaker.

"Unfortunately, Bringer and I have experience with this sort of circumstance," Sanders added.

My adrenaline spiked to the point that I considered getting out and sprinting.

I bailed out of the vehicle before Anson came to a complete stop.

CHAPTER 13

I'd no sooner stepped from the SUV when gunfire erupted all around us. Multiple rounds penetrated the body of our vehicle as everyone scattered for cover.

I looked up. One of the tactical team members ahead of us was the source of the gunfire.

"Hey, we're friendlies!" I yelled.

More rounds rained upon us as I rushed forward, throwing up a shield before me.

As the guy paused to reload, I grabbed him with my talent and propelled him onto the ground.

More shots rang out from nearby and I heard numerous rounds impact turf, followed by a nearby gasp. I turned to see one of the officers who had accompanied us fall to the ground, clutching at his chest.

Following the probable trajectory of the incoming fire, I spotted another tactical team member along a section of concrete wall, his assault rifle pointed toward us.

Once again, I reached out with my abilities, propelling him back against the wall with a thud. He slammed into the wall hard and fell unconscious onto the ground.

We were late. Our mystery target had already arrived.

"Pull everyone back! Now!" I ordered.

"What the devil—" Hill shouted.

I turned and headed back toward our group.

"Don't you get it? The team's been compromised by that woman," I said. "You've got to get everyone the hell out of here now."

"What about those in the warehouse?" Hill demanded. "We can't very well let them just walk away."

"Shit," I muttered. "We're just going to have to take that chance. I can't fight our target if I'm busy fighting all of your people, too."

"He's right, sir," Gibbons spoke up. "We should pull back."

"All right," Hill said. "I'll give the order. Please try not to kill any of our people, if you can manage it."

I gave him a nod and looked at Sanders. "You pull back, too."

She looked none too pleased, but retreated with the group.

"And Hill, try to form a larger perimeter, if you can," I said.

"Aye. If we can," Hill replied.

I turned and headed toward the closest warehouse, opening my thoughts to see if I could detect anyone before they started firing at me. As a precaution, I raised a shield around me.

I continued at a slow pace, listening with both my mind and ears.

...almost in my sights.

Sights?

I halted in my tracks.

Great, probably a sniper.

I evaluated my position and anticipated possible firing positions before stepping forward.

Rather than hearing the rifle shot, I felt the round's impact against my shield. I turned in that direction and saw the bullet suspended before me. My shield held it in place.

Another round slammed into my shield within an inch of the other, and I visually followed the line of fire back to the sniper, who was lying atop a nearby building's sheet metal roof.

I dropped my shield and the suspended bullets fell to the ground.

Controlling my rising anger, I reached out and lifted him into the air. He twisted and shouted as I spun him around and then dropped him to the ground before me.

He hit the ground heavily and I heard the air rush from his lungs. I bent down, stripped the rifle from his grip, and punched him squarely in the face while buffering my fist with a light shield.

His head snapped backward and he slumped to the ground, unconscious.

In addition to being highly effective, my new technique saved me a lot of future bruised knuckles.

I proceeded forward, raising my shield and opening my thoughts, trying to concentrate my focus before me and to the sides for maximum effectiveness. A number of voices immediately made their presence known.

…any more coming?

…have told us by now.

…long before we can leave for the port?

…much like scaring children, really.

…already tired of sitting around waiting.

It seemed as if the thoughts came from ahead of me, somewhere inside the nearest warehouse.

However, I sensed that one person—the one thinking about scaring children—was off to my left and not far from me. That was the one I was most interested in, for the moment.

As I moved in the direction of the source, I felt a strange sensation, like an itching deep inside my head.

Feeling brave enough to find me?

I stopped, startled.

It was a woman's voice. Her thoughts were so clear in my mind that I almost thought she was actually speaking aloud to me.

I slowly moved forward, making my way past stacks of

crates, shipping containers, and large freight trucks.

As if sensing her proximity, I felt drawn to a smaller nearby warehouse, and not the largest central warehouse, the former focus of the tactical operation.

The sliding main doors were ajar a couple of feet, so I peeked inside.

Getting warmer.

I stopped, the itching sensation prevalent in my head again. Once more, the woman's voice in my head was as clear as if she stood beside me.

I hesitated and stepped inside. No interior light fixtures were turned on, but the warehouse was slightly illuminated by daylight from windows interspersed along the walls.

Opening my mind further, I concentrated on detecting thoughts.

…should be interesting.

Wait! He's listening to me!

I paused.

Pain ripped through my head jarring my teeth.

How dare you try to get inside MY head?!

I gripped my head in both hands and pressed on my temples, as if trying to get inside to the pain and rip it out.

I concentrated and tried to construct the strongest shield that I could manage.

After a moment, the pain subsided to a tolerable degree, though I felt intense strain from trying to maintain my shield at that level.

"So, you're stronger than I gave you credit for. So much stronger than the puppets dancing around this city," said a woman, who now stood before me. "Still, it's not going to help you."

She had long, dark hair and was wearing the sweatshirt and jeans that Sanders had previously described. What surprised me was that, unlike her thoughts in my head, her voice carried a slight European accent.

"Who are you?" I asked. "Are you part of Continuance Corporation?"

"You're very inquisitive, aren't you?" she countered. "You don't know me, but I know you. You're Logan Bringer."

"And I don't even deserve to know yours?"

She shrugged. "Marlis, but my friends call me Lis. Not that it really matters to you much longer. Shame really. You're sort of cute."

"Ever visited Minsk, Lis?" I asked.

The edges of her mouth rose. "You do get around, don't you? It's no harm to say that I visited there for a short time."

"Well, I hope the food was good where you were staying," I said. "Because the décor left a lot to be desired from my perspective."

She frowned.

"Say, by the way, which cell was yours? Was it the one with the Crayola pictures on the wall?" I pressed. "I sort of liked those."

Her jaw tightened. "Screw you! You have no idea what we've been through."

"Do tell."

"What are you, some kind of shrink?"

"Why stay there, I wonder?" I asked. "Say, was that where your abilities were manifested?"

"I don't like talking to you anymore," she said, reaching up to massage her temples with her fingertips.

Intense pressure formed inside my head, almost like a vise pressing on my brain, but my shields held.

Concentrating on her, I put all my strength into insulating my mind.

"You're good," she said. "But not very observant."

I frowned and heard someone behind me.

Glancing over my shoulder, Sanders stood with a pistol pointed at my head. Her hands shook as if she couldn't hold onto her weapon.

"Meg?" I asked.

"N-No," she said, gritting her teeth.

A tear ran down her cheek as her pistol fired.

The shield I conjured before me was so weak that the tip of the bullet actually touched my forehead before I managed to stop it.

The mental force of the impact against my shields broke my concentration.

The assault resumed in my mind. Searing pain ripped through my brain, dropping me to my knees.

I struggled to maintain a mental barrier as Meg cried out with anguish. Her pistol fired again and again at me.

My shields felt battered, and it was all I could manage to stay conscious to hold them in place. All the while, I heard Lis' voice screaming in my head.

I'm going to blow your brains out from inside and out! You're going to explode soon!

I felt so violated and angry that I lashed out in all directions with my skills, careless of who I affected.

Meg's body flew across the warehouse and rolled across the floor. I turned and Lis staggered backward, though remained on her feet.

The pain inside my head doubled and I rocked backward on my knees, nearly toppling over.

I thrust both of my hands outward toward her in a last-ditch effort, channeling every ounce of energy I could manage, and felt an invisible sensation of impact as my abilities met her own shields.

Her body flew up into the air and away from me, slamming against the far wall of the warehouse.

Lis fell onto the concrete floor and rolled, coming to a rest against the wall. I reached out with my mind, but sensed no conscious thoughts emanating from her.

My legs buckled, and I dropped to the floor onto my forearms and knees while my hands trembled. I balanced myself for what felt like forever. My nose bled and my vision faded in and out.

Finally, I willed myself to crawl toward Meg.

When I reached her, she was lying face down on the concrete. I gently rolled her over and thankfully felt a pulse, letting out a deep breath that I hadn't realized I'd been holding.

"Oh, thank God," I muttered.

She stirred with a moan.

Then her eyes flittered open and she made an odd wheezing noise as she struggled to breathe.

"Logan," she whispered, fresh tears streaming from her eyes. She reached up with both arms and held onto me. "I'm so sorry, Logan…I couldn't stop myself. I'm so, so sorry."

She started crying in wracking sobs, like a child who had woken from some terrible nightmare.

"It's okay, Meg," I said softly, trying to soothe her.

"…tried not to hurt you," she mumbled. "Couldn't stop myself."

"I know, I know," I said, holding her in my arms. "It's not your fault. Everything's okay now."

"No…it's not," she said between sobs. "I feel dirty inside my head. I hate myself!"

"Meg, stop," I urged. "You're okay now."

I didn't know what else to say; I was barely holding myself together at that moment. I just held her in my arms, so grateful that she was alive.

My entire body felt weak and wracked with pain, but still I held onto her as if my life depended on it.

I needed her.

It was macabre timing for that sort of revelation, and it cut deep to my core.

After a few moments, I lay her onto the floor.

"Stay still," I said. "You'll be okay."

Ignoring the throbbing pain in my head, I struggled to my feet and half-staggered over to where Lis lay.

Anger welled from deep inside me as I stared down at her.

How many people had died needlessly that day because of her?

Heat formed in my right hand. A fireball swirled above my palm.

I raised my hand and paused.

"Burn in hell, bitch."

Someone grabbed my arm from behind.

"Logan, no!" Sanders screamed.

"What do you mean, no?" I demanded, pulling free from her grasp. "She's evil! She ruined however many people's brains and damned near killed us both."

Meg's face looked pale, almost white, and her eyes were terror-filled.

"P-Please don't, Logan," she urged, still gripping my arm in her hands. "I know you're angry. I am, too. But we need answers and she may be the only lead we've got so far."

I took a deep breath as I considered what she said.

Then I nodded and extinguished the fireball, wisps of flame harmlessly falling to the concrete floor beside me.

Only then did she let go of my arm.

"Thank you," she said, her hands still shaking.

I reached out and drew her into my arms, holding her closely.

"I'm so sorry, Logan," she said, her arms wrapped around me. "I could never forgive myself if something happened to you."

"It's okay now," I said. "It was her doing, not yours."

Then the scope of our situation flooded into my head all at once, as if my mind was clearing from a fog-like state.

"Oh, shit! The warehouse," I said.

"We're in the warehouse," she muttered.

"The other warehouse," I said, taking her by the hand and pulling her behind me.

CHAPTER 14

"Okay, okay, I'm coming," she insisted, pulling free from my grip.

"Stay close behind me," I urged. "I mean it."

"All right," she said.

I glanced back over my shoulder at her and she nodded.

"Go," she said.

I approached a standard-sized door with small glass window in it and peered inside.

Seeing nobody, I tried the door handle and found it locked.

While not unexpected, it annoyed me.

Given the urgency of the moment, and anticipating that the element of surprise was lost at that point, I took a deep breath and attempted to raise my abilities once more.

My head throbbed with pain, but I reached out with my abilities until I sensed the door. I pressed my shield against it and felt it meld onto the surface. Then I drew my hands backward and to the side.

The door creaked, its hinges protesting, and then popped loose amidst the loud snapping of metal.

I dropped it to the ground and stepped inside the building, Sanders close behind me.

I listened, but heard nothing at first.

Then I heard the echoes of vehicle doors opening and

closing, then engines revved to life.

Sanders and I rushed through the building until we reached the warehouse's main bay.

A van and two small cars pulled away through an opening in the warehouse's large bay doors and out of sight before I could raise my abilities to stop them.

Honestly, at that point it was all that I could do to stand upright. My legs felt all wobbly and unreliable.

"Shit," I muttered.

I leaned against a nearby stack of crates and then felt Sanders encircle my waist with her arms to steady me.

"We have to stop them," I said.

"Come on," Sanders said. "Maybe we can get word to Hill. He might have even stopped them by the time we get to him."

I leaned on Sanders as little as possible, though I felt like my energy reserves were just about spent.

Had I already used up all my mojo?

Where was a cola vending machine when you needed one?

We hobbled outside the warehouse and made our way toward the gated entrance.

Then I recalled one of the many thoughts I had overheard earlier.

"They're headed for the port," I said.

"What? How do you know?" she asked.

I didn't even have time to reply before she said, "Oh, never mind," she said. "Of course."

Sanders still seemed a little out of it. Then again, we'd both just been through hell together.

As we exited through the main gates, I heard a helicopter circling overhead. Three tactical team members lay dead near the road.

"They blew past the perimeter team," I said, waving up at the helicopter to get the pilot's attention.

"Huh?" Sanders said, looking around. "Oh, crap."

"Yeah," I said. "Big load of crap."

Within minutes, a police SUV raced toward us. Hill,

Gibbons, and two tactical team members exited all at once, their weapons drawn.

"They got away in multiple vehicles," I said.

That's when Hill saw the bodies of his men.

"Damn," he said. "We lost contact with this team. Thought they went inside to support you. At least, that's what we'd hoped."

Gibbons helped Sanders expedite me to the SUV.

"You've got a chopper in the air," I said. "Didn't they see them escaping?"

"We only have access to three helos," he countered. "This one arrived on scene in time to see you and Agent Sanders."

"They're going to the docks," I said. "You need to seal the ports."

"Will do," Hill said. "Did you see the vehicles?"

"I got a good look," Sanders said.

"Give me the descriptions and I'll relay them," Gibbons said.

Sanders nodded.

"What about the woman?" Hill asked, sounding somewhat anxious.

"She called herself Marlis, Lis for short. We left her back in the smaller warehouse to the left. She's still alive, but unconscious. I'd recommend getting in there fast with a medical team. Whatever you do, keep her heavily sedated," I said. "She wakes up and people are going to die again."

"Very disturbing," he said, walking alongside Sanders. "I'll see to it personally. Are you injured?"

"I'll live," I said as Sanders and Gibbons helped me into the back seat of the SUV. "But I'm going to need an energy drink or Coca-Cola ASAP."

Hill and Gibbons gave me the most incredulous of looks.

* * *

I lay on a leather couch in Hill's office, drinking from my third bottle of sports-formula energy drink. Sanders perched on the edge of the couch with a bottled water.

She looked like hell, though she'd never hear it from me.

I was sure I looked just as bad, if not worse.

Our encounter with Lis had taken a lot of out me…out of both of us.

At least my nose bleed had stopped and my head felt like it was a part of me once again.

Sanders placed her cool palm to the side of my face and I looked up at her.

"Feeling better?" she asked.

"Yeah," I replied. "You?"

She shrugged. "I'll be okay."

I reached up and grasped her hand.

Then something struck me.

"I told you to fall back with the others," I said. "Why did you follow after me?"

She slipped her hand from mine and looked away. "We're partners. We stick together. You needed backup, so I waited until I thought it was safe to follow you."

Well, at least her intentions were well placed.

"Thanks," I said.

"For what? Almost killing you?" she retorted, a pained look evident in her eyes.

I reached out to take her hand again. "No, for caring enough to back me up in the first place."

A look of surprise crossed her features.

Hill walked into the room and Sanders quickly pulled her hand away.

I sat upright on the couch.

"You two look somewhat better," Hill said. "We scoured the port and ensured that no ships are permitted in or out of any docks, but nobody has been apprehended yet."

"How many other ports are there?" Sanders asked.

"Surely, you jest," Hill replied. "We're a port-based nation. Take your pick."

I exchanged a sardonic look with Sanders.

"I'm sorry," Hill amended. "That was out of line. You're

in a foreign land, operating on little or no logistical information. The truth is, we'd be lost without you and we're grateful for your help."

"Happy to pitch in. If you don't mind me changing the subject, what's the status of Marlis?" I asked.

"She's been secured in an undisclosed government location, and heavily sedated per your recommendation," Hill replied. "Beyond that, I can't say. I'm afraid the matter has been taken out of my jurisdiction."

"That would be Digginsby's territory, I presume," Sanders suggested.

A wry expression crossed Hill's features. "Actually, DAC Digginsby has been recalled to London. Bit of a sticky wicket, I'm afraid. As such, I've been temporarily granted operational authority here in Cardiff, though I'm confident someone from the Yard will be here soon to oversee further investigations."

Again, Sanders and I looked at each other knowingly. It was ironic how the dynamics of office politics held true, no matter what part of the world you were in.

"It's for the best, I'm sure. We have our hands full with local affairs as it is, you understand," Hill continued. "Still, as for DAC Digginsby, it was a difficult set of circumstances and things could've gone up or down on a whim."

"Digginsby's a scapegoat?" I asked.

"Hm, yes, well, some might see it that way," Hill said.

"How would you classify it?" Sanders asked.

"I'm sure it's merely a readjustment in command structure," Hill replied, casually looking out through his office window. "One mustn't make too much of these things."

"Uh-huh," I said. "Nicely worded."

He looked at me. "One also has to be careful what one says, as well as how one says it, if you catch my meaning."

I chuckled. "Yeah, I, for one, get it."

"In truth, Bringer's merely humoring you," Sanders said. "He's never been very good at subtlety."

I gave her a dirty look, but she ignored me.

"Err, quite," Hill said.

"What next?" I asked, eager to change the subject.

Hill looked at me. "We're combing the region for clues, eyewitnesses, new leads, and what not. For now, there's not much more you can do until we uncover something useful. I recommend the two of you check into your hotel and get some rest. Rest assured, we'll call as soon as we learn something."

That was a suggestion I was all too eager to heed.

CHAPTER 15

I awoke in the middle of the night, having broken out in a cold sweat, with my arms stretched across opposite sides of the bed. I took a deep breath and let it out slowly as I flexed my achy arms and rubbed my forehead.

The room was dark and acrid, as if someone had burned popcorn or toast.

However, my mind was too jumbled with an array of thoughts to focus on that.

No, not thoughts; voices.

...always have to pick up the damned trays all the time? And what's with the bloody lights tonight?

...should tell her that I'm married? Nah...

...never get to sleep at this rate.

...can't believe I almost killed him yesterday.

I felt startled at picking up Sanders' stray thoughts from the room next door.

I realized that our encounter with that woman—Marlis?—had shaken both of us up, though I had neglected to consider it from Sanders' point of view at length.

I imagined that, for an FBI agent, protecting one's partner was top of the list in importance. It was no different with the soldiers assigned to my fire team when I had been overseas.

On our way to the hotel after leaving Hill's office, I had

tried to reassure her that it wasn't her fault, but she had fallen silent and refused to talk more about it.

What more could I do for her?

I reached over to switch on the lamp next to my nightstand, but the bulb appeared to have burned out.

Slowly, I rolled out of bed, feeling many muscles in my body protest with aches and pain.

I wandered into the bathroom and had to flip on nearly every light switch before a dim bulb above the shower finally popped on.

What gives?

Something wasn't right.

I splashed water on my face and toweled it dry before turning back toward the bedroom.

That's when I saw them. Black scorch marks on the carpet next to my bed, illuminated by the dim light emanating from the bathroom.

"What in the *hell?*"

I walked over to the opposite side of the bed to find similar markings on the floor. I grabbed my mobile phone and used the screen's illumination to follow the scorch lines, each leading to the nearest electrical outlet.

I picked up the phone to dial Sanders' room. Fortunately, the phone was still functional.

"Sanders, get in here," I said.

There was a knock just as I was pulling my pants on. I hurried over to open the door.

"What's wrong?" Sanders asked. "And why is it so dark in here?"

I used the light from my phone to show her the scorch marks.

"You did this? How? Why?"

"Yes to the first question," I replied. "And 'beats the hell out of me' to the others."

"So, you must be the reason the lights have been flickering on and off for the past hour," she said. "I wonder why your sheets weren't scorched."

"Dunno," I said. "Maybe I generated a shield in my sleep or something."

"Are you hurt?" she asked.

"Nope. The question is, are you okay?"

She frowned. "Yeah, why wouldn't I be?"

"No reason."

"Bringer, you're acting really strange, even for you."

I called the front desk to report a problem with the lights. I couldn't help wondering what they'd say about the damaged carpeting.

It was more than an hour before the hotel resolved the lighting issue, and the night manager met with me regarding the carpeting damage.

"I don't know," I said. "It was that way when I woke up."

He looked at Sanders, who gave him an innocent look in response.

Hey, I hadn't lied to the fellow, after all. What I said was essentially true.

"Very odd," he said. "In light of things, we should relocate you to another room for the remainder of the night."

"Nah, I'll just stay with her," I said.

Sanders flashed me a surprised look before regaining her composure.

"Um, certainly," she said.

To the man's credit, his raised eyebrows were fleeting. "I see, then. Very good, madam. Please contact the main desk if we can do anything else for you tonight."

As he left the room, Sanders shook her head and walked toward the door.

"What?" I asked.

"Never mind. Collect your crap and come next door," she said.

"Hey, you angry with me?" I asked. "I can always get another room, you know."

She never even looked back. "Shut up, Bringer."

I grinned despite myself, then sobered over the

145

realization that I had somehow channeled electricity in my sleep. The last time something like that had happened was when I had moved objects.

No, that was just before I manifested the ability to move objects.

I gazed over at the nearest electrical outlet.

* * *

I fell asleep on the sofa in Sanders' room, but we were both awakened by an alarm on her notebook computer.

Minutes later, we were both peering at the screen at the multiple images of Wainright, Tevin, and Denton. Each of them looked as tired as I felt.

"Well, you three look like you've been through the wringer," I said.

"Frankly, it's been a long day," Tevin said.

"What the hell are you two still doing in Wales?" Denton demanded.

"Helping the Brits," I said. "We're allies right? Besides, we were able to follow up on a lead. And hey, while we're at it, just how did you know—"

"Sanders filed a report," Wainright interrupted.

I looked sidelong at her.

"Listen, *one* of us has to file the paperwork around here, you know," she said.

"All right, whatever makes you happy," I said.

"Say, are you two getting along okay?" Denton asked.

"Us? Fine," Sanders said.

"Golden," I said, refusing to look at Sanders.

"Mm," said Tevin. "Listen, we're getting a lot of heat from up the chain about your protracted absence abroad. We've already stretched the rules considerably for your investigative trip to Belarus."

"Hey, vacation, remember?" I said.

"Yes, well, that went over with fanfare and fireworks," Tevin replied.

"The brass isn't happy that you're abroad essentially

unsanctioned," Wainright said. "They want you back here in the U.S. ASAP."

"And did you tell them that we're actively pursuing suspects, which is more than I say for the lack of leads we've had so far," Sanders said.

"Yeah, and while you're at it, tell them we took another telekinetic out of play, too," I added.

Tevin took a deep breath. "Yes, I heard. But it's not as if we have direct access to any evidence or suspects over here."

"We're working on that," I said. "Though I'm sure it doesn't help that your so-called brass had rebuffed British requests for assistance. Given what they were facing, the limeys were damned lucky we came along when we did."

"The three of us couldn't agree more," Wainright said. "However, things are rather dicey at our end. I haven't heard of paranoia this thick since back in the days following 9-11."

"Well, you can tell those bureaucratic bastards back home that, just like after 9-11, we're taking the fight abroad before it hits home shores," I said.

Tevin chuckled. "Oh, if you only knew how much I'd like to."

"Be that as it may, those *bureaucrats* happen to the people in charge," Wainright said. "We're already on the outside of those in the know around here, so I'd hate to antagonize them further at this point."

I frowned. "Has something else happened since we last talked?"

Denton shook his head. "Boy, and how."

"I'd feel more comfortable if it was just politics as usual. Unfortunately, things seem to be ratcheting up further," Tevin replied. "I thought things might cool off after Habeas Corpus was suspended in some parts of the country and martial law declared. Now, with a slight uptick in firearms-related incidents and a lot of press coverage about so-called doomsday preppers, there's further talk of the government rationing fuel and ammunition."

That wasn't a good sign.

I had to admit that I never thought I'd see the day those things would happen on a nationwide, federalized scale. Still, the government kept assuring Americans that it was for their own protection.

"Hard to believe that people are accepting this level of craziness," I said.

"The more vocal ones who aren't are being placed on watch lists," Denton said. "We've been receiving updated suspect lists nearly daily for some time. Believe it or not, two of the people on yesterday's list are sitting congressmen."

"Yes, it's all rather disturbing. The overt naysayers and demonstrators—many of whom hadn't voted for President Graydon in the last election—are being investigated," Wainright said. "Some are being taken into custody and held for further assessment."

"I never thought I'd see anything like that," Sanders said.

The flexibility of our democracy was definitely being challenged.

I tried not to dwell on it, but it bothered me almost as much as any telekinetic terrorist threats from Continuance Corporation.

"You make it sound like a political grab for federal control," Sanders said.

"It's best that we not characterize it as such," Tevin said, caution evident in his tone. "Or openly talk to the press about it, either."

Sanders and I exchanged glances.

No matter. Politics aside, we had a job to do.

"Unless you have something else for us to go on back home, we're staying until either we get those outstanding suspects or we get word that they've moved on to somewhere else," I said.

"But orders from up the chain are—" Denton protested.

"I'm with Bringer on this," Sanders interrupted.

Honestly, I could have kissed her at that moment.

"Do your best to find them," Wainright said. "I'll take the heat for now. I'm just not sure how long I can mitigate it before the crap hits the fan."

"Thanks, Wainright," I said.

"You two be careful," Tevin said.

"And, and uh, pick me up a Doctor Who collectible while you're there, too," Denton said.

I nodded. "Sure thing. I'll see what I can do."

As Sanders secured her notebook computer, I couldn't help but wonder how much worse things might get back home.

CHAPTER 16

When Sanders and I insisted on remaining in Cardiff, tensions mounted. Scott and Strutt weren't pleased.

"Why stay? What do we do now?" Strutt asked.

"Wait," I said.

"Wait?" Scott demanded. "Wait, hell. We need to get our asses stateside."

Waiting wasn't a savory prospect for either Sanders or me. We tried contacting ACC Hill, but he was busy in meetings of some kind.

Then I called Agent Fiskall.

Within the hour, an unmarked sedan drove Sanders and I for over an hour through Welsh countryside to an upscale office building on the outskirts of a town named Bridgend.

Our initial impression of the building changed once we took an elevator car down to a level labeled Restricted. We entered a small technology-laden control center manned by a half-dozen men and women wearing business attire.

Agent Fisk met us at the door. "Welcome to one of our MI-6 operations centers. Here are your guest badges. Just swipe them over the panels near doors to gain entry."

Sanders and I clipped the badges to our shirts.

"Wow, keys to the city and everything," I said. "This is

how to treat guests."

"Actually, those will only let you into the bathrooms, this room, and the elevator," he said.

"Well, it's something, anyway," I said.

"From this room we can tap into all government-monitored cameras in the UK," he said. "We're pouring over thousands of images, but we haven't found anything yet. Mind you, we're only one team out of more than a dozen who are actively working 'round the clock on this. Still, more sets of eyes help."

"Thank you for letting us come here," Sanders said. "We would've gone stir crazy back at the hotel, and we couldn't reach ACC Hill."

"Happy to have you," he said. "Let me give you a brief tour and then you can observe our operation, if you like. You might spot something helpful."

Fisk gave us a brief tour. We spent the next three hours observing technicians use computer-assisted recognition routines to comb over faces and vehicle identification tags.

I was more of an action sort of guy, so hours of watching and waiting quickly wore my patience thin. I was half-tempted to go walking the streets of Bridgend just for the exercise.

By the time Fisk retrieved us for a quick lunch, nothing useful had turned up, and I was starting to wonder if it ever would.

"This is the boring part of my job that they rarely bother to mention in those James Bond films," Fisk said. "I'm happy they didn't tell me this until after my training or I might've stayed in the SAS."

I liked Fisk.

We were halfway through a meal of fish and chips when Fisk's smartphone rang.

"Fisk," he said. "What? Where?"

His eyes practically lit up.

"We've got them," he said.

* * *

A military helicopter picked us up outside the intelligence center and flew us southward across country.

As I looked down at the countryside below, I realized that Wales was a rather beautiful place that I wouldn't mind spending more time in.

"Where are we headed?" I asked.

"A quaint little seaside town along the Bristol Channel called Barry," Fisk said. "The targets are near a place called Jackson's Bay."

We landed in the middle of the town, near a large staging area filled with military and law enforcement vehicles. Fisk led us directly to a command post where ACC Hill and other leadership waited.

"So sorry," Hill said to us. "I didn't hear you'd called until I was on my way here."

"No worries. We were just checking in," Sanders said.

Hill nodded and introduced us to a number of key participants.

"What's the status?" I asked.

"Our targets are inside a home near the bay," Hill said. "We have the area under tight control and we're ready to go in and take them into custody. But we were waiting on you, just in case they have more people with abilities in their group."

"Something tells me they would've already used them by now if they had," I said.

"Never can be too sure, though," he said.

"True," I agreed.

"Here, Agent Sanders, take this," Fisk said.

He handed Sanders a 9mm pistol and two spare, loaded magazines.

"Just in case, you understand," he said with a wink.

"Thank you," Sanders replied.

The three of us got into a police SUV and followed multiple law enforcement vehicles through the town toward the bay.

We drove past a heavily guarded checkpoint and stopped a short distance beyond it.

"On foot from here," Fisk said. "We don't want to tip them off."

A man wearing police tactical gear ran up to us.

"Sirs, the targets are still inside the home," he said.

"Better let me go ahead first, just in case," I said.

"I'm going with you," Sanders said.

I started to protest, but she gave me a more than threatening look.

"Don't even," she said. "I'm going."

"I'm Hurst," said the tactical team member. "I'll be leading you to a white home with blue trim."

He handed a small radio to Sanders and led us a short distance down a street before we turned onto another curved street leading in the direction of the bay area.

He stopped alongside a panel van and peered around the side.

"Just four homes down from here," he said.

I followed his gaze to the house in question. It looked ordinary and blended into the rest of the neighborhood quite nicely.

The streets were completely deserted, perhaps cleared by the authorities, though I wondered how they might have managed that without being noticed.

"We'll move in as soon as you either signal us via the radio or motion to us," Hurst said. "We have snipers watching from all exterior angles, so you should be in our sights at all times."

I nodded and walked out from behind the panel van with Sanders beside me. She had tucked the pistol behind her, inside the waistband of her pants.

"We're just going to walk up and ring the doorbell?" she asked.

"Why not?" I replied. "That should really shake them up."

As we casually walked toward the house, I opened my mind to receive thoughts.

...hope Bringer knows what he's doing.

I tried not to smile over that.

...going on out there? Not a lick of traffic.

We were only a house away when a jumble of clear thoughts poured forth.

...he better hurry up and get here.

...don't like sitting about.

...make them pay for Lis.

I wondered if that person knew what had happened to Marlis.

...time for something to eat before we leave?

...wish the news coverage would settle down.

...wonder what sex with her would be like?

"Seriously?" I asked. "At a time like this?"

I wanted to meet whoever was thinking that last thought. Even more, I was curious who they wanted to have sex with.

"What? What is it, Bringer?" Sanders asked.

"Uh, nothing," I said. "Just a passing thought."

"You're really weird sometimes," she said.

...really freaks me out sometimes.

"You don't know the half of it," I said.

We walked up the sidewalk and onto the front porch.

I reached out to depress the doorbell.

...finally! He made it!

...outta here now!

I frowned. "What?"

Inside, I heard upraised voices and even a couple of subdued cheers.

"Somebody got through the perimeter," I murmured.

"What? When?" Sanders whispered.

"Just now," I replied.

The question was, how?

I turned toward Sanders. "Send them in now."

I frantically waved my arms above my head and motioned to the front door as Sanders called on the radio for everyone to move in.

The distant sounds of booted feet on pavement followed as Sanders readied her pistol.

I held out my hands, palm outward, and imagined a giant wrecking ball swinging forward.

The front door smashed inward in a shower of splinters and pieces, taking part of the door frame with it.

Shouts came from inside as I stepped past the debris and into the main entryway.

"Nobody move!" I yelled, progressing into the house with Sanders close behind me.

As I rounded the corner into the living room, gunfire erupted before me as I spotted two men with assault rifles. My shield caught numerous rounds, leaving the bullets suspended before me.

Before I could react further, the gunmen ducked into the next room.

On reflex, I reached behind me to grab Sanders' left hand and extended my shield around her

"What—" she protested.

I dragged Sanders forward with me, reaching out with my mind.

A wave of disjointed thoughts tumbled through my brain, nearly making me reel.

"Everyone hold hands!" a man yelled.

Hold hands?

The clashing noises of glass breaking and doors being breached filled the air around me as tactical team members yelled for everyone to freeze.

"Hey!" Sanders exclaimed as I pulled her behind me.

I maintained my shield as I moved into the adjoining room, a combined dining room and kitchen, to see a group of eight men and women holding hands.

"Drop your weapons!" yelled one tactical team member to my right.

"Get on the floor!" yelled another.

One of the group members, a young man with a goatee,

grinned wickedly.

"You're too late," he said.

I thrust a wall of force forward with my mind that briefly touched something that felt foreign, sending a wave of queasiness spreading throughout my body.

Then the people before me simply vanished.

.

CHAPTER 17

"They bloody disappeared!" someone exclaimed.

"Everyone stand back!" I yelled, releasing Sanders' hand.

I generated a fireball in my hand, enlarging it to the size of a beach ball as men cursed and retreated from all sides.

"Shit, Bringer!" Sanders yelled.

I moved forward with the fireball held before me until I was standing where the group had been.

One thing became certain: they weren't invisible…they were gone.

"Well, crap," I muttered, extinguishing the fireball.

Embers dropped to the floor, hissing against the tiles.

"All clear!" I yelled, stamping out a few stray embers with my shoes.

"What the bloody hell was that all about?" Fisk demanded from behind me.

"They're gone," I said.

"Gone? That's not possible," Fisk said.

"Try telling a man who generates fire that something's not possible," I said.

The limits of possibility had been severely strained with me in recent weeks.

I exited the house, walking past dozens of stern-faced British authorities, until I stood alone in the front yard.

I rubbed at my temples, trying to will away a growing

159

headache, as I contemplated what had just transpired.

Teleportation.

They knew how to teleport.

"How in the hell am I supposed to counter that?" I asked aloud.

"Bringer?"

I glanced back over my shoulder at Sanders, whose complexion appeared as pale as snow.

"Are you okay?" she asked.

I inhaled a deep breath and slowly exhaled.

"No," I said. "But you're the one who looks like you've seen a ghost."

"What you just did—" she began. "What I felt. That was unnerving. Then when those fugitives disappeared, it felt like the floor disappeared from beneath me. It was all I could do not to throw up."

I frowned. "Yeah, I felt that, too."

She reached out to gently touch my shoulder.

"Is it always that way for you?"

I considered her question as I watched a police SUV pull up at the curb. ACC Hill appeared none-too-pleased as he exited the vehicle.

"Sometimes, but mostly I'd gotten used to it," I replied. "Until today. That was something new."

"Agent Sanders, Mr. Bringer," Hill greeted with a stony expression. "So, they've escaped?"

Something in his tone irritated me and I focused my complete attention on him.

"No, Hill, they damned well *disappeared*," I said flatly.

He appeared taken aback and his eyes widened.

"Logan," Sanders quietly prompted as she touched the small of my back with her hand.

That's when I realized I'd conjured a small fireball that completely encircled my clenched right fist.

I extinguished it.

"My apologies," Hill said. "I certainly wasn't accusing anyone of anything."

I gave him a curt nod.

"I'll just go inside for a moment," he said, walking past us, but giving us a wide berth.

A number of police officers and tactical team members stared warily at us. I gazed at them in a single sweep, and to a one, they found somewhere else to focus their attentions.

* * *

"What do you mean, we're being recalled?" I demanded.

Sanders and I sat around a large conference table with agent Fisk, ACC Hill, and other taskforce members inside the same office building that housed the restricted MI-6 monitoring center.

Hill appeared unhappy about the revelation.

"I assure you, it wasn't my idea," Hill insisted. "This came directly from the foreign minister's office only moments ago. Apparently, your President Graydon has issued an executive order recalling you back to the United States. His personal request to the Prime Minister could hardly be rebuffed, relations being what they are."

"Why not?" I asked. "Hell, Graydon disregarded your government's request for assistance early on."

"Honestly, the precise details were sketchy, except that it was conveyed as a matter of your nation's imminent national security," Hill said. "Perhaps they've located a terrorist cell similar to the one here."

I looked at Sanders, who shrugged.

"Call Wainright or Tevin," I said.

"Will do," Sanders replied, rising from the table with smartphone in hand.

"I can't believe they would do that given our current situation," Fisk said, intently watching Sanders exit the room. "We've got fugitives running about…God knows where."

I didn't know why, but the way Fisk watched Sanders made me feel just a little jealous.

"Yes, and that's the question of the hour, isn't it?" said

the gentleman next to me. I think he'd said he was from Scotland Yard.

"They could be anywhere," I said. "And I don't even mean the UK…I mean anywhere on the planet. Who knows how far of a range that man's ability has?"

The room fell eerily silent.

Hill cleared his throat. "Yes, well, we can only go back to what we were doing for now; monitoring the country's surveillance systems and asking for the public's help. The more eyes we have on this, the better."

"And what do you plan to do when you find them?" I asked. "If you try cornering them, they may simply disappear again."

"We could always shoot them on sight," Fisk suggested. "Safely taking them into custody may be well outside our capability."

There were murmurs of agreement at that. It was hard to argue with such straightforward logic.

And I didn't have any better of a suggestion.

Sanders entered the conference room and returned to her seat beside mine.

"Wainright said that it's a political necessity," Sanders said.

Political necessity?

"That's all he said?" I asked.

"That's all he was willing to say at the moment," she clarified.

"That's bloody unhelpful," Fisk said, to which more murmurs of agreement circulated the table.

"Well, be that as it may, we'd better see that you're packed and on your plane home," Hill said. "Though I'm very sorry to see you go, Mr. Bringer, both you and Agent Sanders have rendered welcome and honorable service to both Crown and country. I can't thank you enough."

That was something, at least.

* * *

Two hours later, our plane lifted off from Cardiff International Airport amidst a British fighter jet escort.

I made my way forward to the cockpit to visit with our pilot.

"That's a nice gesture," I said. "You don't get to see that every day. Makes me feel sort of important."

"That's a fact, Mr. Bringer," the pilot replied. "Haven't had that honor since my transport escorts in the Middle East."

"A fly boy, eh?"

"Yep. Made Lt. Colonel before I got out," he said. "You?"

"Nah, ground pounder," I replied. "Army fire team in the desert. Call me Logan, by the way."

He reached up and shook my hand. "Pleasure. Call me Bob."

I liked the guy right from the start.

"Army aside, I'm honored to have you on board, Logan," he offered with a grin, to which I chuckled. "By the way, these guys seem to have a slightly different course in mind for us to follow. We've been informed that U.S. fighters will eventually take over for them, as well."

"Thanks. Nice to meet you, Bob," I said before returning to the rear cabin.

It made me wonder if we were being protected or just kept under watch.

"They don't appear to want us to wander off," Scott said.

"Funny, I came to that same conclusion once I thought about it," I agreed.

Hours later, after U.S. fighters had taken their places off each wing, we landed at Ronald Reagan Washington National Airport, located along the Potomac River.

Instead of disembarking at the terminal, our jet stopped out on the open tarmac. Men wearing dark suits and earpieces stood outside two limousines and a pair of dark sedans.

"Welcoming committee," I announced. "Maybe it's either Bernard or Wallace."

"No, it's neither," Strutt said. "I just got off the phone with Mr. Bernard and he's waiting back at the office in Nevis Corners. He seemed surprised that we landed here, in fact."

"Well, stay here with the jet. If we're not back to our plane in three hours, you need to fly back to Nevis Corners and update Bernard on events until I can meet up with him," I said, though my attention was on whoever was awaiting us in those limousines.

"Will do, sir," he replied.

I turned to the young man, who had done us good service on our excursion overseas. I reached out to shake his hand.

"Good job, Calvin," I said. "I appreciate your help. You were invaluable."

He beamed over my use of his first name. "My pleasure, sir. It was memorable, for certain."

I turned to Scott and he nodded back at me.

"Skip the handshake, for now," he said. "Something out there tells me we're not done yet."

Nevertheless, I shook his hand. "Thanks, but I need you to stay behind with Strutt and make sure he gets back to the home office safely to meet with Bernard. Besides, I'd bet your own perspective will shed additional insight on things."

The tall bodyguard returned my handshake. "Will do. Until later, then."

I nodded and turned to Sanders. "Ready?"

She followed me to the cabin door where we each thanked the captain and crew as we exited.

"Get the rest of our team back home safely, Bob," I said.

"Will do. Watch your back, army," the captain replied.

"Sierra hotel, fly boy," I replied.

As we walked down the steps to the tarmac, Sanders teased me, "You're so chummy with everyone nowadays."

"Just the ones I like," I replied.

A man wearing a charcoal gray business suit stepped

forward. "Mr. Bringer, Agent Sanders," he greeted. "I'm Chad Welch, aide to Senator Ben Conway. He'd very much like to meet with you, Mr. Bringer."

"He would, eh?"

"The senator's waiting for you in the front limousine, sir. Agent Sanders and any others can ride in the second limousine."

"There's only me and Agent Sanders," I said. "And Sanders is my partner, so she can ride with me."

Welch appeared surprised, but he nodded. "As you wish."

Sanders gave me a look of sincere appreciation and followed Welch to the first limousine. I followed Sanders, shamelessly appreciating the view that I recalled Agent Fisk had admired about her.

One thing was certain: I couldn't fault Fisk for his impeccable taste in women.

Sanders and I sat beside each other, facing the rear of the vehicle where Senator Conway sat while Welch sat in the front compartment. As the car proceeded forward, I quietly observed the senator, waiting for him to initiate further conversation.

He leaned forward and reached across to shake our hands. "I'm Ben Conway. It's a pleasure to meet America's latest heroes in the war against terror. Your recent exploits are all the rage in the press at the moment.

"Senator," I replied. "Your reputation precedes you."

Sanders reached up to push a lock of hair over her ear. It was something I noticed she did when she was either irritated or nervous.

I opened up my mind.

...hope Bringer's careful what he says.

...sort of man are you, Logan Bringer? We'll soon see.

"I hope you like what you've heard about me," he countered.

"Let's just say I'm not a close follower of politics, so I might not be the best judge," I said.

...cautious player.

That's Bringer...king of understatements.

I tried not to smile over Sanders' thought.

"I was invited to a meeting with the President this morning along with his national security team," Conway said. "The public's fears have risen considerably since you left the country, Mr. Bringer. As such, I hope you'll pardon the alacrity regarding your abrupt return home."

"Abrupt? Alacrity? Dangerously faulty cars have been factory recalled with greater finesse," I said.

Sanders tucked a lock of her hair back in place.

The senator inclined his head toward me. "Perhaps. However, the nation needs you here more than abroad. You're our only line of defense against telekinetic terrorist threats."

...more needed than most think, in fact.

...where is he going with this?

"You mean you've identified some new targets of interest?" I asked.

"America needs you to be readily available rather than far away in Britain," he said.

"They're allies and their need seemed immediate," Sanders said.

"Yes, but I understand that your latest contacts have since disappeared on you," he said.

What did he know? Or was the senator baiting me?

"It was...unfortunate and unexpected," I replied. "It was something we haven't seen before. And if I may say, you certainly sound well-informed about the details."

"Mr. Bringer, I'm Chairman of the Senate Armed Services Committee, as well as a member of the Senate Homeland Security and Governmental Affairs Committee. I also regularly advise the President," he replied. "I'm aware of a host of details, particularly concerning national security matters."

"Speaking of details, perhaps you could tell me why, as the only telekinetic defense of the nation, our rapid response team at the FBI was recently overlooked for emergency funding in favor of the CIA," I prompted.

The senator stared back at me.

…somewhat more than a mere soldier.

…huge-ass bonus points for Bringer.

I had to force myself not to laugh or look sidelong at Sanders over her stray thought.

"And you said you didn't follow politics," the Senator said.

"I don't," I said. "But I do keep tabs on what's going on in my own back yard."

"The issue was a matter of limited funds being distributed toward the maximum point of leverage and needs," he explained. "I'm confident that the FBI would be considered for additional funding if a critical need arose."

I leaned forward slightly while maintaining eye contact with him.

"Senator, a woman who can control other's minds nearly cost me my partner. Then, a few hours ago, I watched as eight people disappeared right before my eyes," I said. "We don't even have a clue as to where they've gone—maybe Timbuktu—maybe here in D.C. for all I know. Now, as for me, I'd personally like to know how does that rate on someone's critical needs list?"

"I can see that you're a man of action, Mr. Bringer. I like that," the senator replied, completely evading my question. "How would you like to be part of our team?"

…the hell is he talking about?

I was pretty much in line with Sanders' thought at that moment.

"*Our* team? Just who the hell's team do you think the FBI is on?" I countered, leaning forward.

"True enough," he replied. "What I mean is I'd like to give you unfettered access to decision-makers, help you react quicker to the threats we're facing."

"How's that possible?" Sanders asked. "We're already working directly with Deputy Directors Tevin and Wainright on the TASIT taskforce."

The senator looked at Sanders as if she were a child who had spoken out of turn.

I didn't like that one bit.

"Ah, yes, your Telekinetic Anti-terrorism Surveillance and Interdiction Taskforce. It was useful in the earliest days of the investigations, but matters have grown beyond that scale since then. We're talking about threats on a global level, not merely a domestic law enforcement matter. In your defense, Ms. Sanders, I can't expect you to understand everything that's happening well above your pay grade," Conway said. "Suffice to say that key decisions are now being made beyond the scope of Tevin and Wainright. I'm talking about Mr. Bringer reporting to Burt Dulles, Director of the CIA. Dulles and I have been working very closely on the latest threats."

…Dulles appreciates the scope and scale of things as they are.

…Wainright and Tevin were right!

I glanced over at the shocked expression on Sanders' face.

"How about simply inviting TASIT into the fold at upper levels?" I asked. "We're the most experienced team regarding the threats."

"Well, certainly *you* are," the senator stipulated. "That's why I'm inviting you to the table. Besides, I'm better positioned to meet your needs if you can't acquire immediate support through regular channels. I do have the confidence and ear of the Oval Office, after all."

Conway seemed like the sort of man who liked the sound of his own voice.

"What do you think about changing teams, Sanders?" I asked.

"Er, Mr. Bringer, I regret that Ms. Sanders was not part of my proposal," Conway interjected.

…kind of misogynist asshole is this guy?

Sanders certainly seemed to have Conway pegged.

"I think I've already said that Agent Sanders is part of

my team, not to mention my partner since the start of this investigation," I said.

"In the interest of clarity, Bringer was brought onto my team," Sanders said. "I was originally assigned to investigate the bombing of the Wallace building."

Conway looked at me and then at Sanders. "Be that as it may—"

"If she's not part of the equation, then I'll have to decline your offer," I said.

A slight smile crossed the senator's face.

...hadn't seen that before. Now, I understand.

"I hadn't realized that the two of you had grown so close while working together over such a short period," he said, his eyes falling upon Sanders. "Though, it's easy to understand why, I assure you."

…may require a change of plans.

…about to come unglued! Can't shoot a senator…

"Sanders is one of the most competent agents I've met since—"

"Yes, I'm sure that's the case, Mr. Bringer," Conway cut me off, raising one hand. "I'll need to consult with others before I could modify my proposal. Still, I hope you'll give the premise of my offer serious consideration until we speak again."

"I will," I said. "Just one more question."

His eyebrows rose. "Yes?"

"Where the hell is this limo taking us?"

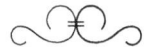

CHAPTER 18

Senator Conway was just full of unpleasant surprises. His limo pulled up to the front steps of the Capitol.

"Mr. Bringer, you and Agent Sanders are expected to attend a closed-door joint session hosting House and Senate security committee members," Conway said.

"I didn't think the House and Senate committees met in joint session," Sanders said. "Isn't that historically against protocol?"

"Agent Sanders, these are truly historic times," Conway replied. "I'm happy to let the lawyers argue it later for posterity, but for now, I'm trying to keep this country intact."

As for me, I didn't give a damned about protocols, lawyers, or posterity. I just wanted the whole thing to be over and done with so I could return to hunting down my enemies.

"Senator, why are we wasting time in a committee meeting?" I asked. "You could learn just as much from a field report, and I frankly don't have the time to deliberate with politicians."

Conway shrugged. "Mr. Bringer, we politicians are the ones holding the purse strings, and you can't fight a war without money. Besides, you might find it instructive to determine where the pulse of the country's at right now."

I caught part of a stray thought from him.

…then come around and start seeing things my way.

Conway practically oozed multiple agendas. I sure as hell didn't intend to turn my back on him.

Passenger doors on each side of our limousine opened in unison and we all exited the vehicle.

Conway walked to my side of the limo and reached out to shake my hand. "I appreciate your cooperation, and please consider what we've talked about. Now, if you'll excuse me, I have some important last-minute business to attend to before the session is underway," he said. "I'll see you in there. My aide, Mr. Dulles, will assist you from here."

He turned and I watched him practically leap onto and up the flight of concrete steps leading toward the Capitol entrance.

"Mr. Bringer?" asked Dulles as handed me a sheaf of papers.

As I thumbed through the papers, it looked more like the rough script for a court drama, heavily laden with terminology that I could only begin to describe as legalese.

"What's all this crap?" I asked as our limo pulled away.

"Your agenda and information on protocol and rules of conduct," Dulles replied. "There's also map to help lead you to the correct chamber."

"Tell me there's not a quiz on all this," I said.

Dulles appeared unamused. "Please try to be on time, Mr. Bringer," he said. "The session will start promptly."

I watched as he hurried to catch up with his boss.

"That guy's all personality," I said.

Sanders touched my arm. "Bringer, though I'm not much on men in shining armor riding to my rescue, thanks for speaking up for me back there in the limo," she said.

"Are you kidding? We're a team, you and me," I said. "Hey, I, for one, admired your sense of restraint during our chat with Conway."

"It was hard. He's a misogynist asshole," she said. "He's lucky there's a lot at stake here or I'd have punched him squarely in the face."

I chuckled over the vision of that. And yet I harbored little doubt she'd follow through on that, too.

"Yeah, I'd have paid handsomely to see that," I said.

"Listen, I'd hate to think that I'm holding you back from an opportunity here," Sanders said. "Maybe if you were on the inside with them we'd make more headway."

Her eyes held a sad look, and I wanted to pull her into my arms and embrace her. Instead, I reached out and grasped her by the shoulders.

"Hey, you listen to me. We go together or not at all, got it? You've got my back and I've got yours. We're so much more than a team…we're partners."

Her look of appreciation was priceless.

"Yeah, partners."

"C'mon partner," I said, taking the steps before us at a run. "Let's go kick some bureaucratic ass."

We'd no sooner made it into the building when I stopped short, Sanders halting beside me.

"What is it?" she asked. "Do you sense something?"

"Damn, this place is bigger than life in person," I said. "You don't get a true sense of this place on the news."

"You've never been here?" she asked.

"Are you kidding? Washington, D.C. is the last place I ever wanted to hang around," I replied. "Granted, it embodies all the long-haired history that would give a nerd a hard-on."

"Bringer, I spent a season here volunteering as a Congressional page while in college," she said.

I gave her a cautious sidelong glance. "Well, nerds are okay people, too. Though I was always more of an in-the-field sort of guy."

"You have such a way with words, Bringer," she said. "And by in-the-field, I suppose you mean blowing things up?"

"Yeah, what else?" I countered. "Explosives were my specialty, after all."

She shook her head at me and reached out to take the

Capitol map from me. "C'mon, Sergeant C-4," she said, taking the lead.

When we reached the Capitol Rotunda, I spotted my old friend Paul Criswell standing amongst a cluster of other politicians.

Paul was a former sergeant and the fire team leader in my unit during my tour in Iraq. We had become best of friends after trading off saving each other's lives on multiple occasions during combat. And while I had returned home to an unwelcome brain cancer diagnosis, Paul had skyrocketed into the role of a freshman congressman from New York.

I was fortunate that he did. Not only had he somehow assured my placement into Nuclegene Corporation's experimental treatment program for my cancer, he had also helped me understand some of the convoluted political machinations at play since the explosion of the Wallace Building.

As we neared him, I waved to get his attention. He smiled when he spotted us, then excused himself from his peers and rushed to meet us.

"Hey, there's my favorite sci-fi experiment," he said, embracing me in a fraternal hug. "Hello, Agent Sanders. Are you keeping this guy out of trouble?"

"Hello, Congressman," she replied. "And, as for Bringer, it's a full-time job, I'm afraid."

"Yeah, Paul," I said. "I figured I'd come to your home turf and wreak havoc for a change."

"Better not," he said with an arched eyebrow. "Not these days, anyway. While I'm one of the committee members attending the session that you're here for, I'm in the minority party and a junior member on my committee, so don't expect me to be able to bail you out of too much trouble."

"Bail *him* out? With both of you in the same Capitol together?" Sanders asked. "I have the feeling that we're all in trouble now. Can the Republic survive it?"

I looked sidelong at her. "Paul's renowned for his schmoozing. He always managed to get invited to all the good parties, so I should've known that Mr. Politics wouldn't miss out on something like this," I said to Sanders.

"Careful there," he said. "You never know, my political connections might inevitably come in handy."

"Speaking of politics, I'm not sure how much you know about what happened in the UK, but one presidential phone call from Graydon was all it took for the Brits to put our asses on the plane to get here," I said.

His expression turned serious. "Yeah, I heard a little about that. Very little, I'm afraid."

"I'll fill you in on the details, if we have time," I said. "And we had an interesting limo ride with Senator Conway on the way over here today."

"Oh, really?" Paul asked. He looked around to see who was standing nearby and then glanced at his watch. "We've got some time before things start, but let's not talk about any of it standing out here."

"Well, then, show us to your office," I suggested.

* * *

Paul's office was small and devoid of any elaborate amenities, though it looked professional enough.

"Nice digs," I said. "Though I have to admit, I expected a bit more glamor."

"Well, it beats working out of the back of a Humvee," he replied. "But you should see the Minority Whip's office."

A television displayed one of the twenty-four-hour news channels where there appeared to be breaking news.

"…a moderate 5.6 magnitude earthquake that struck central Oklahoma earlier today," said a female newscaster. "While there were only minor injuries, numerous reports are still coming in regarding damages to homes and businesses.

"This is yet another quake to strike this region, attributed to the decades of oil and gas fracking that have dominated the state," the newscaster continued.

"Unfortunately for residents and business owners,

private insurance companies are legislatively exempted from having to pay on policies related to man-made events that mimic natural disasters. In addition, the oil and natural gas industry is protected from liability due to legislation passed years ago by the Oklahoma State Legislature. This raises the question of whether private industry should be held accountable for acts attributed to their interests. Some residents are outraged over—"

"Private companies continue to run amok," Paul said. "Meanwhile, I really feel for all those private citizens who are going to have to secure private loans for repairs to cover the damages."

"Yeah, poor bastards," I said.

"You're all heart, Bringer," Sanders said.

"Hey, sorry, but I'm not the one who elected the idiot politicians who've protected the oil and gas industry," I said. "The way I see it, when it comes to voting, you pretty much get what you deserve if you keep re-electing idiots."

"Unassailable civic logic, as always," Paul said. "It might be sunnier if more than thirty percent of the population actually voted. People have lost faith in our elected systems."

"Aw, you're not going to get all civics lecture-y on me now, are you?" I asked.

"Wait, look," Sanders said, pointing to the TV screen.

"…where our reporter on Capitol Hill managed to catch up with one of Oklahoma's legislative members, Freedom Party co-chair Senator Penelope Savage, just moments ago," the newscaster continued.

Senator Savage's face filled the screen.

"Senator, do you have any comments regarding today's earthquake?" the reporter asked.

"My thoughts and prayers go out to the people of Oklahoma at this challenging time," she said. "It's a very unfortunate event."

"Senator, what about the question of whether the oil and gas industry should take some responsibility for the series of earthquakes that have plagued the state in recent years?"

"It's important to note that the oil and gas industries are a major part of our state's economy, as well as integral to our nation's national security and oil independence. As for liabilities, I'm afraid that's a matter for state officials to confront," she smoothly replied.

"But Senator, shouldn't Oklahomans have the right to seek redress for damages from corporate-made disasters?" the reporter asked.

Senator Savage held up her hand. "The people of Oklahoma are resilient and no strangers to disasters and tragedy. For those who may find it too harsh, there's nobody forcing them to reside in the state. Of course, I'll continue to pray for those who were adversely affected by this tragedy. Now, if you'll excuse me, I'm focused on matters of national security at this time."

I turned to Sanders. "And you said that I was all heart?"

"Shh," Sanders admonished.

"What about the recent terrorist activities that took place in Wales?" the reporter prompted. "As a sitting member on the Senate's Homeland Security Committee, what can you tell us about our government's response? Is there any intelligence indicating that a similar attack is imminent here in the U.S.?"

"Intelligence is still being gathered, though the potential for further terrorism is always possible," she replied. "However, I can't comment further at this time. In fact, I'm on my way to a closed door session right now. Again, if you'll please excuse me."

The camera feed continued as the senator walked away with two of her aides trailing after her.

Sanders looked at me. "Okay, so maybe you're not the least compassionate person I've seen today. The ice lady has you beat."

"This is going to sound a little crazy, but I wish that all we had to worry about right now was earthquakes," Paul said. "You'd better tell me what you can about what happened abroad before the session begins."

We gave him a high-level recount of our exploits in both

Europe and Wales, including our limo ride and conversation with Senator Conway.

"Granted, Conway's been pressing political buttons much harder on the Hill than I would've expected," Paul said. "Still, it sounds like we're in the midst of some sort of territorial grab over national security. I've had my suspicions, but what you said appears to confirm it. That being said, I'm not part of Conway's grand Freedom Party movement, either."

"Thank goodness for that," I said. "What a group of extremist whack-jobs."

"Be careful," he cautioned. "Those whack-jobs are pretty close to singlehandedly running the country right now. The President counts many of them as key political supporters, if not close personal friends."

"Who constitutes the Freedom Party exactly?" Sanders asked.

"They're a tight-knit group and almost exclusively right-wing Republicans," Paul replied. "Initially, they started out as a radical fringe of the GOP, but in recent years they've gained surprising momentum and public support, though mainly in southern states and throughout parts of the Midwest."

"Do you think they're trying to break away from the Republican Party and form their own?" she asked.

"Not as far as anyone can tell," Paul replied. "They'd lose immediate access to the veritable treasure trove of GOP funding if they did that. Rather, they claim they're just trying to put the party back into good form. As it is, they control most of the GOP leadership positions, so they're not far from having full control of the party."

"Congressman, do you know where Senator Conway ranks in the President's most-favored list?" Sanders asked.

"He's definitely at the top of the list of Graydon's most trusted advisors," he replied. "He's also one of his close personal friends."

"Whoever these idiots are, it looks and sounds like they're trying to turn the country upside down," I said. "And given all that's been going on, it wouldn't take much more to accomplish that."

"Between the federalization of law enforcement and martial law being declared, things look pretty unsettling right now," Sanders agreed.

"Unsettling, yes," Paul said. "But the nation's not falling apart at the seams just yet. There's still a group of us in the middle and left who are trying to put together our own coalition. We've even made contact with a handful of more moderate Republicans. At this stage, I'm feeling hopeful."

"Perhaps," Sanders said. "However, do either of you remember how Rome fell?"

Paul shrugged. "A big empire got harder to manage as it spread across the world. Add to that, hosting a series of crazy or power-hungry Caesars didn't help."

"True," Sanders said. "However, Rome's biggest failure was from a corrupted Senate who ignored the needs of the Roman people and instead focused on their individual power struggles. Rome's fall came from within. I'd rather not see that happen here."

I stared at her. "I didn't realize that you moonlighted as a history professor."

"I minored in history and political science in college, thank you," she said.

Paul and I exchanged surprised looks.

"Stick with her, Bringer," he said. "If you're lucky, maybe something will rub off on you. You could stand to grow a little smarter."

Sanders beamed over that.

"Fun-ny," I said.

"Say, aren't you two bringing legal counsel with you?" Paul asked.

"Legal counsel? Hell, I'm just off a plane from overseas. I had no idea that I'd end up before a committee today," I replied.

He frowned.

"Are you saying that I'm going to need legal counsel?" I

asked.

"Let's hope not," he said.

That was hardly reassuring.

A knock at the door sounded and one of Paul's staff peeked inside.

"Congressman, the session begins in less than twenty minutes."

"Thank you," he said. "Looks like it's time to put on our stage faces."

"Sorry, I only have the one face today," I said.

"Then I hope it's the polite one for a change," he said. "I don't want to have to try and coax some senator out of contempt charges against you."

"Hypothetically, would you suspect any particular senator of that?" Sanders asked.

"Oh, given who'll be in attendance today, you could pick most anyone who hails from the 'R' side of the aisle," he replied.

* * *

As we approached the entrance to the meeting chambers I caught sight of both Wainright and Tevin, neither looking especially pleased.

"I'm heading on in," Paul said, waving to us.

Sanders and I walked over to Tevin and Wainright.

"Why the long faces?" I asked. "You look like you're attending a funeral or something."

"Because, unlike you, we're not invited to speak," Tevin said.

"At least Sanders is with you," Wainright said.

"You're kidding, right?" Sanders asked. "You think either of us is actually prepared for what lies ahead?"

"Yeah, you two are the ones co-leading our team," I said.

"Yes, but neither Wainright nor I were in Wales with you," Tevin said.

"Well, at least Sanders has worked the FBI bureaucracy

before. She won't be like a fish out of water," I said. "She's damned sure got both a better eye and memory than me."

"Gee, such praise. Where's my recorder when I need it?" Sanders asked.

I glanced at her and she returned a smug look.

Honestly, she was starting to get under my skin, and in a good sort of way, too.

"You two had better go in now," Tevin said, glancing at his watch. "Good luck, but be careful what you say and how you say it. Wainright and I will try to muscle a couple of seats behind you, just in case you need us."

"Thanks," I said. "You know, you're the second person this afternoon to suggest being careful about what I say."

"Oh, and one more thing," Tevin said. "The panel is comprised largely Freedom Party members, so expect to hear some dogma with their questions. Don't let them bait you with any of it."

"Great. Just what I wanted to hear," I said.

"And for God's sake, Bringer," Paul urged. "Watch the hell out for Senator Savage from Oklahoma. She's one of the worst of them."

"Yeah, I just got a sense of that from her TV interview a few minutes ago," I said.

"She practically defended an earthquake," Sanders said.

"Careful," Wainright cautioned. "She can cause a few, too."

"Ha, no pressure," I said.

"We'll get it done, Bringer," Sanders said, lightly patting me on the back.

"Mr. Bringer!"

I turned to see Senator Conway's aide, Chad Welch, power-walking toward us.

"They're ready for you now," Welch said.

As promised, Wainright and Tevon were able to secure seats directly behind us in the first row of the gallery. It felt somewhat reassuring, knowing they were behind us for moral support.

As the first order of business, Sanders and I were sworn in. Then the proceedings were under way, though not without some protracted political posturing and bloviating preambles on the part of several senators and congressmen.

Finally, attentions turned to us.

"Mr. Bringer, I hope that you realize how unusual it is—some might say, historic—for a mixed congressional and senatorial group to come together like this," said Senator Conway. "These are equally historic times that require unprecedented actions on the part of our nation, including its governmental and political systems. The very course of the human race appears to be changing right before our very eyes, as your presence here today attests."

I was suddenly wondering if I shouldn't indeed have attempted to secure the last-minute services of an attorney. As things stood, it was just Sanders and me opposite some of the most powerful politicians in the country.

Hindsight was a harsh mistress.

In the absence of better options, we just had to deal with matters as they unfolded.

React creatively to whatever I encounter.

In combat, that was a dangerous enough prospect, perhaps more so in the politically charged arena we were thrust into.

"Given the highly classified and sensitive nature of topics discussed in this hearing, and as chairman of this joint senatorial and congressional panel of inquiry, I invoke the rule of closed session for this hearing on the basis of matters of national security," said Conway.

"Second," said a congressman on the panel.

"All in favor?" Conway asked.

All panel members voted for the proposed closed session.

"As voted, we will now enter a closed session," proclaimed Conway. "Will the Sergeant at Arms please clear the chamber of unauthorized members and secure the room at this time?"

A murmur went up through the crowd as the vast majority of audience attendees left the room. Unfortunately, both Tevin and Wainright were dismissed, as well.

I stared directly at Paul seated among his peers and discreetly pointed to Tevin and Wainright.

Paul nodded.

"Motion for Directors Wainright and Tevin to remain," said Paul.

"Seconded," said a congresswoman.

Senator Conway paused and then finally nodded. "Agreed. Mr. Wainright and Mr. Tevin are requested to remain while in closed session, including previously sanctioned attendees."

I gazed around the room at high-ranking uniformed military members, as well as some individuals wearing business attire, none of whom I personally recognized.

Then my eyes fell upon Special Agent Yasmine Prichard from the CIA.

"Guess who?" I whispered to Sanders.

She glanced back over her shoulder. "I should've expected as much," she said. "Prichard's boss, CIA Director Burt Dulles, is seated beside her. And I'm fairly sure that the two fellows sitting behind them are the Director of Homeland Security and Hal Wilkes, the President's National Security Advisor."

"All the popular kids," I said.

I tried to open my mind to listen in on interesting thoughts, but the sheer volume of mental chatter from people in the room nearly caused me to reel where I sat.

I quickly shut off my mind.

A gavel sounded before us, and Senator Conway said, "This joint committee is now in session.

"Mr. Bringer, while I'm sure that everyone in this room is well aware of your special abilities, would you please state for the record precisely what those are, including a brief recount of how you came to have them?" Conway asked.

I cleared my throat and recounted at cursory levels what

had transpired during my brain cancer treatments at the Nuclegene facility, including my experiences following the manifestation of my telekinetic abilities.

However, I pointedly left out any description of my ability to read minds. Being under oath meant I faced criminal penalties, if this were discovered.

Nevertheless, despite being a serious omission, it felt safer for me to withhold that information. I wagered that the success of our continued investigation, and perhaps even my life, might depend upon it.

A series of clarifying questions arose from various committee members, though I thought I did a competent job answering them.

Sanders was asked to explain her background with the Wallace Building bombing case, as well as the unorthodox manner in which she and I began collaborating together on it.

We were both asked to recount our experiences tracking various members of the terrorist group associated with the Continuance Corporation, as well as those with telekinetic abilities who we had encountered to date. We finished by covering our recent experiences in Europe and Wales.

"Mr. Bringer, would you please enlighten us in more detail regarding your recent exploits in eastern Europe?" Conway asked.

I paused to consider how best to proceed. The last thing I wanted to do was risk a contempt charge.

"Sanders and I followed up on some leads related to the investigations into possible terrorist activities related to the Nuclegene bombing," I replied.

"Agent Sanders, am I to understand correctly that the nature of your journey was officially declared to be a vacation?" he asked.

"Yes, for the purposes of Customs declarations, it was," she replied.

Muted sounds of amusement came from some of those on the panel. However, the expression on Paul's face was quite serious looking.

"But, Customs aside, wasn't your declaration of a vacation merely a ruse to avoid requesting official approval through your proper chain of command. In essence, isn't it true that you conducted a fact-finding mission on behalf of the Bureau?" he asked.

My temper began to rise.

"Well, the inspiration for our journey began as a vacation," she replied.

I admired her clever wording.

"And is it correct that, in fact, you were conveyed overseas via a corporate aircraft that is owned and operated by the Nuclegene Corporation?" he asked.

"Yes, that's correct, Senator," she replied.

"Do you have any personal or professional ties to the Nuclegene Corporation, Ms. Sanders?" he asked.

Sanders paused.

"That would be me, Senator," I replied. "You see, I was just hired by the Nuclegene Corporation, and it was my first official employee vacation."

Laughter erupted from a number of the politicians on the panel.

Senator Conway hammered his gavel. "You're out of order, Mr. Bringer."

"My apologies, Senator," I said. "However, I thought you'd be far more interested to know what we discovered while vacationing in Belarus."

Sanders nudged my ankle.

"Thank you, but we'll ask the questions here, Mr. Bringer," Conway cautioned.

I held up my hands, palms outward. "Of course, Senator. My mistake. Please excuse me. It's my first time before Congress."

There were a couple of muted chuckles, even as Paul pressed his palm to his forehead.

"Vacation aside, Agent Sanders, what were your findings in Europe?" Conway asked.

Sanders described what had occurred in Belarus in

remarkable detail.

"How was it that you ended up in Cardiff, Wales?" Conway asked.

"We were following a lead provided to us while in Belarus," Sanders replied.

"And what did circumstances did you confront upon your arrival in Cardiff?" Conway pressed.

During the next hour, Sanders and I alternated explaining the events that occurred while we were in Wales. In the process, we repeated some of our earlier testimony.

I described what I had encountered in the field, including the woman with mind-control abilities who I had been able to incapacitate.

That led to a rapid series of clarifying questions that challenged my abilities to keep up. On a number of occasions, I wasn't able to complete my sentences before another politician pressed us with additional questions.

I grew curious about what some of the politicians before us were thinking, and I dared to open myself to surrounding thoughts again. Like before, a barrage of mental dialogue assailed my brain. Only, this time, a wave of nausea threatened to overcome me.

I quickly closed off my mind again. My entire body felt drained and my mind fatigued.

I looked down at the tabletop, focusing my attention on a blue ink pen lying before me. At that moment, I doubted that I even had the strength to levitate it, even if I tried.

My electrolytes had bottomed out. I couldn't recall the last time that I had eaten, much less drank anything other than coffee or water.

In my anticipation of the proceedings, I had made a young soldier's potentially deadly rookie mistake: I hadn't monitored my ammunition as it was getting low.

"Mr. Bringer, are you quite all right?" Conway asked.

Sanders placed a supportive hand on my shoulder as I reached out to fill a glass with water from a nearby pitcher.

A fat load of good water was going to do me under the

circumstances. At least it might clear the growing dryness in my throat.

I took a long swallow of the almost lukewarm water.

"I'm fine, thank you," I said.

I felt Sanders' breath at my ear. "Need something fizzier?"

I gave a slight nod.

Sanders requested a brief break, to which Conway approved.

"These proceedings will pause for a ten-minute recess," Conway said. "However, the chamber will remain closed to the public. All those present are reminded that their oaths remain in order and the material discussed here remains confidential."

"Bringer, are you all right?" Tevin asked, leaning forward.

"He needs to replenish his electrolytes," Sanders said.

"I'll see what I can do," he replied.

I swept the audience and saw that a number of those in attendance were closely observing us, including Yasmine Prichard.

I sat up and steeled my resolve to appear unfazed. I focused my attention on Paul, who stared back at me with a concerned expression.

He quickly made his way down to our table. "You're doing relatively well so far, Bringer," he said. "Be more diplomatic, but don't let them bully you too much."

"Sort of a fine line you drew there," I said.

He shrugged. "It's a nuanced process, not a contact sport."

That was hardly reassuring.

Paul returned to his seat while I drank both of the bottled colas that Tevin had acquired for me. Another cola was placed before Sanders, but she moved it between us.

"It's yours if you need it," she said. "I'm fine with water."

I smiled sidelong at her. "Thanks."

"Welcome, partner," she replied.

The proceedings soon reconvened.

"These proceedings are once again officially in session," Conway said. "We'll continue with questions from the panel. Senator Jubilee Pennyroot, your time begins now."

"Thank you, Senator Conway," he said. "Mr. Bringer, as you would seem to be the only resident superhero present, would you mind explaining to us mere mortals precisely how you subdued your nemesis in Wales? But before you do, I'd like to point out that I've read as much speculation as facts from the so-called special government team that's been assigned to lead the investigation…"

Someone handed a slip of paper to me from behind. The note indicated that Senator Pennyroot was a Republican who hailed from the state of Louisiana, and was a key member of the Freedom Party.

The senator had an accent that was a strong Southern one mixed with just a slight amount of authentic Creole that, in all honesty, was quite entertaining compared to the stately, almost bored, sounding voices of his colleagues. Nevertheless, his highly-charged political preamble almost put me to sleep as I struggled to remember his opening question.

Fortunately, Sanders scribbled a hasty note for me on her notepad before the senator finished his loquacious opening remarks.

Basic facts only, she wrote.

That's about the time that the colas I had consumed offered the promise of rejuvenation. A feeling of near-electricity surged through my body.

"Mr. Bringer?" demanded Senator Pennyroot. "Are we boring you, sir?"

Sanders nudged my shoe.

"Sorry?" I asked, reveling in the energy that coursed through my body. "Could you please repeat your initial question, Senator?"

There was a muted wave of snickering that quickly

subsided as Pennyroot turned to give his peers a cold stare.

"Mr. Bringer, are you touched in the head? How did you subdue your attackers in Wales?" he asked.

Pennyroot's sarcasm pissed me off.

I took a deep breath as a renewed wave of reassuring clarity washed through my brain. My nerves felt almost tingly.

Staring directly into the senator's eyes, I opened my mind and sharply focused my attention upon him.

...sort of idiot does he take me for? ...don't care what voodoo magic he claims, I won't stand for impertinence from some dumbass former army grunt.

Pennyroot stared at me as if completely vexed.

"Well, first off, there were numerous attackers in Wales, Senator," I said. "First, there were the citizens whose minds had been controlled that I helped subdue with the help of local authorities. Then there were the various tactical team members firing high-powered assault rifles at me, though they were friendlies whose minds had also been corrupted. Fortunately, I managed to curtail casualties while countering their attacks."

The room fell completely silent. I couldn't even hear people breathing.

"Then there was a suspect, a woman whose abilities had corrupted all those innocent minds," I continued. "I propelled her against a warehouse wall, rendering her unconscious. The last I heard, she was placed in a medically-induced coma, and I'm not sure when, or even if, she'll regain consciousness. Honestly, at this time, I'm not sure if there's anyone in the UK who could stop her if she did."

Then I folded my arms before me and waited.

Nicely done, Sanders scribbled on her notepad.

It felt as if nobody was going to say anything until Senator Conway finally spoke.

"Well, Senator Pennyroot, it appears that your time has expired," he said. "Shall we continue?"

I focused again on Pennyroot's thoughts and nearly drew a blank before one thought surfaced.

…is this damned devil sitting before me?

What could I say? *Yep, that's me.*

"Senator Savage from Oklahoma," Conway said. "You have the floor, Senator."

I felt a chill form in the air surrounding me.

"Mr. Bringer," she began. "The recounting of your adventure in Wales sounds like something out of a Hollywood-worthy film. While very energizing, I'd like to move beyond the spectacle. It's time to ask some hard questions."

CHAPTER 19

I focused on Senator Savage's thoughts, which were even more inflamed than Pennyroot's.

…won't mince words with me. I'll have you dancing circles before you know what hit you. The time of obstructionism will end…

"Today, Mr. Bringer has informed this panel about his recent adventures in both Europe and Wales," Senator Savage began. "However, I'd like to remind my peers that we're also here to learn how well prepared our nation is for what may lie ahead. Some of my colleagues in both the House and Senate seek to thwart important legislation intended to protect our country from threats, both telekinetic and conventional."

Oh, I couldn't wait to hear where she was going with a preamble like that.

"Our nation has a proud heritage of adapting to changing world circumstances and facing enemies who fashion improved weapons of war to use against us. Swords of yesterday were replaced by firearms and finally strategic nuclear weapons. But what of tomorrow? There will simply be guns of another form," Savage said. "We must never forget that both our latest 'guns' and the Bible made America the great nation that it is today. And we shouldn't forsake either in this age of global threats. Instead, we must devoutly pray for success and stick to our new-and-improved guns, no matter their form, as we move forward with bold initiatives to protect our great bastion of democracy."

I tried not to wince over her analogy.

"In recent days, the Freedom Party and its loyal patriots have encouraged support for an initiative coined PEP, or the Patriots Enhancement Program," Savage continued. "As part of this program, and with competent oversight and nurturing, the United States will finally develop its own effective cadre of elite forces with telekinetic abilities, assuring our continued leadership in advocating security and freedom around the world."

I half-expected chanting to erupt, or at the very least some shouts of Hallelujah. Instead, there was an enthusiastic, yet stately, issuance of applause from over half of the gathered body of politicians, including an audible "hear, hear" or two.

However, there was also some uncomfortable shifting of people in their seats and the pronounced clearing of a few others' throats.

I, for one, struggled not to roll my eyes and shake my head. I turned to look behind me at Tevin and Wainright, whose faces remained carefully impassive.

No doubt years of practice preceded their mastery.

I awaited a question from her.

"Mr. Bringer, in the interim, as both funding and infrastructure are secured for this historic PEP initiative, we need to preserve the nation and its security as best we can," she said. "How do you propose that we accomplish that?"

"I'd recommend mobilizing any of the existing telekinetics in our inventory and prepare for what's coming next," I replied. "And the sooner, the better."

"Existing telekinetics?" Savage asked. "Are there actually any other than you?"

I scanned the faces of the politicians before me. "Well, now, you're asking the wrong person. You see, high-level intelligence isn't something that's being actively shared with me or my team. It must be beyond our pay grade or something."

A series of murmurs echoed throughout the room, both from the gallery behind me and among some of the politicians before me.

"Request for clarification on this matter, Senator Conway," Savage prompted.

Conway stared at me and then scanned the gallery behind me. I looked at the array of military officials, who each shook their heads in negative fashion. The CIA and Homeland Security contingents likewise followed suit.

A wry expression formed on Conway's face. "Mr. Bringer, you appear to be the only telekinetic resource that we have available at the moment."

"Really?" I asked. In truth, it really didn't surprise me. "That's damned inconvenient."

"Well, Mr. Bringer," said Conway said. "Given this latest piece of information, what do you suggest we do?"

"Me? I'd recommend you bring this session to a quick close so that I can get my ass back out there to fight who-knows-what."

An uncomfortable silence followed and Sanders nudged my ankle. By contrast, Paul covered his mouth with his palm to disguise his rapidly growing smile.

"Mr. Bringer, are you trying to be flippant about this?" he asked.

I gave him the hardest look that I could muster.

"No, Senator, I'm just trying to make the best out of a bad situation," I replied.

"I see," he said. "Well, we're all trying to do that right at the moment. Do either of you have any final information that you'd like to share with us?"

"Yes, I do," Sanders replied. "Senator, lately, there seems to be a host of competing interests working various angles on the national response to this crisis. It would be helpful if more inter-agency cooperation and intelligence sharing took place."

"We'll take that under consideration, Agent Sanders,"

Conway said.

"Senator Conway?" I asked, leaning forward in my seat toward the microphone.

"Yes, Mr. Bringer, you have something to add?"

"Yes, I do," I said. "My team and I fully intend to stop these terrorists, but whoever isn't part of that solution is going to find that they're part of the problem, and they'll be dealt with accordingly."

"Ah, well, thank you for sharing your candid views with us today, Mr. Bringer and Agent Sanders," Conway said. "This session is hereby adjourned."

Sanders and I rose from our seats and turned toward Tevin and Wainright.

"Well, Sanders, not exactly a resounding amen to your recommendation, was it?" I asked.

"Hardly," she replied.

"Conway and his cronies appear to hold all of the cards," Tevin said. "Sounds like business as usual, I'm afraid."

"Then maybe it's time for us to give somebody else the business end, isn't it?" I asked.

* * *

My first appearance before Congress wasn't my finest moment, but at least I had survived it without suffering any contempt charges.

Nevertheless, it was an event that scarcely furthered the progress of our investigation. In fact, it might have merely obscured it.

We were getting nowhere fast.

For days, Sanders and I operated out of Wainright's offices at the FBI's Washington, D.C. bureau. We met numerous times with both Wainright and Tevin, as well as consulted via video conference with our team back in Nevis Corners.

In the week that followed the hearing, the news cycles

were ablaze with the political ramifications of the telekinetic threat, including the public outcry demanding a viable government response.

Voters didn't tolerate feeling scared or threatened.

The problem was that, when people feel cornered they often resort to desperate, and sometimes stupid, acts that they later regret.

That is, if they lived to.

The Freedom Party was playing everything to the hilt, capitalizing on people's heated emotions, particularly their fears. Senators Conway, Savage, and Pennyroot appeared on camera or in print seemingly everywhere. They were aided in the House by Representatives Fred Rubicon of Wisconsin and Charity Vandersnoot, both key leaders in the Freedom Party.

Then there was President Beau Graydon himself. For a full week, he invited key Freedom Party members to the White House almost daily, hosting them for tactical meetings and social gatherings.

I was never one to follow politics, but after what I heard—and the few thoughts I overheard—from Conway and Savage during the hearing, I began paying closer attention.

"Those Freedom Partiers know a helluva lot more than they're saying," I said, watching the latest news coverage on a nearby television.

"Given how much they've already been saying, that's a pretty scary prospect," Sanders said while typing on her notebook computer. "Can't you turn that off for a little while, Bringer? I'm getting tired of seeing their faces every time I look up. Even variety shows aren't safe anymore. Representative Vandersnoot was on *The Late Show* just last night."

I muted the TV and looked at Sanders. "*The Late Show?* Why?"

"She was voted the most popular woman in politics in a recent online survey, so they wanted to interview her," she replied. "But even that benign appearance turned to the topic of the latest Freedom Party initiative that Savage spoke of during our hearing. Here, I'll show you."

She typed on the keyboard and then swiveled the screen so that I could see it. It was an Internet-based video clip from *The Late Show*.

"…be willing to share with us a little more about why you think the country should stop being afraid of terrorist threats and instead have a big pep rally?" host Tom Mayers asked, to which the audience laughed.

Vandersnoot smiled with alarming ease. "Well, Tom, I'm encouraging Americans to rally behind PEP, not have a pep rally."

"Aww, I love a good pep rally," he said. "So, what are you referring to, then?"

"I'm talking about the Patriots Enhancement Program that my colleagues and I are launching," she said. "It's a rapid-reaction effort to arm the country against the recent telekinetic threats."

"And what does that involve?" he asked.

"Select federal agencies will combine their efforts in conjunction with key government contractors to develop and quickly activate telekinetic defense forces to protect our nation," she said.

"It sounds bold," he said. "But why do you believe this is the best solution? I mean, where's the public mandate to create even more people with telekinetic abilities?"

"Oh, Tom, I believe that there's an inherent mandate, bestowed upon us as God's faithful servants. We're a nation founded on sound Christian principles, you may recall," she said. "Like those brave settlers of our cherished past, it is the Manifest Destiny of our nation to harness our faith, embrace courage, and return our country to a place of prominence and leadership. Once we flourish, we can then help the rest of the world. It's the Christian thing to do, really."

The video ended and I looked up at Sanders. "What the hell was that all about? I'm pretty sure she just said to support

PEP because it's the Christian thing to do."

"Faith plays well as a motivator for conservative supporters in the country, Bringer," she replied.

"And people are actually supposed to buy into that half-assed explanation?" I asked.

Sanders shrugged. "She's pushing all the right buttons for her political demographic."

"Holy crap," I said.

"Don't let her hear you say that," she said with a smirk.

I gave Sanders my least impressed-looking expression. "Vandersnoot be damned. She, Conway, and all those others are into something that we need to look into further."

"Yeah, I've been thinking the same thing, really," she said. "Not an easy thing to do with all of the attention focused upon them, especially for us here in the FBI. We'd barely open a case file before the news got wind of it."

"Not if we keep it between just a few of us," I said.

Sanders' eyes widened and she pointed at the TV.

"What?" I asked.

"Quick, turn up the volume again!"

I fumbled with the remote even as I focused on the headline flashing on the screen.

"…just coming in that Senator Benjamin Conway has been kidnapped from his home here in Washington, D.C. You're watching live helicopter coverage of the senator's property," said the newscaster.

I heard a host of telephones begin ringing, even as Wainright burst into our office.

"Conway's just been—"

"Yeah, kidnapped," I interrupted. "You got scooped by the news already."

CHAPTER 20

"How did the news know before we did?" Wainright frowned as he watched the TV screen.

"Bringer, I think we just found our opening to investigate Conway," Sanders said.

"Investigate Conway? Why?" demanded Wainright.

"Because he just got kidnapped," I said.

Wainright gave me a dirty look, but I responded with an innocent one and pointed at the TV.

Within half an hour, Sanders, Wainright, and I sat in a crowded conference room with four other federal offices taking part via video conference, including Deputy Director Tevin and some of his team.

"What do we know so far?" Wainright asked. "Sound off, people. This is no time to be shy."

"Sanchez, sir. Based upon the latest data, we're less than three hours out from the abduction," said one agent. "The senator's estate video surveillance system went offline at that time. Aside from on-site security, only the senator was on the premises."

"What kind of security? Any causalities?" Wainright asked.

"Templeton here, sir," prompted a female agent while raising her hand. "Hammer and Company is the private security firm contracted to protect the grounds. There was a detail of four armed guards onsite; each was rendered unconscious, though not seriously injured, and no shots were fired. It was clean and fast, suggesting that whoever did it were professionals or maybe ex-military."

"Any eyewitnesses?" asked Tevin.

"Gibbons, here. None to the actual abduction that we know of," said another agent. "Though one witness, a lady who lives nearby, claims to have seen a non-descript black van traveling in the area within the time period the abduction likely took place."

"Is that all she recalled?" asked Tevin.

"She said she couldn't recall the exact time, but a television program she watched soon afterward places it around the time of the abduction, though we don't know if it was before or afterward. The direction she recalled the vehicle traveling suggests it was afterward."

"What caused her to recall that vehicle in particular, Gibbons?" Sanders asked.

"She said it looked like a contractor's vehicle, but there were no business markings on it," Gibbons replied.

"Did she recall at least a partial on the tag, Gibbons?" Wainright asked.

"No," Gibbons replied. "She merely thought the vehicle seemed out of place, nothing more."

"What about video surveillance from the area? Any traffic coverage?" Wainright asked.

Another agent raised his hand.

Wainright pointed at him. "Trent, what have you got?"

"Local law enforcement is still actively working with us to review municipal and private video footage," he replied.

"Mm," Wainright replied. "Put additional sets of eyes on that, if needed."

"Yes, sir," Trent replied.

"Have any demands been made yet?" Sanders asked. She scanned the faces in the room and looked up at the monitors, which displayed faces from the remote sites.

Silence.

"Who would want the Senator?" I asked. "Could it stem from something personal? Maybe a political rival?"

"We're still looking into that, as well," replied Templeton. "Though, preliminarily, neither the senator's staff nor family can think of anyone they would immediately hold responsible. There's no strong evidence of any recent threats against the senator, merely the usual politically-charged hate mail from a few members of the public."

"I'm surprised there's not something more there," Tevin said.

"According to his aides, he was receiving pressure from some liberal groups opposing the Freedom Party or its latest efforts over the Patriots Enhancement Program. However, we're actively following up on each of those, with assistance from local law enforcement within the various jurisdictions," replied Templeton.

"So, we're looking for an elite band of military-trained, left-wing liberals pulling off a precision-based abduction of a conservative U.S. senator?" I asked. "Seriously?"

"Nobody's suggesting that, Bringer," Sanders said. "We're just covering our bases. This is what actual criminology professionals who can't throw fireballs do when you're not around."

"In my opinion, you can get a lot of practical use out of a well-placed fireball," I murmured.

"Bringer might actually be onto something there," Tevin said.

"You've got to be kidding," Sanders said.

"See?" I asked. "Fireballs are handy."

Sanders gave me a flat look.

"Not fireballs, per say," Tevin said. "The senator's abduction is a fiery political development."

"Naturally, but in what way are you spinning it, Tevin?" Wainright asked.

"Think about it. Right now, the last thing the FBI needs is to lose a senator on your watch, particularly one so close to the President," Tevin replied.

"Yeah, we're already on the outs with the administration, not to mention being left out of key intelligence-sharing and funding opportunities under the current crisis," Sanders offered. "The Bureau is hamstrung in the worst sort of way."

Wainright looked at Sanders. "If that were true, Conway's abduction could be politically motivated after all," he said. "But that's a lot of effort to go to just to embarrass us."

"It's only one theory until there are definable suspects," Tevin said. "No matter the motivation, it's more important that we secure the senator's safe release."

"Anything else?" Wainright asked. "Let's get back to it, then. Keep me informed if anything develops."

Sanders and I held back with Wainright until everyone had exited the room. One by one, the remote sites signed off, except for Tevin and Agent Denton.

"Conway's safety aside, we might still be in the wringer over this if we don't get Conway back safely," Wainright said. "The administration will lay the blame on the FBI's apparent incompetence while the public outcry will further the Freedom Party's agenda."

"Don't forget, the NSA has a hand in this, as well," Tevin prompted. "This is a TASIT team operation."

"So, you're already thinking that this event is a political stunt?" I asked.

"I don't know," Wainright conceded. "But I've been in administrative levels of the federal government long enough to be a cynic."

"You're only cynical if it's not true," Tevin said with a wry expression.

"Frankly, both of you gentlemen unsettle me sometimes," Denton said, leaning forward.

"Mark, you'll have access to all of the NSA resources I can muster," Tevin said. "This is still a TASIT team project as far as I'm concerned."

"Thanks, Bob," Wainright said. He ran his fingers through his thinning hair.

There was a knock on the conference room door.

"Come in," Wainright said.

One of the agents from the meeting poked his head inside.

"Sir, Director Tyrone is on the phone for you."

Wainright nodded. "I'll be right there."

"I'm betting your boss isn't making a social call," Tevin said.

"Nope," said Wainright. "That's one thing I'm sure of."

"Sounds like the political wrangling has begun," I said.

Wainright took a deep breath, slowly exhaled, and nodded. "Yep."

I hated to think it, but better him than me.

* * *

Despite Conway's abduction, the Freedom Party moved forward an event planned to rally public and conservative political support around their PEP initiative. They had scheduled it for the Horizon Center two days hence, a venue that supported over 20,000 visitors. The event had originally been orchestrated by Senator Conway as a gathering point for national, state, and local conservative politicians, including numerous prominent financial donors, to further extol the merits of the PEP initiative. Now, the public was encouraged to attend, as well.

The press ran coverage of the senator's abduction around the clock. Conservative channels suggested an association between his abduction and the senator's championing of the PEP initiative.

"Surely, terrorists must be to blame," Senator Pennyroot said during a guest appearance on one news program. "This is an attack at the very heart of our public leadership, but we won't be intimidated by thugs. The rally will move forward, as I'm sure Senator Conway would want. Only now this rally is about more than the PEP program. It's about support for Senator Conway as we remain hopeful for his safe return."

Even President Graydon issued a brief public statement from the White House Press Briefing Room.

"Senator Conway's abduction is a tragic event. One of this nation's great leaders has been taken from us," Graydon said. "I shall marshal all of the powers available to my office, including mobilizing key government agencies, to secure Senator Conway's safe release and ensure that the perpetrators are swiftly brought to justice."

Yeah, no pressure on us there.

A couple of hours following our latest status meeting, we received our first major break in the case.

Sanders and I hurried into Wainright's office.

"One of our system techs, Ms. Lee, has some key leads," Wainright said.

"We have a single image from a traffic camera located at an intersection five miles away from the senator's home," Lee said while standing before a large, wall-mounted video screen. "This is the driver of the black van reported near the crime scene as he proceeded through a red light. You can see the driver's face relatively clearly via the front-facing camera."

The guy had young but rugged features.

"Any tag information, Lee?" Wainright asked.

"No, sir. Due to the damaged rear-facing camera, the image was too granulated to process," Lee replied.

"What about an ID on the driver?" Sanders asked.

"We're running it through the federal database now, sir," Lee replied.

Wainright went to the phone on his desk. "I'd better call Tevin. It's not much, but it's something."

Ten minutes later, the FBI system had a match.

Tevin teleconferenced into the meeting.

"His name is Sam Welder, but he goes by the nickname Thrasher," said Lee. "He's a former Marine who specialized in recon. In recent years, he's a known mercenary, mostly operating in parts of Europe and the Middle East. To the best of our knowledge, he's never been associated with activities that ran counter to U.S. interests."

"Does that mean he's worked for the government before?" I asked.

Lee looked at Wainright, who nodded.

"Welder doesn't hold any current classified access," she replied. "However, some information in his case file is level five confidential and I didn't have the required access to view everything."

"Tevin?" Wainright asked.

"I'm on it," he replied. "Keep talking."

"His last known location was Odense, Denmark, where he has cohabited for the past three years with a woman named Allis Rianka," Lee continued.

"Sounds cozy," I said. "I'd like to visit Denmark."

Sanders flicked the edge of my ear with the tip of her fingernail. "Shush."

"Ouch," I said, reaching up to rub at my ear.

"Does he have any local contacts?" Wainright asked. "Any ties to Senator Conway?"

"His file doesn't indicate any," Lee replied. "However, his record reflects that he's as a lifetime member in good standing with the National Rifleman's Association. He was also a dues-paying member of the Republican National Committee for a ten-year period, where he contributed hundreds of dollars to various conservative candidates. However, his membership expired more than four years ago."

"Well, that hardly makes him an RNC lackey," Tevin said. "And a high percentage of military members and veterans are NRA members."

"I'm an NRA member," I said.

Sanders gave me a hard look.

"We're attempting to locate the black van, though longer it takes, the larger the search area grows," Lee said.

"I'll have our techs run face pattern recognition," Tevin said. "However, it'll take some time, especially as the perimeter widens."

"I'll alert all law enforcement outlets, including Homeland Security and points of entry or exit," Wainright said. "Without more to go on, we'll have to list him as a person of interest."

"That's it?" I asked.

"That's about all any of us can do for now," Sanders said. "We can't say for certain that he's actually tied to the kidnapping, though he's the best lead we have at the moment."

"Are you kidding?" I asked. "A merc residing in Europe shows up out of the blue near a kidnapping scene and we're not sure he's our guy? Why the hell else would he be around here? House-hunting?"

"Bringer, this is just how—" Sanders began.

A single loud knock sounded on Wainright's office door before Agent Templeton entered the room.

"What?" Wainright asked.

"Oh, shit," Tevin said.

I saw the shocked expression on Tevin's face via Wainright's computer screen.

My attention diverted to Agent Templeton.

"Sir, the DoD just passed along a high-priority national-security-level message to all agencies," Templeton said. "The Air Force has lost an EMP device!"

CHAPTER 21

Lost an EMP device?

Yeah, that's definitely oh-shit-worthy.

"Aw, Christ," Wainright said, rubbing his forehead with the palm of one hand. "What next?"

"How in the hell did the Air Force manage to lose track of an EMP device?" Sanders demanded.

"Device, nothing," I said. "That's a *weapon*. Hey, didn't Conway pick a bad day to get kidnapped? He just got trumped by an EMP."

Sanders shriveled her nose and frowned in that cute way that she always does when she's pissed with me.

I could probably stand to keep my sarcastic comments to myself more often.

Nah, they were too good not to share.

Meanwhile, the office transitioned from high gear to near-pandemonium.

"Call in everybody and begin round-the-clock schedules," Wainright said to someone over the phone. "Coordinate with DoD and Homeland Security, and get me a line to the Director asap."

"So, then, what's protocol for something like this?" I asked Sanders.

She just stared back at me. "I'm really not talking to you right now."

Instead, she picked up her smartphone. "Denton, did you hear about the EMP device?"

"Sir, I think you should get our team prepared to mobilize," she said.

I only half-listened to Sanders' phone call. I realized then that I didn't have anyone even remotely useful to call. Instead, my thoughts gravitated to my parents, my sister, and her kids.

Everything that I knew about an EMP explosion could be summed up in just a few sentences. I recalled a briefing about it from my army days.

It isn't the explosion that causes harm to humans, unless they happen to be holding something electronic, in which case they might receive a powerful electrical-type shock. It is the chaos caused by losing electronics within the affected area.

I recalled that an EMP was most helpful when used as a precursor to an invading force. I could easily imagine what something like an EMP blast could do to disable a large city.

Like Washington, D.C., for example?

Then another prospect resonated within me.

Invading force?

"Aw, crap," I said. "I'd better load up on sports drinks."

* * *

Sanders and I hadn't even checked into a hotel when we arrived in D.C. Once we did, it wasn't until around midnight that we finally made it into our rooms, and that was only long enough for a shower, a quick nap, and a change of clothes.

I managed to sleep only because of my sheer exhaustion. An abrupt knock at my hotel room door roused me back to consciousness.

"Bringer?" Sanders called out.

I groaned and glanced at my watch.

It wasn't even five in the morning yet.

As soon as I opened the door, she winced.

"Wow, you look even worse than I did this morning," she said. "And it's not every day a girl gets greeted at the door by a guy wearing underwear. Be still my beating heart."

"Shut up," I said as she squeezed past me to enter my room.

That's when I noticed two large designer coffee cups in her hand. She proffered one, which I eagerly accepted.

After one swig, I moaned with no small degree of satisfaction. Fresh-brewed coffee was just what the doctor ordered.

"Yeah, you're welcome," she said. "Syringe of funny-fluid?"

"Funny-fluid?" I asked while pointing to the small refrigerator nearby. Fortunately, I still had one dose remaining.

"I can't remember what Maria calls that crap we're filling you with," she said, setting her coffee cup aside. "I only know that it helps you."

She retrieved my last syringe and, following a quick rub of my shoulder, she unceremoniously stuck me.

"This is all you have?" she asked.

"Yeah, I need to remember to call Maria and have her overnight some to me," I said.

"Remember, nothing," she chastised. "Do it now. We need to keep you fully juiced and ready for when things finally go down."

She seemed to have gone into full drill sergeant mode. Still, she made a good point. I should have thought of that already.

"Will do," I said. "Thanks."

She spared me a brief sympathetic look before returning to her coffee.

"Hurry up and shave," she said. "We need to get back to Wainright's office asap."

"Any new leads?" I asked as I walked into the bathroom and picked up my can of shaving cream.

"Nothing major yet," she replied. "But Tevin says they

got another facial recognition hit on Thrasher at a gas station on the south side of Woodbridge, Virginia. So far, he's heading south, but it's anyone's best guess as to where he's ultimately going."

I made short work with my razor as I listened.

"Thrasher," I said. "Sounds like the moniker for a bad-ass comic book villain."

"Bad-ass is a keen description of him, given his resume," she said. "It reads like something out of a John le Carré novel."

"Enough about him for a minute," I said. "What about the missing EMP?"

"Still nothing on that," she replied. "But we're supposed to attend an update briefing with Tevin and Wainright as soon as we get to the office."

"Hm," I said, carefully shaving my neck.

"As I started to say, I read a little more about Thrasher before falling asleep last night," she said.

"Aw, I was hoping you were thinking of me," I teased.

"Keep dreaming, Bringer," she said. "Sam Welder ended up with the nickname Thrasher while still in the Marines, where he had an exemplary record. Since then, he became somewhat of the mercenary's mercenary. He's even done contract wet work for the Israeli Mossad."

"Okay, so I'm impressed," I said. "I've definitely got to meet this guy."

"Same here," she agreed. "I'm convinced he's our perp for Conway's abduction. The two questions in my mind are: one, why Conway, and two, who hired him?"

"Forgive me for saying this, but Conway seems like small potatoes compared to the EMP issue," I said.

"On the surface, maybe," she said. "But what if they're connected?"

I hadn't considered that.

"How? Why?" I asked.

"I haven't worked that out yet, but I'm keeping an open mind," she replied.

"So, you think that maybe Conway's abduction was a distraction while somebody snatched the EMP?" I asked.

"I see the caffeine is finally starting to take effect," she said. "However, it wouldn't make sense to wait until the nation's law enforcement agencies are mobilized before choosing to steal an EMP device. That would be the poorest of timing, in my opinion."

I frowned as I walked over to my suitcase and pulled out a fresh pair of jeans and a shirt. "Yeah, there's that. I guess I need more caffeine."

"What we both need more of is sleep," she said, turning away as I pulled on my jeans. "But that's not going to happen anytime soon."

Oh, how I wished she was mistaken about that.

At the FBI offices, Wainright and Tevin started the briefing as soon as we stepped foot into the conference room.

"Okay, people, here's where things stand," Wainright began.

Some of what he said Sanders had already told me back at the hotel.

"Deputy Director Tevin's NSA resources have been invaluable. We're mobilizing federal, state, and local resources to canvas the area each time we receive a new hit on Thrasher's location," Wainright said. "Unfortunately, nothing new has turned up in the past few hours. Tevin, would you please bring everyone up to speed on the latest regarding the EMP device?"

"Certainly," Tevin said. "The Air Force has just shared video from the storage area where the device was housed."

A nearby wall-mounted screen displayed video of a dimly lit bay area where a couple dozen cylindrical nodules, which appeared to be man-sized or larger, were lined up in rows and tethered to individual, raised platforms.

"This video was taken from a sealed underground storage facility maintained by the Air Force in an undisclosed location somewhere in South Dakota," Tevin said.

The video was devoid of people until a lone figure of medium height wearing a camouflage military uniform walked into the frame. Any further distinctive features were subdued by the low light conditions.

For a brief moment, the figure's face was vaguely visible as he turned toward the camera.

"The perpetrator is male, but that's about all we know at this time," Tevin continued.

"Perpetrator? The cameras didn't pick up any of his accomplices?" Sanders asked.

"Nope, just him," Tevin replied. "And this is the only feed that anyone unauthorized showed up on."

"Let me get this straight. One guy managed to walk off with an EMP that size?" I asked.

"Bringer, watch closely," Tevin said. "Here's where things get even more interesting."

The man walked up to one of the devices and reached his arms around it, as if hugging it to his body.

Then both he and the device disappeared.

Sharp intakes of breath sounded throughout the room, including some muttered curses.

"Unbelievable," Sanders said.

"We did manage to enhance the portion of the video once he faced the camera," Tevin said. "Here's a close-up."

"That's the bastard!" I yelled.

"You recognize him, Bringer?" Tevin asked.

"Damned straight I do! That's the guy who disappeared right before my eyes, along with that group of terrorists in Cardiff," I said.

CHAPTER 22

"So, that appears to confirm we're dealing with terrorists, but part of what group?" asked Agent Sanchez.

"Our best guess is Continuance Corporation," replied Tevin.

"Isn't that the organization with all of the rogue telekinetics?" asked Agent Templeton. "Aren't they the ones responsible for the Wallace Building bombing and the attack on our FBI regional office in Nevis Corners?"

"Yes, that's our belief at this time," Tevin replied.

"As to the identity of the perp in the video, is there anything in our databases about him?" Sanders asked.

"Nothing so far in the FBI or state databases," Wainright said. "Tevin?"

"Unfortunately, nothing in the NSA system, either," Tevin replied. "However, we've forwarded the image to Interpol and I'm hoping they have something— anything— that gives us some clue about him."

Whoever he was, what I wouldn't give to have another crack at the guy.

"So, the military won't even tell us where the weapon was stolen from?" I asked.

"Notice the other devices in the storage area?" Tevin asked. "The military's not keen on giving up that location right now, though I believe the remaining inventory is actively being moved to another secure location."

"That type of heist sort of changes the definition of secure location, doesn't it?" I asked.

Sanders nudged my knee with hers beneath the conference table.

Wainright gave me a long look. "In the meantime," he said. "We're putting together three rapid response tactical teams to mobilize at a moment's notice. Tevin and I will coordinate together from here in the command center. We will both act in equal command capacity, as needed. Sanders and Bringer, you're heading up one of the three teams."

"Finally, something to do," I said.

"Any questions?" Tevin asked.

"Yes, sir," an agent who had teleconferenced in asked. "Given our suspects, isn't a likely target the upcoming Freedom Party PEP rally? As such, shouldn't it be cancelled or rescheduled?"

Wainright and Tevin exchanged slight nods.

"He actually said *pep rally*," I whispered to Sanders.

"Grow up, Bringer," she admonished.

"Yes, it's a likely target, and I agree with your recommendation," Wainright replied. "In light of Bringer's recognition of the suspect, Tevin and I will convey your idea to our superiors."

"Anything else?" Wainright asked, casting a frown in my direction.

"Sir," asked Templeton. "Which of the key searches are the tactical teams to be assigned to, EMP or Senator Conway?"

"Either," Tevin replied. "We're covering both, though we'll directly collaborate with the military when engaging in any EMP-related responses."

"That's all for now," Wainright said. "Let's get back to it."

"Sanders, you want to hang around the command center while I work with our team to prepare?" I asked.

"Sure," she replied. "Maybe they'll even let you pick out

some of their toys to play with."

"Ah, you know me too well," I said.

"Just save a few of the good ones for me, too," she said with a quick wink.

Sanders followed Tevin and Wainright as they left the room, headed for the command center. Everyone else trailed after them.

Better Sanders than me.

I was only too happy to have something functional to occupy my thoughts and hands. Tactical team matters felt more familiar to me, reminiscent of my time operating with an army fire team.

I hated to admit it, but Sanders was far better suited to the intelligence gathering process than I was.

Suddenly, she reappeared at the conference room doorway.

"And call Maria about your special refill," she said.

"Oh, yeah, thanks," I said. "Check in with me later, okay?"

Then she was gone again, and I listened as her footsteps rapidly faded down the hall.

I couldn't help but smile.

* * *

I felt both productive and more at ease by the time I met the tactical team that would work with Sanders and me.

When Sanders finally showed up, our team and I were still in an underground armory, one level beneath the building's public parking garage, inspecting the variety of weaponry assigned to the group.

The armory hosted not only weapons, but also an assortment of transportation options. There were the traditional black cars and SUVs with tinted glass that were frequently depicted in Hollywood films and on television, as well as some military-grade vehicles, including armored troop transports, each emblazoned with the FBI insignia.

I had never even realized that the FBI had anything quite like the armory I was standing in. Suffice to say, it impressed me.

"Hey, Sanders, over here," I said, waving to her.

She stopped short of us and took a moment to observe the array of weapons laid out on tables.

"All of these are for the team?" she asked, handing me a cold bottled sports drink.

"Thanks. And are you kidding?" I countered, opening the bottle. "Those are just mine. You guys have to go get your own."

"Figured as much," she said.

"Bringer, you've got the best arsenal in town, my friend," said one of our team members. "Fireballs? Hell, yeah."

"Sanders, welcome to team Alpha," I said.

"Team Alpha?" she asked. "Oh, that's original. Did you come up with that, Bringer?"

"Yeah, yeah, whatever. Alpha, Bravo, and Charlie teams. The military wanted to keep the naming simple, and since we're merely 'assisting' them in responding to the EMP matter, they had the final say," I replied. "Apparently, they're still as much against creativity as when I was in. I personally would've preferred team Fireball for us."

Sanders nodded.

"Let me introduce you," I offered. "Lt. Kris Holt is our team's military liaison; she's an accomplished member of Delta Force and is invaluable in case we locate the EMP weapon."

"Hello, Agent Sanders," Holt greeted. "But, just to clarify, the version stolen is technically classified, and registered, as a non-nuclear EMP device."

"That's used as a weapon," I said, looking squarely at Sanders.

She pursed her lips to curtail a smile.

"Moving on," I said. "Our fireball fan is Mackie Snow, an FBI sniper. He prefers to be called Mackie. Next, Kevin Rain and Dalia Hunter are both FBI tactical entry specialists.

And, finally, Reedus Irons is from the NSA, specializing in tactical combat and surveillance."

I gestured to Sanders. "Everyone, this is FBI Agent Megan Sanders, team co-leader. More importantly, she's my partner."

Sanders gave me a warm, yet fleeting, look of appreciation before greeting and shaking hands with each team member.

After Sanders donned a tactical vest and pocketed additional ammo for her duty pistol, we returned upstairs to the command center.

The command center looked like something NASA maintained at a launch facility. Displays and rows of tables with computer stations filled the room, each location manned by a technician.

I looked to my left at a bank of wall-mounted screens, three rows of four that displayed various news broadcasts. I noticed that one screen showed a news interview with my friend Paul.

"What the—" I said, walking over to turn up the volume on the displays.

"...feel it's necessary to counter this politically charged PEP rally with a conference of House and Senate moderates from both parties who want to come together for the good of the country," Paul said.

"Yes, but Congressman, don't you think this could also be viewed as merely a desperate political stunt to try to divert attention from the more popular Freedom Party efforts?" asked the interviewer, Joe Scarborne of Central News Network. "After all, the Freedom Party polls very high among Americans."

Paul didn't appear amused. "I appreciate that some might feel very strongly about the Freedom Party and the energy of many of its members, Joe," he said. "However, I know for a fact that Americans are being swept up in both fear and fervor over recent events, and it's important that balanced, diverse views are heard and considered. I'm trying to build a coalition of senators and representatives, both Republicans and Democrats, who'll thoughtfully consider our options before leaping blindly forward into potentially dangerous legal and legislative waters. For example, a recent legislative effort by Freedom Party members to further strengthen and centralize presidential powers seems both reckless and potentially dangerous to our federal government's delicate mechanisms of checks and balances."

"Some have referred to you and your peers as obstructionists for blocking legislation that many view as essential to protect the public from recent escalating telekinetic terrorist threats," Joe said.

"I prefer to think of it less as obstructionism and more as observing sensible legislative process," Paul said. "At the very least, multiple views should be heard and considered before rushing to pass hasty legislation."

"Do you have any idea how many members of Congress are planning to attend your rally, Congressman?"

Paul nodded. "Thus far, approximately eighty House members and another thirty or so senators have committed, including Vice President Spade, who has been a refreshingly steady voice in the Senate during recent debates."

"Some political insiders have suggested that Vice President Spade is on the political outs with President Graydon," Joe said. "There have been unconfirmed reports that he's no longer invited to many closed door meetings with the President. In fact, leading up to Senator Conway's abduction, there was speculation that the President might replace Spade with Senator Conway on the ticket for Graydon's presidential reelection campaign."

Outstanding, I thought. *As if we needed any more pressure to find the bastard.*

"Congressman, Central News has received unconfirmed reports that an EMP weapon has recently been stolen from a military storage facility," Joe said. "Can you confirm that for us?"

"Really? Well, I'm afraid you'd need to consult with the

Justice Department or Defense Department on that, Joe," Paul replied.

"No time for TV, Bringer," Sanders said. "Hey, isn't that Congressman Criswell?"

"Yeah," I said.

"...really shouldn't speculate on how the President chooses to conduct his future campaigns," Paul continued. "I'm focused on returning balanced, deliberative tones to both the Senate and the House."

"What's going on?" Sanders asked.

"It sounds like Paul's marshalling politicians to counter the Freedom Party," I replied.

She whistled. "That sounds like political suicide to me; like standing in front of a tidal wave, really."

"Maybe, but if anyone has even a remote chance, it's Paul," I said. "If it were me, I'd probably just end up shoving a lot of fireballs into faces."

"Ah, so more of an Emperor Nero approach, then," she said.

"Bringer, Sanders, we've got something," Wainright called from across the room.

Wainright and Tevin stood before a huge screen before the command center that displayed a topographical map of the eastern part of the U.S.

"Got a lead on the EMP weapon?" I asked.

"No, not yet," Tevin replied. "But we've logged two recent camera images that flagged positive for facial recognition on Sam Welder. He's changed vehicles and is currently driving a brown Suburban with tinted windows. The vehicle is registered to a florist based out of Montclair, Virginia. It's likely stolen, but local authorities are confirming that now."

"Any sign of Conway?" Sanders asked.

"Not yet, but our best guess is that he's being detained in the Suburban," Tevin replied.

"Sirs," said one of the technicians sitting before a nearby terminal. "The Virginia Highway Patrol has located an abandoned black van believed to be the one driven by Welder. It's located near an I-95 service road."

"Mobilize resources to blanket the I-95 corridor as far south as Richmond," Wainright ordered. "I want immediate air and ground coverage. We're not letting him trek all the way across the country."

"Bringer, Sanders," Tevin prompted. "Stay close to your team and keep everyone on ready status. And you'd all better pack a go-bag just in case we have to relocate you to a forward holding position. We're also readying Bravo and Charlie teams."

Sanders and I headed straight for the armory to join up with our team.

CHAPTER 23

Despite the enterprising lead, our team had remained on standby for twenty-four hours, during which time the trail for Welder went cold. Regardless of Tevin's ability to bring one of their intelligence satellites into use to comb the east coast, thus far we'd failed to even locate the brown Suburban that Welder was last seen driving.

Maybe he had ditched it already and was in another vehicle. It seemed to take forever for the NSA's software to scan what had to be hundreds, or maybe even thousands, of cameras from Washington, D.C. to as far south as Florida and as far west as Georgia.

"What about using military drones to help in the search?" I asked Sanders, who had just sat down after retrieving some fresh coffee for us.

"Thought of that already," she replied. "Tevin said the military has deployed available drones to scour the country, seeking their lost EMP device. Hell, we're lucky the NSA was able to retain use of a satellite to search for Welder."

"The big PEP rally is tomorrow," I said. "And Conway's going to miss it."

"You really like saying PEP rally, don't you?" Sanders asked.

"Hey, I was trying to be serious there."

"Well, you're right, of course. If something doesn't break

soon, Conway's going to miss a lot of things," Sanders said. "That's even if he's still alive."

"You see, the thing I don't get about this whole situation is, why take Conway in the first place?" I asked.

"He's only one of the most powerful politicians on Capitol Hill, including one of the heads of the Freedom Party, and a close personal friend and advisor to the President," Sanders said. "Isn't that more than enough?"

I rubbed at my forehead. "Yeah, yeah, I get that he's all important and everything. What I mean is what good does taking him actually do anyone? The President's still going to make tough decisions, and we've seen how the Freedom Party and their PEP program is barreling right along without him."

"Hell, Conway might even be more of a figurehead as a captive than he was in front of the cameras," I continued. "If it's for propaganda, nobody's taken responsibility, and if it's for money, there haven't been any ransom demands."

Sanders stared at me. "Yeah, I actually thought about that last part, too. This definitely isn't the typical kidnapping case."

I pondered further on what Sanders had said, and then spent the better part of the afternoon playing cards in the ready room with Mackie, Rain, and Hunter while Sanders stood by in the command center.

Around eight o'clock that evening, I rejoined my team in the armory to make another review of our equipment and the two vehicles that we had equipped to use upon activation.

"Anybody want to tell me why there's a cooler full of sports drinks in the back of this SUV?" Hunter asked. "Are we going to the lake or something?"

"That cooler's mine," I said. "You can get your own."

Mackie took him aside and whispered something to him that I couldn't hear, but I saw Hunter nod and then give me a curious look.

A few minutes after we started our equipment review, each of our smartphones received text messages.

"Finally. We're deploying," Mackie said.

"Bringer!" called Sanders as she ran across the bay toward us. "Ready the vehicles!"

I waited until she was within conversational earshot.

"Where to?" I asked.

"The airport," she replied. "We found Welder."

"The airport?" Mackie asked. "They tracked Welder to the airport?"

"No, the vehicles will be loaded onto a military cargo plane that's waiting for us," she replied. "They got a solid hit on Welder's location, but it's in Hawkinsville, Georgia."

"Where the hell is that?" I asked.

"The middle of nowhere, actually," she replied. "You'll see soon enough. Let's get our bags loaded and get going!"

* * *

By the time we touched down at Robins Air Force Base, unloaded the vehicles, and got on the road to Hawkinsville, it was almost eleven o'clock.

Sanders briefed us on the road, using a secure radio frequency to speak to the remaining team members, who trailed us in the other vehicle.

"State and local FBI agents are establishing a discreet perimeter at a five-mile radius while waiting for us to arrive. We're trying to keep a lid on this, prevent the press from finding out, to avoid tipping off the suspects, though nobody should expect that to hold for very long," she said. "Welder is supposedly held up in a small complex of three buildings. The complex once operated as a sheet metal manufacturing plant, though it's been primarily used for extended merchandise storage for the past three years. It's currently owned by Blevins, Inc., a plumbing parts supplier."

"Well, I hope they're insured," I said.

Mackie and Irons both chuckled sardonically.

"Remember, priority one is safely retrieving Conway," Sanders advised. "Apprehending suspects is optional only."

Really?

That was a first since Sanders and I had worked together. Normally, live suspects are the order of the day.

I looked sidelong at Sanders.

"Not my call," she said. "That comes from the top."

During the drive, we reviewed NSA satellite images of the target area on our tablet computers, as well as digital maps identifying local landmarks, roads, and structures.

Hawkinsville was a small town and the area surrounding it had a rural feel. The biggest concern was sections of dense trees interspersed throughout the area, disrupting our view of all terrain.

Admittedly, we could use the trees to our advantage for cover.

Sanders and Lieutenant Holt agreed upon team member placement. We also coordinated with Bravo team, which was on standby via helicopter.

We reached the perimeter around 1 a.m. The law enforcement presence was definitely cursory. I only saw one highway patrol vehicle and two unmarked SUVs, likely federal units, parked along the roadside.

Fortunately, I didn't see any press around the area yet.

"Tactical team?" asked an agent, wearing an FBI jacket, as he stepped up beside our vehicle.

"TASIT taskforce, Alpha team," Sanders replied while displaying her badge and ID.

He waved us through and we parked a few miles ahead, but still a half mile or so away from the target area.

Each of us accepted earpieces, microphones, and night vision goggles. Next, we conducted a weapons check.

Well, except for me; I was a walking weapon already.

Mackie slung a .308 sniper rifle over his shoulder before hefting the 50-caliber sniper rifle in his arms.

"You're taking the fifty, too?" I asked.

"Nothing's getting away from us tonight," he replied. "Man or machine."

"Take out any perimeter targets first," Holt reminded

him. "Then establish a position with as many of the entrances and exits in front of you as possible."

He nodded and hurried into the tree line and disappeared.

"Irons, you advance beyond the property and then use your best judgement on approach," Holt said.

"Check," Irons replied. He chambered a round in his assault rifle and proceeded down the road ahead of us.

"Sanders and Bringer, I'll stay furthest back where I'll be available to you as a floater," Holt said.

"Got it," Sanders said. "We'll move forward, but will wait for Mackie's report before proceeding beyond cover."

"Good luck," Holt said, adjusting the night scope on her assault rifle.

Sanders and I quietly made our way up the road toward the target property while Rain and Hunter followed, flanking us on either side.

The moonless night made everything feel almost claustrophobic, and the night vision goggles were difficult to adjust to.

Mackie, Holt, and Irons checked in with us every few minutes, noting their position advances. Sanders confirmed our location as we proceeded forward.

"One suspect outside the center building, smoking a cigarette," Mackie said.

"Try to hold until we get into position, but you're not to permit him ingress back into the building. Got it?" Sanders asked.

"Copy that," Mackie replied.

By the time our group of four reached a shallow roadside drainage ditch next to a culvert just outside the property line, it felt like an eternity had passed, though it had only been about twenty minutes by my watch. And we were still nearly a hundred yards away from the buildings.

"Holding in the tree line east of the complex," Irons reported. "Awaiting orders."

"Copy that," Sanders said while squatting beside me.

"Bringer, can you read thoughts from here? Maybe detect how many people might be in there?"

"I'll try," I replied.

I opened my thoughts and imagined a bubble extending forward ahead of me.

...keep smoking that cigarette, came Mackie's thoughts.

...door will we enter through first?

That had to be Irons.

...hate waiting for the phone to ring.

Okay, that wasn't one of ours. Likely, it was the fellow standing outside smoking.

Then I sensed a series of mental impressions rather actual thoughts, and I wondered if the concrete composition of the buildings was hampering my abilities.

"There's a sense of others inside the buildings, but I can't tell how many," I said.

"Which buildings?" Sanders asked.

"I don't know. Maybe if I get closer," I replied.

Sanders paused. "Bringer needs to advance to determine which buildings are active. Mackie, take out the smoker if he moves."

"Copy that," Mackie replied.

Then Holt and Irons acknowledged.

I exited the drainage ditch, crouching as low to the ground as possible while slowly advancing forward.

I made it about thirty feet and tried sensing thoughts ahead of me.

...think there's someone out there, came a strong thought.

Through the night vision goggles, I saw the silhouette of a man ahead standing erect.

"Crap, I think the smoker's detected me," I whispered.

"Copy that," Mackie said.

I watched as the smoker fell to the ground.

"Target neutralized," Mackie said.

"That starts the clock, people," Holt warned.

"Moving forward," I said.

"Hurry, Bringer," Sanders urged.

Damn, everything suddenly felt rushed.

I stood up a bit more and methodically walked toward the buildings while reaching out with my thoughts.

It was an imprecise effort, to say the least.

"Multiple targets in the center building closest to me. Estimate more than three, but less than eight," I said. "No targets in the building to the west, and only one in the east building. I can't tell who's who, though."

"Mackie, choose your position for best coverage of the back and side doors to the center building," Sanders ordered. "Irons, breach the east building. Holt, take a position between the center and east buildings to cover exits and support Irons. Rain and Hunter, breach the center building with me. Go."

I admired how impressive Sanders was in the field.

She came up on my left as Rain and Hunter quickly passed us on their way toward the front door of the building before us.

After removing her night vision goggles, Sanders readied her pistol while Hunter placed plastic explosives around the lock and door handle of the windowless metal door facing us. Rain readied his assault rifle.

Sanders nodded and a loud bang sounded amidst a momentary flash.

I formed a shield before me and thrust it ahead of me, knocking the door inward.

We charged forward into the building.

CHAPTER 24

"FBI!" Sanders yelled.

"Drop your weapons!" Rain yelled.

Chaos and gunfire erupted around us as I moved through a front office area, forming my shield before me to provide us some cover.

"One suspect down," Hunter said.

In the hallway before me, a person bearing a rifle stepped out from behind a tall filing cabinet and fired at us.

Multiple rounds hammered my shield, sending short jolts through my head. I imagined a sphere and punched forward at the assailant.

He flew violently into the air and backward down the hall, impacting the wall at the end and collapsing onto the floor. He didn't move after that.

"One down," I said.

"East building breached," Irons said. "Sole suspect down."

"Holt, in position," the Lieutenant said.

Following behind me, Sanders fired to my right multiple times, hitting a suspect using a desk for cover. He crumpled to the floor.

"One down," Sanders said. "Take the doors, Bringer."

I used my shield to bust open a door to my right, which Rain entered. I did the same with the door to my left, which

Hunter entered.

"Clear," Rain said.

"Clear," Hunter said.

Continuing forward, I tried to reach out in all directions with my thoughts to sense others nearby, but detected nobody else.

"This part of the building's empty," I said.

"Hunter and Rain, clear the remaining rooms," Sanders ordered.

I turned and headed back into the main office and reached out with my thoughts to where I sensed more people.

"At least three beyond that door," I said, pointing to a door at the back of the office.

"Breaching another room," Sanders said. "Cover exterior exits."

Holt and Irons each acknowledged.

I pushed my palm outward away from me and the door flew off its hinges and into the room before us.

I rushed forward, generating a shield before me with Sanders close at my heels.

"FBI!" Sanders yelled. "Nobody move!"

"Hunter and Rain on your six, Sanders," Rain said over the comm.

It was a large storage bay and there were crates and boxes stacked everywhere. Large shelves created rows and lined nearby walls.

I hurried down the nearest aisle in the direction of the individuals whose presence I sensed.

Three distinct, yet simultaneous, voices sounded off in my head.

…hurry already.

…happening so fast.

…right on schedule.

"Three people," I said, quickening my pace forward while churning a small fireball in the palm of my right hand.

As I barreled forward, I heard footsteps peel off in

opposite directions behind me, presumably Hunter and Rain.

I sensed Sanders' presence at my back and to my left.

Hurry, Bringer, came her voice in my head.

Sanders and I came to a large, open area in the middle of the bay where three people stood next to a big cylindrical-looking object positioned on a metal stand.

The EMP!

My eyes went to the men before us. Sam Welder shouldered an assault rifle and fired.

Sanders stood well off to my left and her weapon went off at the same time Welder's did. His rounds hammered at my shield while Sanders' rounds caught him squarely in the chest, staggering him backward slightly.

"Cease fire!" I yelled, unsure what one stray bullet might do, given the bomb before us.

A man standing beside Welder grasped Welder's shoulder.

It was the terrorist who had disappeared before us in Cardiff; the man on the video who'd stolen an EMP weapon.

The two men promptly disappeared.

"Dammit!" Sanders yelled.

My eyes fell upon the third person, handcuffed to the bomb platform.

Senator Benjamin Conway.

He appeared only shaken, which surprised me given the circumstances that had just unfolded before him.

An unwavering politician.

Hunter and Rain each appeared out of opposite corners of my peripheral vision.

"Oh, hell," Rain said.

"Sanders? Rain?" Holt demanded. "Status."

"No team casualties and Senator Conway is safe. We're in a bay of the central building," Sanders said. "However, two suspects escaped."

"Negative, Sanders," Mackie said. "Holt, Irons, and I have every exit covered. No sign of hostiles."

"Guys," I said. "The two suspects just teleported outta

here."

Radio silence.

"Oh, and Holt, you might want to get in here. I think we found your lost EMP weapon," I added.

"Copy that," Holt replied.

"Hunter, Rain, clear the building," Sanders ordered.

Conway appeared relieved, if not amused. "Great timing, Mr. Bringer. I'm glad to see you."

I offered a cordial smile in return while opening my mind and concentrating on him. "Our pleasure, Senator."

...have planned this better myself.

I immediately wondered what he meant by that?

"You okay, Bringer?" Sanders asked while she removed the senator's handcuffs.

"Huh?" I asked. "Yeah, just relieved to see the senator alive."

There was something just a little too unnerving about Conway, much more than just his radical politics. However, I couldn't formulate things fully yet.

For now, it merely reinforced why I didn't like the guy.

"Are you unharmed, Senator?" Sanders asked.

"Me? Fine," he replied. "I think they intended to set this off with me attached to it."

"Why? Were they making a statement or something?" I asked. "Hey, do you have a pacemaker?"

Sanders gave me a hard look before turning her attention to Conway. "Senator, I have to ask, did they make any demands of you?"

"Strangely, no," he replied. "Though it's hard to fully understand the twisted agendas of terrorists."

He paused. "However, there's something I think you should know. I'm sure I overheard one of my captors mention activating this device, though I have no way of knowing for certain whether that's true or not."

"Activating the device?" Sanders asked, half-stunned.

Lieutenant Holt entered the bay and quickly inspected the device.

"Good. This is our missing EMP, and it appears intact," she said, patting the device's metal surface. "Good work, everyone."

"Holt, can you tell if this thing's live?" I asked.

"Live?" she asked with surprise. "As in, armed? Unlikely. You can't easily prime these manually and there are other built-in safeguards. For one, you'd need the proper codes."

She quickly went around to the opposite side of the device while removing a Swiss Army knife from her pocket, which she used to carefully open a small, square side panel.

"Oh, Christ," she said. "This isn't possible. It's on a countdown to detonate!"

"What?!" Sanders demanded.

"According to this, we've got just over twenty-four minutes before it goes off," Holt said. "I don't understand. Nobody's supposed to be able to do something like this."

Holt rapidly pressed various buttons over and over again.

"Don't you have shutdown codes or something?" Sanders asked. "There must be fail-safes and overrides."

"Yes, I'm using the shutdown codes," she said. "But it's not accepting them or any other prescribed overrides. The interface is disabled and it's still counting down. It's not supposed to do that!"

Holt hastily removed what looked like an oversized smartphone from a pouch on her web gear.

"This is Lieutenant Kris Holt," she said. "We have a condition Red Hot on the missing EMP. Countdown twenty-two. Advise."

"I think it's time to leave," Conway said.

"Don't worry, Senator, we're going to get you out of here," Sanders said, dialing her smartphone. "Sanders here. Priority One. Send in Bravo Team to extract the senator ASAP. The EMP device is onsite with an active twenty-minute countdown. Override codes ineffective. Recommend evacuation of immediate area."

God, I admired how Sanders had nerves of steel at a time when most people might have crapped themselves.

Hell, I still might.

I stared at the long, smooth-surfaced oval-shaped object before me. Stenciled on the side of the object were the words "Property of United States Air Force" in large black block letters.

It was ominous-looking, even in its simplicity.

Well, isn't this just a giant sack of shit for a gift?

"Senator, I'll escort you outside for the extraction," Sanders said.

"No, let Bringer," he countered. "No disrespect intended, you understand."

"Certainly, Senator," she replied, appearing somewhat taken aback.

"Holt?" I asked. "You need me here?"

The Lieutenant looked back at me with a determined expression. "There's not much any of us can do at the moment."

I nodded. That wasn't a hopeful response on her part. Not that I had any brighter ideas.

I cast a worried glance at Sanders before escorting Conway to the front of the building and then outdoors. The night seemed oddly calm compared with what was actively unfolding back inside.

"I shouldn't just be standing here," I said.

"I needed to talk to you," he said. "And I'd like your complete attention."

I stared at him while pulling my earpiece out and pocketing it. "This isn't really a good time."

"Convenience is rarely an option," he countered. "These are admittedly trying circumstances, Mr. Bringer. However, very soon now, gridlock will give way to progress, political impasse to continuity. There have been occasions in this nation's history during periods of conflict when the politics of obstructionism yielded to a united and common vision: the Mexican War, Pearl Harbor, the Twin Towers on nine-eleven."

I couldn't help wondering if one of his captors hadn't

actually hit him on the head a little too hard.

"Senator, this is no time for reflection," I said. "We're in deep shit here, if you hadn't noticed."

"You've dealt with explosives during your time in the military, haven't you, Bringer?" he asked.

Improvised explosive devices were one thing; this was something altogether different.

"Nothing like this," I said. "I was in the army where we only dealt with tactical weapons. This is strategic, super-sized."

"This isn't beyond you, though, is it?" he asked. "Or rather, perhaps I should say, beyond your unique set of abilities."

I gave him a hard look. "Listen, I'm not freaking Superman."

He shrugged. "Perhaps not. But for now you're the closest thing we have, and I have confidence in you, son."

If that was true, then the planet was in a helluva lot of trouble.

I opened my thoughts and focused on him.

The time is nearly at hand. A new tomorrow is coming.

"Mr. Bringer, I'll make certain that nobody will blame you personally if you fail to stop that device from going off," he said. "Just give it a try. I wish I could be here to watch you."

...see what you can do, Bringer, came another stray thought.

...eventually make more just like you.

His last thought sent a cold shiver down my spine.

"But you have your PEP rally," I said dryly.

...just in time for stage two, he thought.

His eyes practically glistened as he stared back at me.

...dark sense of humor...knew I liked him.

"In less than twenty-four hours, the world's going to change, no matter how things turn out here," he said. "You'll see."

Okay, now the guy was really creeping me out. He must have made one too many stops at the proverbial punch bowl.

"What's changing in twenty-four hours?" I asked.

"Everything," he replied. "The fate of our nation is in the balance and everyone needs to carefully choose the correct side."

...soon there'll be no other sides to choose from.

"I don't understand, Senator," I said.

"Don't you see? Surely, a man with your experience will. This is an important, pivotal moment. Our next move in this global chess game is critical," he said. "There are too many pieces floating about, but I see that matter being simplified very soon. There's a light and dark side, and I'm what you might call a bishop of the light side. I'm at the side of the king, helping to inspire and direct the other pieces."

"And I suppose that I'm just another pawn," I said.

His eyes widened in a slightly unnerving fashion. "Oh, no, Bringer. Far from it, in fact. You're a rook, a very important battle piece. Understand? The question is, are you playing for the light side or the dark side?"

"I'll consider that," I said.

"Good man," he said. "I know you will."

The sounds of rotor blades grew louder until a helicopter touched down in the middle of the empty parking lot nearby.

Two tactical team members exited the chopper and rushed toward us.

"Mr. Bringer, Captain Evans, Bravo Leader," said one of the men, shaking my hand. "We'll convey the senator to Robins Air Force Base ASAP, sir. Good luck here!"

I nodded and watched the senator as he hurried with the two men and boarded the chopper, which began lifting up before the side door was even closed.

I removed my earpiece from my pocket and reinserted it.

"Senator's on the chopper and away," I said. "Another chopper inbound for us?"

All I heard in response was silence.

"Team? Sorry, I pocketed my earpiece," I said. "Everyone okay?"

"Bringer, you might have had your earpiece out, but you were still hot mic'd," said Sanders. "Now, get your ass back in here!"

I bolted back inside the building.

CHAPTER 25

When I arrived back at the bay, everyone was standing around the EMP weapon, except for Mackie.

They all looked at me with wide-eyed stares.

"What's the sitrep here?" I asked, hurrying over to rejoin the group.

"Have a nice chat with the senator?" Sanders asked, her eyebrows arched.

"Oh, charming," I replied. "So, I'm guessing you all probably heard that, too?"

"Guy's a fuckin' lunatic," Mackie said over the comm.

"Where are you, Mackie?" I asked.

"Retrieving one of our vehicles and then hustling back to you," he replied. "And I'm waiting to see your play Superman. Got any miracles up your sleeve?"

I looked Sanders, who shook her head.

"Any luck on an override?" I asked.

Holt's face appeared ashen. "No," she replied. "It's up to us. A couple of the techs at base are suggesting we try to remove the front cone so I can disconnect the primary control mechanism."

"And why aren't you doing that?" I asked.

"We've got six minutes left," she said. "It takes ten to open the cone, and that's if I had the proper tools, which I don't."

I swallowed hard. "What are we looking at?"

"Best case with this size of unit?" Holt asked. "It knocks out all electronics and power grids within a hundred miles of this place."

That was the best case?

"And…people?" I asked.

"There'll be large numbers of electrocutions and shock-related injuries, including killing anybody using pacemakers or other medical devices," she replied. "Even worse, nearby aircraft are going to crash and vehicles will stop, causing numerous accidents and impacts. A lot of people will die."

"Communications will fail, including Internet, cellular, and landlines," she hastily continued. "The backlash through the grids will be catastrophic, maybe taking years to fully recover from."

"Feel like trying to be Superman?" Sanders asked with a pleading expression in her eyes. "It really couldn't hurt."

As I stared back at Sanders, I felt like I was floating in place, as if my soul had momentarily departed my body.

A moment later, I felt whole again, and just plain angry.

"Son of a bitch," I said, stepping up to the device. "Everybody step back. In fact, I'd feel even better if you all just went outside."

"Conway was right. Looks like the world really is going to change," Rain said, staring at the device.

I gave him a hard look.

"Not if I can help it," I said.

"Bringer," Sanders prompted. "Can't you just drain it or something? Maybe something like you did with the electricity in Seattle."

I frowned. "Drain it?"

Actually, that seemed like a pretty sound idea.

"Way to go, Sanders," I said, looking sidelong at her. "Now, haul your pretty ass and the rest of our team out of here."

She nodded. "Everyone outside," she ordered.

Concentrating on the bomb before me, I reached out to

touch its cold metal skin and used my talent to try pulling power from it. A steady thrum of tingling coursed over and through my body.

Pulling energy from the weapon was a slow, laborious process, and one that hardly felt like it was yielding viable results. Yet my body's temperature began to steadily climb, as if I were standing directly beside a fireplace.

Before long, I felt as if I was going to burst into flame, so I stopped.

Siphoning its energy wasn't the answer. But maybe the opposite was.

"Bringer, please don't get yourself killed," Sanders whispered in my ear.

Her voice made me lurch. I thought she had gone already.

"We need you. I need—" she added.

I turned my head, our noses nearly touching. Her eyes filled with emotion.

I wanted to open my mind to her thoughts, but somehow I didn't dare.

There was no time.

"Hey," I said. "See you soon. Now, get outta here."

She nodded, and, after a moment's hesitation, she turned and ran for the exit.

Good girl.

Refocusing my efforts, I generated a shield and began drawing electricity from any nearby receptacles, and then reversing the energy flow around and into the device as fast as I could.

My skin felt tingly at first, and then itchy like ants were crawling all over it. I increased my shield and tried to imagine energy dancing across it.

Soon, my skin merely felt tingly again, if not slightly warmer.

My telekinetic senses reached out, gathering energy from somewhere in the ground deep beneath me. I drew it up toward me and then channeled it across my shield, through the device.

Fleetingly, I hoped Sanders would somehow be far enough away if my new approach failed, though that seemed dubiously hopeful given Holt's prognosis.

As I poured energy from around my body into the device, I imagined a raging river washing water down a narrow creek bed.

Energized emanations from the device felt as they were accelerating in time with my efforts.

Was I merely giving it more energy for its reaction?

I wished that I knew way more about what the hell I was trying to do.

Once in, all in.

With one effort, just like inhaling a deep breath, I drew additional electrical energy from the environment around me and funneled it directly into the weapon.

Something inside the bomb surged, and I instantly wrapped my shield around it, like an eggshell.

Something both intensely hot and bright exploded before me as I tightly squeezed my eyes shut.

It felt as if every nerve in my body ripped apart, even as my blood boiled and my brain burned.

Then darkness overwhelmed me.

* * *

I awoke abruptly and my body jerked as if a truck had impacted it. Then I felt my back grow cooler and my ears rang with a high-pitched sound.

I opened my eyes and inhaled as stale-tasting air flooded into my lungs.

All I saw was darkness.

Then I realized that I was lying on my back on the concrete floor. Every muscle in my body protested as I rolled onto my stomach and tried to rise from my place on the floor. A wave of nausea washed over me as throbbing pain ratcheted my brain.

As I slowly, achingly, rose to my knees, my nose felt ticklish. I reached up and felt thick warm moisture on my fingertips.

My nose was bleeding.

Once again, I had forced my mind and body to do too much.

How much longer could I keep doing that before I was out of commission for good?

Maria was probably going to kill me.

No need; I'm doing a pretty good job of that all by myself.

I projected my senses toward the EMP weapon and stumbled forward in the darkness until my palms fell against it cold metal skin.

As I probed at it, it felt empty inside; devoid either of power or activity.

With effort, I conjured a small fireball in the palm of my hand and looked at the device.

Its outer shell and casing appeared intact, and it felt cool. The LED display was dark.

That's when I let out the deep breath that I didn't realize I'd been holding.

Perhaps the building's electrical power was the only casualty. At least, I hoped that was all.

I used the reddish-yellow illumination from my waning fireball to make my way toward the nearest building exit, extinguishing the flames as I walked outside, appreciating the feeling of cool night air against my face.

My vision blurred, so I squinted my eyes as I stepped away from the building, waiting for my vision to clear.

The throbbing pain in my head abated slightly.

I thought that I heard the distant sound of a helicopter, and I made my way around to the front of the building.

"Sanders?" I called out. "It's over."

Someone hollered, "Woo-hoo!"

"Hell, yeah!" Rain shouted.

I heard someone running and then caught sight of Sanders as she leapt atop me, her arms wrapped around me.

We both fell to the ground together.

"You did it, Bringer!" she yelled. "I knew you could. I just *knew* it."

"Yeah, just lucky I—"

She planted the biggest kiss of my life on me and, aching body be damned, I was only too happy to return the gesture.

CHAPTER 26

After Holt reported the all clear, federal and state authorities rushed in alongside military forces to take control of the site.

"I don't know how you did it, but thank you," Holt said, shaking my hand. "It's an honor to serve alongside you."

She remained onsite with the remainder of our team as Sanders and I boarded an extraction chopper bound for Robins Air Force Base in Atlanta.

Onboard, Sanders sat beside me, but neither of us said anything to each other. It was all either of us needed, I suppose.

Sometime during the ride, I dozed off.

Once at the base, we were put up in guest quarters for the night. Within the hour, our go-bags were retrieved from our tactical vehicles, hauled in via chopper, and delivered to our rooms, courtesy of the FBI.

The next morning, Sanders and I ate a quick breakfast together in the mess hall, though neither of us mentioned the post-tension kiss that we had shared.

In truth, I was afraid to jinx it, and nervous that she might have discounted it as nothing more than a spontaneous burst of relief.

I didn't feel that way about it then, and I felt even more strongly about it upon reflection.

After breakfast, we used a conference room in the base's headquarters building to teleconference with Wainright, Tevin, and Denton.

I let Sanders do the honors of explaining everything, right up to my lone efforts with the EMP weapon.

"It pales to merely say, well done, Bringer," Tevin said. "But, really, how did you manage to disable the device?"

I took a deep breath and exhaled. Sanders stared at me with a curious expression, though I'm not sure I could do my deeds the sort of justice of description that it deserved.

"Sanders suggested the idea that I try to short circuit it," I said. "Actually, it sort of worked."

"Sort of?" Sanders asked with a frown.

"Yeah, I think it still went off, though," I said. "But it must've been less powerful by then, because I was able to contain it within my shields. Though at the time I thought it had burned me to a cinder. That's about the time I blacked out."

Sanders gave me a wide-eyed look. "You didn't mention—"

"I know," I interrupted. "We haven't had time to talk about that yet."

She gave me a meaningful look. "That's something I would have thought you'd make time for."

I returned her look in kind. "There's a couple of topics to make time for."

Her eyes widened and she quickly looked away at the wall-mounted monitor before us.

"Bringer, as for the EMP," Tevin said. "Do you think you actually contained the full blast from the device?"

I frowned. "Maybe…maybe not. I can't say for certain. It was, after all, a first-time for me."

"And, hopefully, a last time," Sanders said.

"It felt…more powerful than anything I've ever sensed before," I said.

My memory of it was still so vivid that I almost thought I felt my temperature begin to rise again. I felt like I was in a trance and my skin started to itch.

The lights momentarily flickered and the screen blinked.

"Bringer," Sanders said.

I snapped back to the present and my mind cleared. My skin tingled and I rubbed my palms against the fabric of my pants.

Sanders looked at me. "Did you just—"

"Bringer?" Wainright asked. "There was a fluctuation in our signal for a moment there."

I looked at Tevin's tense facial expression on the screen.

"Bringer, do you think you could recreate that effect if you had to?" Tevin asked.

"Huh?" I asked.

Sanders reached out to touch my right hand, still perched atop my thigh.

"Never mind. Don't think about it too much, okay?" she asked.

"Yep. Better forgotten," I agreed with a nod.

"So, again, well done, Bringer," Wainright said. "I'm not sure if the military brass are going to want to ask you about that or not, but—"

"Maybe my memory won't be so good if they do," I offered.

"Good answer," Tevin said.

A previous topic quickly resurfaced in my mind.

"Of course, now that we've dealt with one potentially lethal bomb, we all really should talk about the other," I said.

"The other?" Denton asked. "I thought there was only one device missing."

The look of recognition on Sander's face was priceless.

"Senator Conway," she said. "And his little chit-chat with Bringer."

"Chit-chat?" Wainright asked.

"Bringer and Conway had a—let's call it highly unusual—conversation outside as they awaited his helicopter extraction," Sanders replied. "The entire team overheard what was said over the tactical comm system."

"Really?" Tevin asked. "Was it one of those conversations that could prove dangerous for those with loose lips?"

"Precisely, and I think that most of the team already feels that way about it, as well," Sanders said.

I shook my head. "Guys, Conway's one chirp away from being a cuckoo clock."

"Bringer, I was going to say you have such a way with words, but in this case, I have to agree with you," Sanders said. "I thought something was odd when I asked him what his captors expected from him, and he replied, 'nothing.' That's strange on its own, let alone that his captors were likely affiliated with the Continuance Corporation."

"So, you had a peculiar conversation with him under tense circumstances," Wainright said. "Maybe it was just the stress he was under at the time. We can't build a case on something that was said off-handedly like that."

"No, Sanders is right. Conway seemed far too at ease with what had happened to him. And it wasn't just what he said," I noted. "I picked up some of his thoughts while standing beside him."

I repeated most of them for the group's consideration.

"Damn," Wainright said.

"Admittedly, those raise numerous red flags, Bringer," Tevin said.

"Yeah, but what are we supposed to do about it?" Denton asked. "So, maybe it sounds as if he's got some grand plan in mind. Not only are thoughts not admissible as evidence, but Conway's also more than just influential. He's powerful, with a wide reach. With someone as well-placed as him, lesser opponents might get squashed underfoot like bugs."

Sanders nodded. "Denton's right about that."

I glanced at her, but she immediately looked away from me.

"You're suggesting that we should just let him carry on unabated?" I asked.

"I think the suggestion is that we proceed cautiously moving forward," Tevin said. "That's sensible even under the best of circumstances, and particularly where high-level politics are concerned."

I thought about the words that Conway had used, as well as the thoughts that I intercepted from him.

"He kept alluding to the world changing," I said. "Starting today, in fact."

Sanders looked sharply at me. "Yeah, that's right."

"The PEP rally might be pivotal for both him and the Freedom Party," Denton said. "If it's successful, they're well-positioned to secure contested Congressional positions during the mid-term elections."

"Something else still bothers me. Why was Conway abducted and then taken to a remote location outside of Atlanta?" I asked. "More so, why hide an EMP weapon there with him where there are no major targets in the vicinity?"

"Both equally good questions," Sanders said.

"I dunno," Denton said. "Maybe they couldn't get the EMP device anywhere near someplace more critical. I mean, places like Washington, D.C. or New York are high-visibility areas."

"Yeah, but the person who stole the weapon seems to be able to teleport in and out where he wants," I said. "What's to limit him to Hawkinsville, Georgia?"

"That's a damned good point," Sanders said with a nod.

"The intelligence guys at NSA have started calling him The Teleporter," Tevin said.

"Just great. Now we're giving the bad guys cool nicknames," I said.

"I hear yours is Superman," Tevin said.

I tried not to grin.

"I think I like Captain JFM better," said Denton.

I'd almost forgotten about that one: JFM for Just Freakin' Magic.

"Wait just a minute, guys. What if the idea wasn't to disrupt but to distract instead?" Sanders asked.

"Distract?" Wainright asked. "Distract who?"

Then a sordid thought occurred to me.

"Denton, a moment ago, you said something about the Freedom Party running away with the next election," I said.

"Yeah, so?" he asked.

"That's especially true if there's no more competition," I said.

"What?" Tevin asked. "What do you mean by that?"

Sanders looked at me as if lightning had struck her.

"What if it's not about the PEP rally," she suggested. "What if it's today's caucus at the Capitol with those opposing the Freedom Party."

"That's a big hypothesis that could have disastrous political consequences for everyone if we're wrong. It's already like tap-dancing in a minefield around here as it is," Wainright said. "And don't think your brownie points for retrieving Senator Conway and thwarting an EMP explosion would save you from the fallout over a major misstep like that, either."

"Last night, I picked up on a distinct thought from Conway," I said. "It was, 'soon there'll be no other sides to choose from.' What if all of it was to distract everyone from the real target?"

Sanders expression darkened. "What if someone's going to attack the caucus of moderates? The Vice President's also supposed to attend."

"Guys, either you're geniuses at drawing up conspiracy theories, or the world's about to go to hell today," Denton said.

"The caucus begins in a little over an hour," Tevin said.

"We can mobilize extra security for them," Wainright offered.

"Paul's there," I said, feeling nearly dumbfounded over the thought of my friend's life being in danger. He had already nearly lost his life in Nevis Corners trying to help me.

"We've got to get back to D.C. right now," I said.

"Bringer, it's going to take you hours to get a flight and

make it back here."

An idea struck me. "We're already on an air base. And I'm sure they have fast planes parked around here some place."

* * *

Tevin pulled some NSA strings with the base commander, and before I knew it, Sanders and I were outfitted with flight suits.

And I was correct about fast planes, though I didn't realize it at the time. Robins Air Force Base hosted a squadron of the military's newest and fastest stealth interceptor aircraft, the Ghost Eagle.

The circumstances were even better than I could've imagined.

"You look good in a flight suit, Sanders," I complimented.

"And you look like a kid at Christmas," she said. "Try not to drool into your oxygen mask."

As they were two-seater fighter jets, we were flown in separate planes, each seated in a copilot's seat, located directly behind the pilot.

Taking off was a breathtaking experience all its own.

Once in the air, I thanked my pilot, Major Connors, for helping us out on short notice.

"Aren't you two the agents who shut down that EMP that I heard about on the news?" he asked.

"Yeah," I replied. "That's us."

"Actually, it was Bringer," Sanders said over our shared channel.

A feeling of satisfaction washed over me.

"Nice job," Connors said. "Hell, after that, you don't owe me any thanks. I'd fly your ass all the way to China and back if you asked me."

"Don't give him your phone number, Major," Sanders said.

Both pilots laughed.

I tried to smile, but was too worried about arriving in D.C. in time to stop what I feared was imminent.

To my surprise, we broke the sound barrier after reaching altitude and landed at Andrews Air Force Base just outside of D.C. within the hour, more than beating what would normally have amounted to as much as a nine-hour process for us.

Wainright had an FBI helicopter ready for us as soon as we exited our planes. After a hasty change out of our flight suits, we flew directly to the Capitol complex.

Additional security, including some of the FBI agents from our TASIT team, quietly mobilized so as not to cause a panic.

On the helicopter, my thoughts were far away until Sanders gently touched my elbow.

"Hey, we're almost there," she said, glancing at her watch. "By now the PEP event is well under way and Congressman Criswell's Capitol-based event began fifteen minutes ago. So far, nothing's happened. They say no news is good news, right, Bringer?"

"Sure," I replied, though I wasn't feeling nearly as hopeful. "That's what they say."

Too much crap had happened up until now. Add to that, our enemies, whether Continuance Corporation or others yet to be identified, had track records of being both unpredictable and lethal.

Maybe I was just becoming paranoid.

Of course, people like Senator Conway had a way of encouraging that feeling in me.

"Agent Sanders," the pilot prompted. "We'll be landing on a helipad near the Capitol Building. We're less than five minutes out now."

I only hoped that my luck could hold out that long.

Then something changed.

"Negative, WAC, I'm carrying TACIT taskforce members inbounds on a critical security support assignment," our pilot said. "Copy that. Bureau 7, out."

Sanders unbuckled her seatbelt and leaned forward. "Problems, Taggert?"

"There's some logistics snafu with Capitol Security," she replied. "They're diverting us as a matter of protocol."

"Wait, what sort of snafu?" Sanders asked.

"Not sure, Agent," she replied. "Washington Air Control is rerouting us away from Capitol grounds. We'll have to land at our D.C. bureau helipad."

"But—" Sanders protested.

"Wait one damned minute," I said, unbuckling my seatbelt.

I darted forward while pulling Sanders backward, and leaned between the pilot and copilot.

"Hey," Sanders protested.

"You tell them that we're putting this bird down in front of the damned Capitol, right now," I ordered. "Otherwise, I'll personally thrust a fireball up their ass so hard they'll feel it in the afterlife!"

CHAPTER 27

Taggert looked sidelong at me, and her expression was cool. "No need, sir," she said. "It's an open mic. They heard you loud and clear."

"Nice job with mics again, Bringer," Sanders said, giving me a slight shove.

"Copy that, WAC," the pilot said. "Bureau 7 inbounds directly to the Capitol."

She banked our chopper and reached out to flip a switch on the control panel before her.

"There," she said. "The mic to tower is cold, and we're back on our original course."

"Thanks," I said, sitting back in my seat. "Can you please try to get us as close as possible?"

"Roger that," she replied. "I can put you on the front steps, if you want."

"Thanks, Taggert," I said, looking outside at the looming Capitol Grounds.

The helicopter made a hard bank and angled forward. It felt like we were increasing speed.

"My pleasure, Mr. Bringer. Going in hot and fast," she replied. "Brings back memories from flying helos in the Navy."

I definitely liked Taggert.

I looked over at Sanders, who had already dialed

someone on her smartphone.

"This is Agent Sanders," she said. "What's the sitrep in the Capitol?"

* * *

Unbelievably, and as promised, Taggert sat us down on the green grassy area directly before the Capitol Building.

"Nice job, Taggert," I said, opening the copter's side door.

"Good hunting," she replied.

Despite the height of the copter, I couldn't help but hunch over slightly as we ran toward the Capitol steps, the whirring of the rotor blades overhead.

I scanned the area as I ran and Taggert took the chopper airborne and away before we were scarcely twenty feet from it. I saw individuals walking about, though it seemed like light crowd traffic for a weekday in Washington, D.C., especially compared to how busy the city had appeared on our approach.

I likewise didn't see a press presence outside, which made me wonder about the success of Paul's venture.

Strange.

Sanders was trying to intently listen to someone on her phone.

"Bringer," Sanders said. "Security teams are out of proper place throughout the area. Apparently, Operations lost contact with them. Secret Services, FBI, and Capitol police are mobilizing now."

I heard the sounds of multiple sirens in the distance.

"Let's go," I said.

We rushed to the steps leading up to the Capitol building, which I took two at a time at a dead run.

Impressively, Sanders was right at my heels. Truth told, she was probably in better cardio shape than I was.

"Something's wrong," Sanders said. "There should be more people here. It's the Capitol beat and there's not even a single reporter around."

"I thought something felt odd," I said, though I wished I had been mistaken.

"Here we go again," Sanders said.

"This time, no bad guys are getting away," I vowed.

It still pissed me off that The Teleporter had managed to escape me twice already. I thought that I'd had a shot at him the previous evening.

Who knew when I'd finally meet up with him again?

Besides, I still didn't know how he controlled his disappearing acts, much less what the scope of his abilities was.

As soon as we breached the main entrance doors and passed through them, I knew that something was definitely wrong.

Nobody was manning the security posts or visitor inspection areas.

There wasn't anybody in view.

Nor did I hear any commotion or gunfire. Frankly, it was eerie. The place seemed deserted.

Sanders drew her weapon. "Where is everybody?"

"Yeah," I replied. I opened my thoughts and scanned the area before us, but I sensed only a handful of contacts. "There's a few people in the vicinity, but not anywhere close."

"Lockdown, maybe?" I asked.

A single gunshot echoed in the distance.

"Oh, hell," I said. "Your turf, you lead."

"This way," Sanders said, hurrying down a corridor.

Warning sirens went off, as well as a series of rapid beeps that must've been code for something important.

We rounded a corner into a wide, historic-looking hallway. The next thing I saw was a speeding fireball flying directly at us.

I conjured a shield before us just before it impacted, sending a shockwave through my head as flames fell harmlessly to the marble floor.

There was power behind that one.

I conjured a fireball in reply, but Sanders grabbed at my shoulder.

"Bringer! Don't burn down the Capitol!"

Aw, shit.

I shook my hand to dispense my burgeoning fireball and strengthened a forward shield as another fireball and some bullets struck, ricocheting off it.

The fireball struck a stone wall beside us and a large portrait burst into flame.

I propelled my shield before me as I charged at our attackers, gaining speed and momentum as I went.

"Stay close!" I yelled.

I only caught part of what Sanders said as I concentrated on strengthening my shield.

"...to tell me twice," she said.

The sounds of continued rapid gunfire preceded more bullets and another fireball striking before me.

I wasn't backing down.

No retreat!

My shield slammed into four people at once and bodies went flying left, right, and backward.

Sanders fired from behind me as I repeatedly pounded my fist into the face of the telekinetic guy.

A woman fumbled with an assault rifle as she lay on her back before me. She raised it at me, but Sanders fired first. The woman's body went limp and her head thumped back against the floor as her weapon fell from her grip.

The man I was pummeling managed a glancing punch to my head as I coated my fist with flames and slammed it into his face one final time.

I followed that strike with one to his chest and his body burst into flames. Before getting burned, I generated a shield before me and awkwardly staggered backward into Sanders.

"Hey!" she said, wrapping her arm around my waist to steady her balance. "Fiery hand!"

I rapidly shook my hand, extinguishing the flames to

avoid singeing her.

Additional gunfire from behind us caused me to pivot in a semicircle just in time to deflect rounds coming downrange at us.

It appeared to be two Capitol police officers bearing assault rifles.

"Woah, good guys here!" I yelled as Sanders held up her badge.

"FBI!" she yelled. "TASIT taskforce!"

They ceased fire.

"Sorry, Ma'am!" yelled one officer.

"All hell's breaking loose!" yelled the other one.

We hurried over to them and they appeared half-scared for their lives.

The sirens and warning buzzers abruptly ceased.

"What's your situation?" Sanders demanded. "Who's in command?"

"Who knows," said the younger officer, who had to still be in his twenties.

"We've lost control of much of the building and the command center's compromised," the older officer said. "Attackers everywhere and some of them are wearing our uniforms. Offices just went on lockdown, but who knows if that's even safe."

"Don't know for sure who's even on our side," said the younger officer named Cooper, according to his nametag. "The radios are offline, so Atkins and I were just trying to link up with anybody we recognized and trusted."

"Stay with us," Sanders said. "Where are the delegates and politicians, Atkins? Are they secure?"

"Last I heard, most managed to make it to the Senate Chambers before everything went chaotic," Atkins said. "You can't imagine the insanity."

"What insanity?" she asked.

"Hell, this sounds crazy, but I saw two of our officers get tackled by some guy in black fatigues and then they all disappeared," he said. "I can't even find half the people who showed up for duty this morning. They're gone! I haven't even seen more than a handful of dead bodies!"

It had to be The Teleporter.

God, how I hated that nickname.

I've gotta kill him sooner than later.

Atkins nervously ran his fingers through his hair with one hand.

"Easy, Atkins," Sanders said. "You're not going crazy. There's a guy who can…make things and people disappear."

He looked at Sanders as if he was barely holding onto his last semblance of composure.

"Who the frig is supposed to fight somebody who can do that?" asked Officer Cooper.

I held up my hand and generated a flame around it. "Me, that's who."

Cooper practically fell backward as he gawked at me. "You're that wizard guy!"

Seriously? Wizard guy?

"Hey, you two get your shit together and cover our flanks," I ordered, extinguishing the flames around my hand. "And help point out any good guys to us, while you're at it. I don't wanna fry the wrong people."

Both officers gave me a wide berth.

Sanders acted as guide as we hurried toward the Senate chamber.

Gunfire erupted ahead of us and we quickened our pace.

To their credit, Atkins and Cooper held themselves in check. Cooper neatly nailed one assailant as he came out of a side office at us.

There were dead bodies galore in the area leading to the Senate chamber, and most of them looked like friendlies. There was a mix of uniformed personnel, plain clothes agents, and a number of civilians, including some members of the press.

I led the way, rounding a corner to an open area outside the chamber where a half dozen armed men in plain clothes were gathered. Two of them appeared to be setting explosives against the chamber doors.

I quickly backed up and around the corner before they spotted me. I halted my group and held my finger to my lips.

"Six hostiles," I whispered. "Two are setting explosives. I'll go first. Follow and terminate with prejudice."

I generated a shield and started to conjure a fireball, but suddenly extinguished it.

"What?" Sanders asked.

I looked at her. "Explosives and fire?"

She nodded.

I held up my finger for them to wait and turned the corner.

Gunfire erupted as soon as they saw me. I maintained my shield and used my abilities to grab one of the men and cast him against the others, progressively knocking four of them to the floor.

The two men setting explosives turned and fired, but their rounds hammered at my shields.

I projected my shield forward at rapid speed until it clobbered the men, slamming them backward.

"Now!" I yelled.

Sanders, Atkins, and Cooper rounded the corner and fired downrange.

Two hostiles returned fire and I heard Cooper yell out behind me.

I used my ability to grab that assailant and project him upwards into the ceiling. I followed by rapidly propelling him onto the tile floor.

After I heard bones break and he lay unmoving, I released him.

Sanders expertly shot another guy in the head and he crumpled to the floor.

I turned back to look at Cooper, who was on the floor, grasping at his left thigh, which was bleeding profusely.

Sanders and Atkins immediately went to aid him while I walked up to the chamber doors.

"To anyone inside," I shouted. "The cavalry has arrived!

We're here to protect you!"

"Secret Service detail to Vice President Spade here," sounded a reply. "Identify yourself."

"I'm Logan Bringer with FBI Agent Sanders of the TASIT taskforce," I said.

I could hear raised voices before someone yelled, "Everyone quiet!"

Then there was relative silence.

"Bringer? Is that really you?" asked a voice I definitely recognized.

Paul Criswell.

Thank goodness.

"It's me, Paul."

"We're glad you're here," he said. "How do we know it's you?"

"Are you kidding? I even rode backseat in a Ghost Falcon at Mach plus just to get here in time," I said. "Now open the damned door so I can save your ass…once again!"

"You asshole," he said, relief evident in his voice.

I grinned.

Then there was a pause until he added, "Yes, Mr. Vice President, that's definitely him."

* * *

Inside, the room hosted more than four dozen senators and representatives, as well as a meager handful of Secret Service agents and four Capitol officers. A small group of civilians stood nearby, including a couple of reporters.

Sanders and Atkins helped Cooper inside while I watched for uninvited guests.

We quickly secured the doors shut.

Vice President Spade walked over to me and shook my hand. "Logan Bringer. It's a sincere pleasure to meet you."

The Secret Service agent beside him seemed less than enthused.

"My pleasure, sir," I replied, shaking Spade's hand.

Sanders stepped up beside me. "Mr. Vice President, I'm FBI Agent Megan Sanders."

"Thank you, Agent Sanders," he said. "We're grateful."

The Vice President turned to the agent beside him. "Agent Eric Jacobs here is head of my security detail," he said. "What's going on out there?"

Paul stood beside me while Sanders hastily recounted events since our arrival and a bevy of politicians gathered around us.

"I thought more forces would be here by now," Spade said. "Jacobs says we can't hold out here much longer."

"There are barely enough agents and officers to cover potential entrances, but we'll be in trouble if we're attacked in force again," Jacobs warned.

"Everyone better be mobilizing as we speak," Sanders said. "It shouldn't be long now."

I wished that I felt as confident about that as she sounded. It seemed to be taking an awful long time.

"How long have you been holed up here?" I asked.

"We only secured the room about ten minutes before you arrived," Agent Jacobs replied. "The gun battle outside was costly, but we needed to choose someplace large enough to hold us. This was the closest location."

Jacob's estimate suggested that things must have started going to hell during our helicopter flight to the Capitol.

"It shouldn't take this long for backup to arrive," Agent Jacobs said. "Communications are offline. All phone lines and Internet are down, and we can't even get cellular signals, which in itself is damned strange."

Sanders and I each took out our mobile phones. True to his point, neither had signals.

"Okay, that's something new," I said. "Actually, Mr. Vice President, I think cellular signals are the last of your problems right now."

He and Paul had grim expressions.

"I think you're all the targets here today," I said. "But you, in particular, Mr. Vice President."

"Why the hell—" Spade began.

"You can credit enemies in high places...right across town today, if I'm not mistaken," I said.

The Vice President merely nodded, which actually unnerved me, and I turned to look at Sanders, who appeared as surprised as I felt.

"I've had my suspicions recently, but I never thought it might come to something like this," he said. "Or on this scale. This will tear the nation apart."

There were gasps throughout the room and rapid whispering. Suffice to say, the news was received poorly.

Paul stepped up beside the Vice President. "Sir, I respectfully recommend that now might not be the best time for us to discuss this."

He nodded. "I know. But there's never a good time for this, is there? Legally, the difficult thing is proving it."

Sanders and I exchanged knowing looks.

"You might be interested in a conversation I had last night with a certain senator," I said.

Paul and Spade both looked at me.

"I know where you were last night," Spade said. "And who you were busy saving."

"That's the guy," I said.

Agent Jacob's eyes widened, but he remained silent.

Gunshots rang out, preceding screams and shouts throughout the chamber.

Sanders and Jacobs brought their weapons to bear as people ducked for cover.

As the crowds parted, I stared across the expanse of the chamber to the far side and focused upon the three gun-toting assailants who had abruptly appeared.

One was familiar to me; the man we referred to as The Teleporter.

As Sanders and the nearest Secret Service agents returned fire, I reached out with my talent and grabbed the man who had twice eluded me.

But not now.

He seemed to realize what I had done and his eyes settled on me from across the room.

However, rather than him disappearing, this time it was everyone else who disappeared from around me.

My stomach twisted into a knot as I alternated in and out of a state of insubstantiality. I felt suspended in a void.

Then my feet felt grounded again, and he and I were standing in the middle of a dimly lit, stale-smelling basement. There were numerous bodies lying about on top of each other like some macabre abattoir, each corpse devoid of movement and displaying various of hollow-eyed, often horrific, expressions.

There were plain-clothed civilians, Capitol police officers, bodies bearing press badges, and I noted more than a few Secret Service agents.

The man before me thrashed back and forth, like a fish caught on a hook, but I held him firmly in place.

My mind strained to retain control of my abilities.

And then my world spun into nothingness again.

We appeared in the middle of a dining room.

I saw and heard the rain falling against the nearby picture window, and I could smell salty sea air, though it was too dark outside to see anything more distinctive.

However, I realized that we were once more standing in the middle of the house by the harbor that we had raided in Cardiff.

I lunged at The Teleporter and punched him solidly in the face. I grabbed him by the throat and my world spun yet again.

This time, I held onto his neck, even as my stomach threatened to evacuate itself.

The new location was a sunny desert, and a hot dry breeze touched my face as soon as we appeared. The sky was starkly blue against the surrounding sand dunes.

The man's fist impacted the side of my head, catching me off-guard. I squeezed his neck harder, trying to strangle him, if I could somehow manage it.

He kicked at me, his shoe catching the side of my knee, sending pain shooting through it.

My anger rose, and my skin tingled all through my arms and into my back, then up my neck and throughout my head. I heard a buzzing sound and realized that something smelled like it was burning.

His body caught fire and his skin sizzled like bacon on a skillet. I let go of him and he fell to the sandy ground in a burning heap as greasy wisps of smoke swirled into the air around me.

He was definitely dead.

I felt very gratified. I had finally beaten the bastard; a thorn no longer plaguing me at every turn.

His teleporting days were finally over.

Then I realized an urgent problem.

Oh, shit. How am I going to get back?

I looked around but saw only dunes of sand.

Endless, hot sand.

Grabbing my mobile phone, I tried to call for help, but there was no cellular signal.

I slowly turned in a complete circle and stared at nothing but tall hills of shifting sand dunes.

I was stationed in the desert before. I didn't enjoy it much then and my appreciation for it hadn't grown with time.

Face it. I was in a world of hurt.

CHAPTER 28

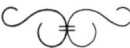

I climbed the nearest dune to gain a vantage point and spotted a small cluster of structures directly to my south, just downhill from where I stood.

Upon inspection, the site was abandoned and was comprised of merely a handful of single-story buildings built using particle board and old lumber.

It reminded me of the hastily assembled orientation sites that I had trained at during my time in the army. The layout mimicked that of a small village or depot.

Bullet holes riddled the buildings and burned residue ringed gaping breaches, though nothing alluded to who might have attacked the site. Given the deteriorated appearance of the facades, the place didn't appear occupied in quite a long time.

Though flimsy at best, my immediate need for shelter was met. However, more pressing was a lack of water and food.

I climbed to the top of the tallest nearby dune, only to see sand stretching out all the way to the horizon in all directions.

Any remaining semblance of optimism evaporated beneath the sun's hot rays, making me regret any quip that I'd ever made regarding the preferred dryness of a desert heat.

My plight was stark. I had no idea where I was, so I

didn't know if heading any particular direction would bring me closer to aid or further into whichever desert I was stranded in.

It was a big planet and there were a number of deserts to choose from.

I had rarely felt more helpless, except perhaps when cancer had ravaged my body.

I cautiously examined my surroundings via short excursions, being careful not to lose my home location where at least I had meager shelter. On two occasions, I became mildly disoriented and nearly lost my way. Each time, I barely found my way back.

During my brief journeys, I kept checking my phone but never received any signal, no matter my location.

There were no cactus or other foliage, and I noticed no aircraft or sounds of civilization. From the peaks of even the tallest dunes, a sea of sand greeted me.

I sent fireballs high into the night sky, as high as I could project them. And still, nobody came.

No aircraft.

Nobody.

Three days later, I lay beneath the shelter of the sturdiest of the structures, feeling desperately thirsty and completely alone.

I'm doomed.

I didn't want to die.

But then, who in their right mind really did?

While contemplating and facing my imminent demise, I experienced moments of sober clarity. My thoughts frequently drifted to my parents, my sister Lexi, my niece Kristie, my nephew Jake, and my partner, Meg Sanders.

I felt solace in knowing that, while I was never a touchy-feely person, my family knew that I loved them.

At least I made sure to tell them that on frequent occasions.

However, Sanders—Meg—was another topic entirely. There were things I still wanted the opportunity to say to her.

God, such strong feelings of damnation from things left unsaid.

A hard lump formed in my throat.

I lay on the shaded sand, which felt strangely cool despite the arid air.

If I make it out of this, I never want to visit a beach again for as long as I live.

I choked back a bitter laugh, suspecting that I didn't have a terribly long life left to live.

My parched throat yearned for moisture and my stomach ached for sustenance.

That night, the air nearly chilled me as I experienced a series of frequently surreal, and other times vivid, dreams. Memories from my life prior to gaining my abilities blended into horrific visions of near-fatal battles that had transpired since.

I fancied the idea of my family meeting Meg for the first time, followed by the memory of when I had first stopped a bullet from penetrating her skull, just outside my home in Nevis Corners. Visions comprising contrivances of my imagination continued to mix with recollections of actual moments in time.

The next day, I didn't move very much. I either stared blankly up at the particle board ceiling or quietly lay with my eyes closed, my thoughts wandering aimlessly.

I honestly just wanted things to be over and done with; meet whatever end came next.

Anything had to be better than where I was.

I tried to visualize a happy place; somewhere and sometime in my life when I had felt most content.

I remembered holidays spent with my family and friends. Then there were my days in college, as well as good times spent while I had been in the military.

Ultimately though, one moment in time eclipsed all the others. My sister, Lexi, had come to stay with me for a couple of weeks at my Nevis Corners house after I had finished my last chemotherapy treatment, just prior to beginning the experimental program at the Nuclegene clinic.

Around that time, my best friend, Travis Cooper, had relocated to Nevis Corners just to be closer to me if I needed any help. Between them, Lexi and Travis had kept my spirits up and spent quality time with me.

My brain cancer had just been officially declared terminal and I had been reconciling the prospective end to my life. And yet, despite how miserable I had felt, I had kept hanging on to each day, making each moment special.

Like some prison inmate awaiting the chamber on death row, each moment had been precious in its own way.

Together, we had watched more movies and sports events on television than I had my entire life. We'd eaten what junk food I could stomach, and even drank the oddest flavors of beer, some merely because those were the ones that I could keep down.

Through it all, I had never lacked company or support. My parents, nephew, and niece had visited, but Lexi and Travis had remained at my side seemingly around the clock. I had wanted for nothing.

I remembered one moment in particular and focused upon it. I had been laying on the couch, a beer in hand, watching the Iowa Hawkeyes in a Big Ten title-winning game against the Wisconsin Badgers with Travis and Lexi. I hadn't felt ill that entire day, and I had even managed to eat nearly a third of the pepperoni pizza we had ordered.

For some reason, that day—those memories—as simple as they were, had felt like fleeting moments of perfection in my life. It had felt like the best of the last days of my time left on Earth.

Good times.

The best of times.

I could almost taste the zesty pizza sauce, followed by what must have been the coldest of beers. I remembered the penetrating warmth of the house as snow fell outside, and how my couch had felt like the most comfortable spot on the globe.

I remembered wanting to lie there forever, that moment

never passing; frozen in time.

That damned comfy couch…

Moments of perfection were fleeting; just like life.

Fleeting and then over before you even realized that it had passed.

My story was ending, but I would live in that perfect moment instead.

My stomach clenched, twisting into a knot, thirst and hunger maddeningly taking its toll on me.

And yet, I felt as if I was floating in nothingness.

I sank further into the void, embracing and clinging to its cold, insubstantial form. It was the only semblance of comfort remaining.

I sank into the welcome oblivion.

* * *

My eyelids fluttered open and I awoke amidst near darkness with a sickening feeling in my guts.

Shifting slightly, my body ached as my bare arms rubbed against what felt like faux leather.

I grasped and squeezed a cushion beneath me and took a deep breath. Familiar scents assailed me as a dry, hacking cough overtook me.

As I rolled my body to the left, I suddenly felt nothing, dropping for a mere second.

My stomach lurched as I impacted stale-smelling carpet.

My mind raced as I pressed my palms against the very real carpeting. But I felt so weary that I could barely move my muscles.

Holy shit!

My eyes started to focus as I struggled to understand where I was. I heard a vehicle passing in the distance as artificial light illuminated the room between nearby blinds.

I looked up and saw dimly lit dining room furniture.

My dining room furniture!

I scrambled to my feet, nearly falling over as I struggled forward toward the nearest wall.

My hand hit a wall switch and my fingers fumbled to activate the buttons. My dining room lit up via the light fixture hanging above my table.

It had to be an illusion, conjured from delirium.

My mind struggled to understand what was happening.

A mirage?

Mirage or not, I half-stumbled to the kitchen sink, frantically turning the knobs until water flowed freely before me.

I drank greedily from the tap before immersing my head beneath what could have only been near-magical water in my half-deluded state.

It was real.

Or I'm dead and this is heaven!

I didn't know how long I stood with the water washing over me, but I finally grabbed at a dish towel hanging beside me and wiped my face with it.

I laughed manically, half-willing to confess that I must have gone insane leading up to the final stages of exposure.

But I wasn't dead.

I'm home!

My empty stomach twisted with pain, but something far stronger pulled at me.

My next lucid thought was, *Sanders!*

I grabbed at my mobile phone, reassured by the complete set of bars indicating the strongest of cellular reception. My fingers trembled as I struggled with the auto-dial functions, something that should have been child's play for me.

I dropped to the floor onto my butt, my legs too wobbly to stand. The line only rang once.

"Bringer? Is that you?" Sanders asked. Her voice sounded small and tentative.

"Meg!" I yelled.

"Logan! Oh, God—" she replied. "Where are you? Are you hurt?"

I coughed, my throat still painfully raw.

"Listen to me," I rasped. "I was trapped in a desert, but I'm back—"

"Back where? Where are you?" she interrupted.

"Sanders, this is crazy," I said, trying to catch my breath. "I don't understand—"

I still didn't believe that what was happening could be real. I managed to get to my feet and awkwardly ran toward the front door.

"*Where are you?*" she demanded.

I fumbled with the door locks and staggered outside onto my front porch. The sun was just starting to rise in the east and the early morning air felt unmistakably cool. A vehicle passed by my house, its headlights on and the driver seemingly oblivious to me.

I practically gawked at the car, as if stunned by the mere substantiality of it.

"Bringer?" Sanders asked. "Say something!"

"Sanders, I'm at my house," I insisted. "I'm in Nevis Corners—"

"What? How?" she demanded.

That's when I realized what must have happened. A cold sensation rushed through my weakened body all at once. I had to lean against the cool brick of my house just to remain upright.

"—took his ability," I muttered, my vision blurring and my head beginning to feel dizzy. "I freakin' *teleported*."

I heard her gasp just before I lost my balance and blacked out.

ABOUT THE AUTHOR

Jaz Primo: Delving into flights of fancy and realms of imagination; eagerly sharing with you.

Jaz lives in the Great American Midwest where he writes paranormal romance, urban fantasy, and young adult literature. He's a history aficionado, Doctor Who fanatic, "pun-master", an all-around fan of vampires, and a caregiver to the world's most endearing cat.

You can easily find Jaz Primo online at the following locations:

Website: http://jazprimo.com

Twitter: @jazprimo

Sunrise at Sunset: Revamped
Sunset Vampire Series, Book 1
(Second Edition)
by Jaz Primo

The Sunset Vampire Series achieved Third Place in the Reviewer's Choice Award for Best Paranormal Series of 2012 (Paranormal Romance Guild).

This new, second edition of the original, has new never-seen-before material, *Revamped* includes a forward by Jaz explaining how this version improves over the original. Additional bonus material includes a new bonus chapter that bridges events between the first novel and the sequel, *A Bloody London Sunset*.

When is a bloodthirsty predator the best protection against a psychotic killer?
When the predator is both a vampire...and the woman you love.

Caleb is bravely overcoming a dark past while having no memory of the beautiful vampire that saved him. Despite a promise to stay away, Katrina is compelled to return to him.
However, a vengeful rival from her past has dire plans for both of them.

Available in trade paperback and all major eBook formats!

Go to http://jazprimo.com/books for purchasing links!

Winner of the Paranormal Romance Guild's Reviewer's Choice Award for Best Young Adult Novel of 2012!

Gwen Reaper
A Young Adult Paranormal Romance
by Jaz Primo

Boy meets beautiful and mysterious, yet reclusive, girl who harbors a potentially-lethal secret.

"A thing of beauty is a joy forever: its loveliness increases; it will never pass into nothingness." John Keats, English romantic poet.
I never thought that my first exposure to real beauty would be tinged with the threat of oblivion…
~ ~ ~ ~ ~
When high school junior Scott Blackstone is forced to move from his childhood home in Springfield, Illinois to small-town Custer, South Dakota, he expects nothing less than to languish in complete disappointment. Instead, he discovers a beautiful and mysterious seventeen-year-old girl named Gwen, who captivates him from his initial, adrenaline-laced sight of her on the shores of Stockade Lake. Scott's pursuit of the elusive Gwen sweeps him into the midst of a potentially lethal family heritage that was birthed in hope, only to be passed into a legacy of guilt and death.

Scott engages in a journey of discovery, tinged with both angst and danger. Like many dire legends throughout history, he is unprepared for the untimely revelation that both love and despair are often two sides of the same coin.

Gwen Reaper
(A Young Adult Paranormal Romance)
is available in trade paperback and all
major eBook formats!

A Bloody London Sunset
Sunset Vampire Series, Book 2
by Jaz Primo

In *A Bloody London Sunset*, a timid spirit rises to assert himself, a forbidden love sparks, and a forgotten past threatens to topple the power of love.

Katrina Rawlings is a vampire who has finally rediscovered happiness for the first time in centuries. But unwanted complications erupt with a vengeance. Decisions of necessity combined with dark memories from a forgotten past threaten her relationship with the love of her life. When a sacrifice must be made, can she endure her decision?

Caleb Taylor's life is finally back on track. He has rebounded from a near mortal injury, both physically and emotionally. Yet, his reality is shaken by the suggestion of a betrayal of trust from the woman he loves. Can the power of love overcome the power of a lie?

Paige Turner is a century old vampire who fearlessly revels in a simple existence pursuing blood, dancing, and sex. Simple needs, and all met in the same manner: hot, fast, and without regrets. But a spontaneous visit leads to heartfelt sacrifice, and unexpected complications strike fear to the core of her soul. Will she survive the revelations?

In the exciting second novel in the Sunset Vampire Series, a trust is betrayed, bonds of friendship are strained, relationships may end, and a tenuous neutrality among the world's vampire population is threatened. With stakes so high, some will not survive A Bloody London Sunset!

Go to http://jazprimo.com/books for purchasing links!

Summit at Sunset
Sunset Vampire Series, Book 3
by Jaz Primo

Does the fate of one innocent human soul outweigh the needs of the entire vampire race? The third, and most exciting, novel in the *Sunset Vampire Series* has finally arrived!

Powerful vampire Katrina Rawlings and her human mate, Caleb Taylor, are once more drawn into dangerous circumstances. Representatives of the most powerful and influential vampires from around the world converge upon a scenic mountain retreat located in Slovenia's Upper Bohinj Valley for a summit of historic proportion. Mystery leads to treachery, and events quickly spiral out of control. With the fates of both vampires and humans in jeopardy, Katrina desperately struggles to reconcile the balance of worldwide vampire power against honoring her commitment to the love of her life. Unwilling to be rendered helpless, Caleb initiates a desperate gamble that leads to a mortal decision. Meanwhile, the sexy and sassy vampire, Paige Turner, spearheads her own mission involving both surprising revelations of heart and grave circumstances for those around her.

In *Summit at Sunset*, unlikely alliances will be sought, eternal bonds of friendship will be tested, unrequited love will be unleashed, blood will be shed, and one pivotal person's fate will collide with destiny.

Available in trade paperback and all major eBook formats!

Go to http://jazprimo.com/books for purchasing links!

Wicked Sunset
Sunset Vampire Series, Book 4
by Jaz Primo

After exploring urban fantasy with Bringer of Fire, and young adult romance with the award-winning Gwen Reaper, author Jaz Primo returns to his beloved and extremely popular Sunset Vampire series with the eagerly-awaited fourth novel, Wicked Sunset.

Security, more than ever, is an illusion.

The world's vampires are on a terrifying course of destruction, putting everyone in mortal danger. Katrina has a confrontation with dire consequences. Caleb, surrounded by darkness, and facing challenges at every turn, makes a surprising decision- that has even more surprising results.
Even his relationship with Katrina, something he could always believe in, may be changed forever. But if Caleb can finally come into his own, he may be able to claim a legacy he never dared imagine.

Available in trade paperback and all major eBook formats!

Go to http://jazprimo.com/books for purchasing links!

Sunset Rising
Sunset Vampire Series, Book 5
by Jaz Primo

In *Sunset Rising*, the exciting fifth installment in Jaz Primo's Sunset Vampire series, life is the ultimate prize in a race against time.

Vowing retribution, Katrina tenaciously seeks out those behind the attack against Caleb, whose research to unravel a centuries old mystery attracts both unexpected competition and mortal danger.

Paige's conflicted feelings erupt, altering the lives of those she loves and leaving emotional disaster in her wake.

Battle lines are drawn as the vampire world's fiercest beings choose sides, rendering those undecided few as hotly contested spoils in a growing war.

In *Sunset Rising*, all bets are off!

Available in trade paperback and all major eBook formats!

Go to http://jazprimo.com/books for purchasing links!

Bringer of Fire
Logan Bringer Urban Fantasy Series, Book 1
by Jaz Primo

Spinning "a wonderful first book in his Logan Bringer series" (Paranormal Romance Guild), Jaz Primo has created a new urban fantasy hero in this story packed with explosive action, danger, and intrigue.

Logan Bringer is a cancer survivor and war hero who should have his hardest battles behind him. But when he develops the ability to move things with his mind, he's hunted by corporations, terrorists, and his own government.

Darkness and corruption are everywhere.

When even his family is threatened, he fights to control his new powers— and becomes more powerful than his enemies can possibly imagine.

Available in trade paperback and all major eBook formats!

Go to http://jazprimo.com/books for purchasing links!

www.ingramcontent.com/pod-product-compliance
Lightning Source LLC
Chambersburg PA
CBHW060538180626
46817CB00002B/627